# ON A HOT SUMMER DAY IN GORAKHPUR

Tanvir Salim

Vitasta
*Let Knowledge Spread*

Published by
Renu Kaul Verma
Vitasta Publishing Pvt Ltd
2/15, Ansari Road, Daryaganj
New Delhi - 110 002
info@vitastapublishing.com

ISBN 978-93-82711-68-1


Disclaimer
All persons portrayed in this book are fictitious. Any resemblance to real persons, living or dead, is purely co-incidental.
Though this is the work of fiction, opinions expressed in it are the author's own. The Publisher is in no way responsible for these.

Cover and layout by Vits Press
Printed by Vikas Computer and Printers

FOR MY CHILDREN

There is no greater agony than bearing
an untold story inside you.
—Maya Angelou

# Foreword

My old gardener Ramji was a short and stout man who lived in one of the outhouses that were not too far away from the *Kothia* or the main living premises, where we lived. It was simply curiosity that often took us there. One day I pointed to a stick that was hanging on the rugged mud plastered wall in his room. He shyly brought the stick down, and to my surprise that was not an ordinary walking stick. It was an old fashion swordstick. It concealed a shining sword, which could not be seen, unless pulled out. Who would have ever thought that the concealed sword had once tasted human blood?

That night I could not sleep thinking how the mob would have killed and burned the policemen at the police post, or the thana, in the sleepy village of Chauri-Chaura, which was not too far away from Gorakhpur. What had led them to kill the ones who were there to protect them? Life is not that simple as it seems from the surface. There is always the rest of the story, of which often we were not aware of. It took me many decades to know what exactly happened in Chauri-Chaura in 1922. The narration was provided by an old and haggard lady, Najbun, who used to help the cooks in my household. She claimed that not knowing what else to do, she hid herself in the hen's coop, when policemen started firing at the protesters. I have seen the world enough to know that the struggle between the have and have-nots will never cease to happen as long as there is injustice, inequality and uneven distribution of wealth. But, during the course of this learning process, I also came to know something which I did not know. There was a surprise waiting for me, which unfolded when I turned some of the yellowish, moth ridden papers of the family archives. The old worn out walls of the *Kothia* have once witnessed one such skirmish, which if it had been documented and archived properly by historians could have been the first uprising against social injustice that brewed in the quiet town of Gorakhpur.

Being what we are, we all have witnessed the perpetual discrimination and prejudices that reside everywhere, including in all of us. No society or way of life can claim sainthood in this regards. Even the best of the religions are only that good as its followers are.Prophet Mohammad, in his Last Sermon was very clear when he stated, 'An Arab has no superiority over a non-Arab and a white man has no superiority over a black man, except by piety and good actions.' But this message of the Prophet Mohammad, which is the essence of Islam, got lost in the Indian subcontinent where some clamored to be more equal than the others.

In this book, for the first time, the inconvenient truth about the caste system amongst Muslims of the Asian subcontinent is brought to the surface. It is sad that contrary to the teachings of Islam, this practice is thriving among Muslims on similar lines as in Hindus. This attempt is not to chide the ones who subscribe to it, but to create awareness, so that the crux of Islam is brought to the surface and the social reform, which is the need of the day and long due, finds some takers.

It is our duty to bring to the surface the untold stories which got lost in the cracks of history, and to let our imagination stroll into the unchartered territories, to give the reader a glimpse of various permutations and combinations, of the endeavors which are attainable, to get him ready for the future so that it may not come as a surprise, as it always does, after the fact.

The planet may be spinning at the same speed, as it did for the past billions of the years, but the subtlety of the population that resides on its surface is witnessing changes every minute. These changes have to be documented, and whether one likes it or not, the burden is on us to narrate it in a manner which we know best. My attempt here is to bring to the readers few of the things of the past and blend it with what ifs of the future.

The world is in great turmoil and the churning is immense. Everybody seems to be in a hurry to score a point over the other. The followers of one particular religion are under close scrutiny, and their actions are dissected and analysed manifold to an extent that they are quick to claim victimhood, whether rightly or not, which is for history to judge.

My special thanks to my family and friends, especially to the friends, Sharique and Ayman, who encouraged me to keep going, otherwise I would have not finished this work, and to my children Saman and Shaaz who were deprived of the time, which otherwise would have been spent with them. And last but not the least to Renu and the editorial team of Vitasta Publishers who believed in my work and worked to make it happen.

# Prologue

The forests of the Terai region are essentially the foothills of the Himalayas. Even in those days, the Doma range near Nichlaul was laden with animals of all shapes and kinds, and the place was aptly considered a hunter's paradise.

The kids were at the Pakri Farm, enjoying their school vacation. All afternoon they were awash with the excitement that generally accompanied the adult's hunting expeditions. The locals, who knew the forest trails like the back of their palms, began to gather. Someone had set out to fetch the petrol for the Jeep, while another was cleaning the barrels of the guns. The locals from nearby villages were busy gathering reports from different forest areas; their discussions vivid with confessions of having seen one thing or another in the forest the past few days. 'That was simply a rabbit.' One jovial youth teased the man sitting next to him, for which the choicest abuse was hurled back at him.

They were on the prowl. It was getting dark and the distinction between darkness and the trees and the shrubs was getting blurry. With the onset of what looked like an uneventful midnight, the kids began to get bored. Thankfully, the occasional howling of the jackals and the horrifying screeching and scampering of other nocturnal animals kept them awake; otherwise they would have dozed off a long time ago. The one on the left with curly hair was fat and bulky, and the one sitting next to him had straight hair, and was calm and skinny. They both were attentive. They were assigned a task, and their task, they thought, was the most essential in the entire excursion. They were given flashlights to look out for animals at night. Their flashlights were tiny compared to the huge floodlights mounted on the Jeep, illuminating the area as if it was broad daylight. Both the kids were competing with each other to be the first one to find something in the jungle.The lean kid had his eyes on the road ahead, but his thoughts wavered. He was thinking about the Hollywood movie *Hatari*, which had released last week and he had enthusiastically watched in a theater in Gorakhpur. He debated with himself, 'Why the hunter or actually the animal catcher, John Wayne, sat on the bonnet of the Jeep?' He gazed in the darkness and smirked. 'I will never do that! What if something jumps on me from the bushes?' This thought itself was enough to send a shiver down his spine and he kept his eyes peeled on the road ahead with the resolve to be more attentive than he was before.

Suddenly, the vehicle came to a crashing halt. One of the locals sitting in the rear of the Jeep conveyed a message in hushed tones to those sitting in the front.

Yes, they could see it. The contours of its eyes were

like little fish, though they were big for eyes, and were very bright. The person driving the Jeep was their grandfather's younger brother, who turned around and asked the kids whether they had seen it or not. One of them lied, and shook his head in the negative because they wanted to see more.The driver smiled, and whispered to them, 'I will show you.' He started the Jeep, made a sharp turn and drove towards the eyes. Now they could see it all. The eyes belonged to a huge animal, sitting on its hind legs, ready to make a jump. The Jeep whirled past it.When all this was happening, the local chap sitting at the far end of the Jeep was trembling with fear and was murmuring the shlokas (verses) from the *Hanuman Chaleesa*, seeking divine help form Lord Hanuman, the mighty god who kept all evil at bay.

The kid's throat had turned dry and he managed to rasp out, 'Was that a lion?' The man who was holding the gun whispered back to him, 'No, that was a tiger; there are no lions in this part of the jungle.'

How wrong he was! Once upon a time, there were lions in this region, and in the future too, there will be.

the [illegible] … they were lucky for [illegible] and were very [illegible] … The person among the kids was their granddaughter [illegible] … and asked the [illegible] … which … [illegible] … One of them [illegible] and shook his head in the negative because there was nothing to see [illegible] … and whispered to them … saw you … [illegible] … made a sharp … and [illegible] … towards the eyes. Now they could see it all. The eyes belonged to a huge animal [illegible] … body was ready … [illegible] … all this was happening … [illegible] … with [illegible] … and the [illegible] Lord Hanuman, the mighty [illegible] … day.

The kids, however, had turned dry and [illegible] … The man who was holding the [illegible] … there are no limits in this part of the jungle.

[illegible] … and in the [illegible]

THE KENNEDY Airport in New York City was as crowded as ever. It was like a vast sea of faces in which almost everyone had a bored expression while waiting for their flight's announcement or for their baggage on the conveyer belt. Amidst the cacophony of various noises, the flights were taking off as usual. Every morning, approximately forty thousand flights took off in the United States. Not too far away, Ahmad was on his way to be submerged in that sea of faces at the airport. He already had that restless and shaken look on his young face. After reaching the airport, he headed towards the lounge, trying to keep his mind clear from any fears or doubts. This was the first time Ahmad was flying on Air India. It was not very long ago that Air India had reintroduced direct flights from New York to New Delhi.

He sat on one of the huge comfortable lounge chairs at the airport thinking about how time had changed everything. As a kid, whenever he flew with his parents, he was required a stopover in Europe. Now, he was going on a direct flight, crossing the vast ocean without his parents. Nobody else showed any interest in going with him. The fact was that he 'had to go' because his father had died in India. The news had flashed on one of the Indian news channels, and his cousin who was watching it called him to give him that tragic news. It was a road accident and it had happened somewhere in the countryside. That is all what the news channels knew at the time, but a cryptic tweet on Twitter gave it a different twist. His father was actually killed in his own home.

Everybody discouraged Ahmad from going, but he was unwilling to listen. His sister, Amna, certainly had a firm opinion when she said sheepishly, 'There is nothing you can do at this stage. You don't even understand the language spoken there, do you?' His little niece got the opportunity to take sides with her mother when she said in her style, 'You will look for the return flight to come back home, to me.' One of his cousins, Bilal, was more blatant. He said in his usual pessimistic way, 'Remember, what Anne called you in the library? "ABCD", and you shot back with ABCDEFGH La, La, La, La, La?' Anne was his class mate and her original name was Anita Patel. She was the daughter of immigrant parents; her father was from Gujarat and mother was from Hyderabad. In fact, to personalise it for her, Ahmad had once added the alphabets EFGH (Especially from Gujarat and Hyderabad) to the customary ABCD (American Born Confused Desi). Bilal had gauged the stress Ahmad was beginning to feel, and was trying to divert Ahmad's attention, but it was all in vain.

Everybody had an opinion and Ahmad politely heard them all. But he had his own, and he knew that he would not waver, and that he would go through with it. His father had never been able to convince him to come and visit him in India, and now he was going of his own accord. Death has the potential to influence destinies to a great extent. Sometimes the dead are more potent than the living. There were traces of guilt, which Ahmad was not able to camouflage by a false smile, which was permanently affixed to his face since yesterday. Only Ahmad knew about the physical challenges his father had faced; he was paralysed on his left side. Maybe because of this handicap his father was not able to escape when attacked.

But what control did a mere mortal have upon the ways of life? When the soul left the body, the process was not reversible. There was no homecoming for the dead. Some say that the soul, after leaving the body, wanders around it, watches its dear ones in mourning, and then slowly gets disconnected and disinterested with the ones who at one time were so precious, and then altogether loses interest in worldly affairs, until it finally floats upwards for its final voyage.

As a fitting tribute to his father, Ahmad felt his left side was getting numb, just like his father's when he was under pressure. But for Ahmad, it was simply a state of mind, a sense of new-found bonding which he had never experienced before. It was telling him that his father is going to be with him always and would be watching over him because he had to carry their family's torch forward.

In the flight, he turned on in-flight entertainment and scrolled through the list of Bollywood movies which were being offered during the flight. He wanted to learn as much of the Hindustani language as he could in the shortest time possible. He knew that he would need it.

His mind was wandering over the past. He was making an attempt to not go into the future, because the future was beyond comprehension. He suddenly found himself staring into a cold vaccum. He was not ready, but who was ever really ready for the death of a parent?

Ahmad was looking at the floor, thinking about the futility of it all; after all, he had failed to reconnect sooner with his father, when he was still alive. He was roving down memory lanes in a quest to bring back the memories he would have to ration for the rest of his life. He wished he had the ability to go back in time, to rewind and pick the most important moments with his father at leisure. How was his departure from this world? Was it calm and peaceful or was it of agony and distress? Was he thinking of Ahmad during his last moments? Was he able to recite the holy verses of the Qur'an before his soul was ejected from his body? There were too many questions floating in his mind and he had no answers for any of those questions.

He clenched his fist, and suddenly heard himself saying out loud, 'Damn!' He looked around sheepishly to see if anybody had heard him. His head throbbed and he felt his eyes burning in their sockets. He closed them to ease the pain. Soon he lapsed into a troubled sleep. New Delhi was still fifteen hours away.

There were many present to receive Ahmad at the Gorakhpur Railway Station. After all, he was the son of the former Chief Minister of an important State of India. Relatives, whom he had never met or heard of, were present. Most of them were there out of sheer curiosity.They all wanted to see the son who had come, which frankly nobody was expecting. He was not going to get a chance to see the dead body of his father because they could not have prolonged the burial, or the tadfeen. Islam encourages burying the dead as soon as possible. From the railway station, he was driven straight to the cemetery.

Ahmad was later told that the crowd at the funeral was unprecedented. The local media called it the 'greatest gathering of all times', and compared it to the crowd that assembled when one of the Mahants or the priests of the local Gorakhnath Temple was buried in the temple's premises in the 1960s. The Muslim cemetery was just a stone's throw away across the temple. He was informed that the road in front of the temple was jam packed, and there was a stampede when the chopper carrying the State's current Chief Minister flew over the temple to land several miles away, in the vacant premises of what decades ago used to be a fertiliser factory. A caravan of a few dozen vehicles, ferrying the Chief Minister, came from the north, and parked inside the temple. From here, the Chief Minister, as did the Mahant, moved towards the cemetery along with thousands of other mourners.

After reaching the cemetery, Ahmad's eyes desperately looked around for a fresh grave. It was easy to find because they had not removed the bamboo barricades, which were hurriedly installed at the time of the burial to prevent the surging crowd from coming too close to the grave. The grave would be left unmarked, and after a passage of time, it would look similar to the hundreds of other graves in the vicinity. If that would have not been the case, then the gravestone would have likely said, 'Beneath this simple stone that marks his resting place, one of the Lions of Gorakhpur finds solace.'

It was past midnight when he finally entered his father's house. The house was thankfully empty save for a few stray relatives whom he had never met before. Outside, the atmosphere was very alive. There were more than a dozen guards along with a couple of police SUVs, which were parked in no particular order. Since the murder investigation was still underway, the house was cordoned off by the local administration.

Ahmad went straight to his father's room. A quick glance around showed him the usual stuff. His picture when he was a baby still hung on the wall along with the picture from his High School yearbook. His sister's picture and that of his mother were on the side table. Maybe his father used to look at them in his lonely moments. But, judging by the type of life his father had lived, it was hard to imagine that he would ever have been lonely. In spite of his busy life, however, his father was lonely; but knowing him, Ahmad knew that he preferred it. Only Ahmad knew that, because like his father, he was a loner too. A ghost of a smile broke on his face and that was the closest he came to smiling in many days.

After a few moments, Ahmad stood in the centre of the room and by some strange mechanism, he felt that he was absorbing the energy residing in the room. His father's energy, a residual energy that seemed to permeate him. This was his day for receiving tribal knowledge which would help him in the days ahead. Ahmad's father wanted to enrich him with the wisdom he had acquired through the trials and tribulations of his life, but had not been able to do so. It was an inheritance left hanging in the air, swirling all around him, waiting impatiently to infiltrate the rightful heir.

At the study table in the back of the room, Ahmad was not surprised to see his mother's old computer, a Compaq Deskpro 386, which was gathering dust. He had fond memories of that machine because he had played many games on it as a child. His father had taken great pains to bring it to India, and had successfully converted it to operate on the latest version of Windows, rather than on the primitive DOS, for which it was originally designed. Ahmad remembered how thrilled his father was after performing that feat. Next to the computer was an old family picture, with him sitting in the rear seat of his father's BMW and his sister sitting next to him. It was taken by his mother during a trip to the Niagara Falls. Those were good times.

Ahmad stood near the computer and looked at the blank screen with a faint smile on his face. Somehow, he felt that the screen smiled back at him. He started to look elsewhere, but again as if by some force, his eyes turned back towards the screen. It seemed like the screen was trying to convey some message to him. He mumbled, 'What is going on? The jetlag's getting to me, gotta sleep.' But the screen was sending him invisible signals and instinct told him to act. Ahmad pushed the start button and the screen started glowing. Many images appeared on the screen, until it finally stabilised. It asked for a password.

Without even thinking, Ahmad typed in his father's last name. The screen responded with a message that flashed in large font, 'Access Denied'. He pulled the chair near the table, and kept staring at the screen, racking his brain. He slowly entered two different combinations of passwords, but they failed as well. He decided to shut the machine off, to fiddle with it at another time. He looked at the screen again, hoping for some guidance, but the screen was not as obliging as he stared at it.

Melancholy and sadness engulfed him. He started to doubt his ability to face the days that were ahead. His eyes were closing involuntarily, and his head dropped on the table near the family picture.

Suddenly, as if jolted out of a deep reverie, Ahmad opened

his eyes and looked at the picture again with a knowing smile, because his father seemed to be certainly guiding him. He slowly typed in 'dentures', a family code and the machine accepted it.

An exciting experience awaited him. It was etched on the hard drive of his mother's computer. All he had to do was to put the pieces from the Backroom Diaries together. Only he could have done it, because nobody else was indoctrinated the way he was. Ahmad was restless. In spite of being sleep deprived, his eyes were wide open. He wanted to know everything and soon he would; because the sound of bugles just blown in Delhi and other places, announcing the mutiny, had reached Gorakhpur on a hot summer's day. The clock had turned back to 1857.

THE YEAR was 1857 and the smell of death was thick in the air. Now it was indigenous and was emanating from every nook and cranny of Gorakhpur. The summer was going to be like no other summer in Gorakhpur, and in any other part of the country before. Gorakhpur then was a somnolent town, so most of the time the roads were empty. But today there was an eerie silence that made the place resemble a ghost town. Nobody was talking to anyone; no one even dared to look into the eyes of others. There was hardly any house in the town where a meal was prepared that day. Everybody had lost their appetite after hearing what had happened at the Main Square in Alinagar. They all felt guilty and had too much going on in their heads to bother about menial tasks like cooking or eating. Not too far away from Alinagar, a middle-aged man, dressed in modest clothes, moved around restlessly in his humble home.

Shakir, who was sitting in the corner of a room, was unable to understand what had happened to make his father so restless. He kept on muttering as he paced around the room; his body language tense. He was definitely very disturbed but Shakir could not, for the life of him, understand about what? In fact, it was not his father alone. Everybody who had gathered at the Main Square was distressed but they tried hard to mask their emotions. After all, one didn't know who to trust; not when an Indian, like them, was the cause of death of one of his countryman. An Indian fighting for the freedom of his country was hung by the British. The hangman was an Indian and the doctor who pronounced him dead was also an Indian. And all this happened on a hot summer day.

Shakir's father looked at him as if to tell him to leave the room, but Shakir did not budge. He had by now learnt of the hanging from the people who came to his house to discuss the matter with his father. Shakir had too much going on in his little mind which was replete with questions about the soul, once it departs from the body. Waiting for things to happen is painful, but waiting for the moment when life would end was unimaginable. What was that person thinking moments before his body would no longer be alive? The trap door would fling open, and his legs would flutter in the air, and instantaneously his head would limp to one side. His eyes will bulge out along with his tongue, which would later be pushed out of his mouth. One needed severe courage to watch what in legal jargon was termed 'to hang until death'.

Quite a handful of men had gathered in the room by now and everyone looked angry and scared. A couple of days ago, Shakir's father was told by one of his elder cousins about the holding place or jail which was not very far from his house. The British were using Shakir's favourite childhood spot to punish the rebels. The pakar tree near the jail, on which he used to play lakhni with his friends, was used for hanging rebels, while the nearby well was used to dump the dead bodies. Scores of people were hanged in the last few days itself.

Babu Bandhu Singh was a zamindar and belonged to the state of Dumari Khaas, but unlike other zamindars of that time, he hated the British. His hatred for them was so intense that he would spew venom against the British before anyone without their asking. He made a major mistake by confessing this to one of his close friends, giving away the exact location of a stockade of firearms stored by his comrades in the process. Unfortunately, that close friend turned out to be a British informer, who was later handsomely rewarded for betraying his friend. Those were the days when betrayal against one's friend and country ensured hefty pockets.

Shakir's father was quite shaken when he was informed about this. With a sullen face, he said to his cousin in hushed whispers, 'Khooni kuan! Kaise ho gaya ye sab?' (Murderous well. How did all this happen?) Originally, this building near the river belonged to the Sattasi Raja Basant Singh, and today it became the last refuge of Babu Bandhu Singh, before he was taken to be hanged. Some others whispered to Shakir's father about the possibility that Shah Inayat Ali Shah of Shahpur Estate, and Kunwar Singh of Jagdishpur Estate, were also hanged in this jail, which later became famous as Moti Jail.

There was stillness in the room as if death had visited there. A hint of suspicion could be seen in each set of eyes. No one could be sure whether the person sitting next to them was an informer or the enemy or not.

They were all awoken from their trance by a gentle knock on the door. Everyone stood transfixed. Shakir's father mustered some strength and started moving towards the door with heavy steps. Shakir's body started to convulse as he broke into hysterical sobs. In those days, a knock on the door was considered inauspicious because nobody knew who would be the next one to be pulled away from the house, and later charged with helping the rebels. Many who were taken away this way with a knock on the door never returned. Shakir's father reluctantly opened the door. On the other side of the door some men stood with sagging shoulders. Mujjan, the one with red beard, spoke in frightened whispers, 'Bhaïyya, Bandhuji ko tarpa tarpa kar maar diya, unka wazan kam ho gaya thaa, isi liye phanda theek se kas nahin paya.' (Brother, Bandhuji was killed with great pains, since he had lost some weight, the noose could not tighten enough.)

Mujjan broke into uncontrollable sobs. Others were too shocked to even react. With each passing moment, their breathing became heavy with rage. Shakir's mother emerged from inside the house and lifted the heavy jute curtain to ensure that everything was fine. With one look at the assembly in the room, she immediately went back inside sensing the gravity of the situation.

Babu Bandhu Singh was hung in broad daylight before a large audience. Those who watched with glee were the usual favourites, the sycophants, who took great pride when the British attended their parties. The man who was hung was one of the Lions of Gorakhpur who had instilled great fear in the British hearts. The British could never have managed to capture this brave son of Gorakhpur had he not been betrayed by his back-stabbing friend. History would remember him for his ultimate sacrifice; he laid down his life to ensure that the future generations eventually live in a free country.

In the early days, Gorakhpur was too far off from the sight of the Mughals, and thus it was inconsequential in their grand designs. It was controlled by local Rajput Rajas, who were later replaced by the Nawab of Awadh, and from there, Gorakhpur became a part of the Subah-e-Awadh (State of Awadh).

Gorakhpur was originally called Ramgarh owing to the large water body Ramgarh Taal on the outskirts. Legend has it that once this place was visited by Mughal Emperor Aurangzeb's sons, Azam and Muazzam. One of the places in the area was named Azamgarh and Ramgarh was renamed Muazzamgarh. It was later that the place came to be known as Gorakhpur because a large number of followers of Baba Gorakhnath, a prominent Hindu saint of later years, lived here.

This small town came under direct British control in 1803. It was nestled close to Nepal, in the United Province, which later became Uttar Pradesh. Compared to other places, there was peace and prosperity all around. The land was fertile, promising food for everybody. Nepal was not too far off, so there was an influx of natives from that country, who ventured with for greener pastures in the town. They were hard-working, honest and hence were in great demand. Since they came from the hill, they were nicknamed Pahari, or from the Pahar or hill. Their honesty and valor got recognition from the British and it resulted in the creation of a separate Gorkha regiment in the army.

Gorakhpur was too far from Delhi to be plundered by the invading armies entering the country from the Khyber Pass, but in spite of poor road connectivity and overgrown jungles, this place was often infiltrated by the Gorkhas from Nepal and the Banjaras from other neighbouring places. It was around 1803 that one of the Nawabs ceded Gorakhpur to the British East India Company.

People of Gorakhpur had a penchant for stories, especially from Lucknow, the land of the Nawabs. Those stories were always juicy and were full of fantasies revolving around begums, nawabs and concubines, a permanent fixture of the colourful life there. Gorakhpur also had its share of such stories with its own flock of zamindar and raees, who were not averse to the lifestyle that was thriving in Lucknow and other places at that time, but those stories were not that magnificent and interesting.

The story of Begum Hazrat Mahal, the wife of Nawab Wajid Ali Shah, reached Shakir's father by word of mouth. One day, Shakir heard his father talking to one of his close friends, Chand, during an afternoon siesta. 'Jumrati kah raha tha ki who mahal mein kothe se layi gayi, aur maloom hai, Nawab ne kya kiya? Usse shadi kar lee, shaadi kar liya us kothe se layi ladki se, aur unko Mahakpari naam diya. Kya naam diya.'(Jumrati was saying that she was brought to the palace from the brothel, and do you know what the Nawab did? He married her! Married the one who was brought from the brothel, and gave her the name Mahakpari! What a name.)

After noticing that he had everyone's attention, Chand continued, 'Boojho kya? Jab Angrez se ladai chid gayee, woh ek sherni ki tarah ladi, aur unki hi koshish se Nawab sahib ka beta Birjis Raj gaddi pe baith saka, nahin to sab chala gaya tha. Nawab khud kisi kaam ke nahin the.' (Guess what? When the battle with the British broke out, she fought like a lioness, and because of her effort, the Nawab's son Birjis was put on the throne, otherwise all was gone. The Nawab himself was good for nothing.) While saying this, Chand made a sour face to show how much he hated the Nawab.

Gangoo stood nearby, shaking his head in agreement.'Wahi cheez Jhansi mein bhi hui. Begum ki tarah Rani bhi bête ke liye lad rahi thi.' (The same thing happened in Jhansi also. Like the Begum, Rani was also fighting for the son.)

Teerath, an old man who had been listening to this conversation from a distance, added his wisdom. He shook his head and said, 'Pata hai, dono hi mein, jis beton ke liye who ladein, khud unke bête bhi nahin the.' (You know, in both cases, the sons for whom they fought were not even their own sons.)

For Phool, who was lazily lying on the cot and listening to everything with a visible distaste, the gallant battles held no interest. He was only interested in those parts of the story where the kotha and the tawaif were mentioned. He wanted to ask more about that kotha in Lucknow from where the begum was transported into the pristine palace, but realised that Chand today was not in a mood to talk about 'silly things'. Shakir's father was pondering over the cunning of the British. 'Poora mulk tabah kar diya. Hum Hukmaraan se ghulam ban gaye.' (Destroyed the whole country—from being rulers we became slaves.) And he was not wrong in saying so.

There was another piece of news from Lucknow which was bothering Shakir's father since the night before. What he heard still echoed in his ears, making him shudder.'Jaante ho, Maulvi Baqar ko tope ke munh se baandh ke udha diya.' (You know, Maulvi Baqar was shot by being tied to the mouth of the cannon.) He had never met or heard of this maulvi before, who was the editor of an Urdu newspaper in Lucknow, but his heart still bled for him.

The people in Gorakhpur were not left untouched by the happenings of the mutiny in Delhi. They participated in their own way by burning a few police stations along with the bungalow of one of the joint magistrates. There were many homes clandestinely participating in the symbolic sending and receiving of the chapatis, which was the signal of readiness for the uprising or resentment that was brewing in the areas closer to Delhi.

The situation in Gorakhpur became explosive in June, and martial law was imposed in the town. Many local rajas supported the rebels. Prominent among them were the ones from Narharpur and Satasi along with many others who proclaimed the end of the British rule. But it was not that easy. The East India Company was able to crush the rebellion with the help from the ruler of Nepal. In this context, the name of Mohammad Hasan, the Nazim of Gorakhpur, and his Deputy, Musharraf Khan, who were the leaders of the rebels, could not be relegated. Their names do not find place in history books, but their sacrifices were no less than by the others. The ultimate sacrifice of these Lions of Gorakhpur would be remembered by the generations to come.

Because of the distance and lack of communication, the happenings in Delhi and elsewhere had no bearing on the day-to-day life of the people in remote villages. Most of them were not even aware that the last Mughal emperor, Bahadur Shah Zafar, was sent to exile or to the kaala-paani, as it was popularly called then. Mothers there were still telling their children stories of the grand lifestyle of Dilli ka Badshah, at the time, when most likely, the king was penning his famous verses 'Lagta nahin hai dil mera ujde dayar mein.'(My heart doesn't bode well in this deserted place.)

This type of news would first come to the higher-ups through the harkaras or the post carriers, but the higher ups were selective in suppressing the news that could damage the status quo. This is how they were trained; trained to maintain the status quo. The country was not prepared for the uprising, and the mutiny which could have changed the course of history, unfortunately, became a damp squib. This provided the British new zeal by which they started pursuing their goal with renewed fervour.

The general populace in Gorakhpur, who were not accustomed to the change, started noticing differences in the environment around them. For the simple at heart like them, it was not easy to comprehend. The white-skinned British were occasionally spotted in Kalepur and Civil Lines areas, and their sighting was generally adored by the locals, who were impressed by their clothes, sophistication, and above all, by the colour of their skin.

The women would converse among themselves behind their pallus, 'Ekdum safed hote hain. Doodh ki tarah.' (They are totally white, like milk.) Another woman lifted her veil and with her eyes fixed to the ground, shyly added, 'Aankhen neeli thi.' (The eyes were blue.) They looked at each other in total amazement. Then they all started laughing and giggling, hiding their red cheeks behind their pallus, feeling a queer thumping in their heart, as if they had committed a crime by looking into the eyes of the British.

Once the British came in direct contact with the locals, the true intentions of these people surfaced. The ones who were appointed to far flung and less significant places like Gorakhpur, were of low order in Britain's social hierarchy. The influential ones got themselves appointed to plump positions in big cities like Delhi, Calcutta and Lucknow. Devoid of any position of influence back home, those posted in Gorakhpur were surprised to see how they had become celebrities in the eyes of the local denizens overnight. They started to enjoy their new-found status. From being ordinary citizens back home, now they were the aqaas or the ruler to the local Indians. No wonder, they were basking in glory and were rightly singing in unison, 'Long live the King and the Queen'.

Gorakhpur started to develop and the development came with a price tag. The open spaces were getting scarce because more and more houses were being built along with roads, schools, hospitals and parks. The rich, who in the past did not care much about what they possessed, became more careful and attentive about their assets. There were big palatial houses with modern amenities owned by some, but the rest of the crowd was still living in the dark ages. Their needs were scant and they were content with whatever they had.

Shakir had heard plenty about the zamindar's haveli, which had a toilet where the arrangement was such that you have to sit, like you sit on a chair, and defecate, rather than squat on the floor to do it. The general populace was still using the outside fields to defecate and the women had to go really early to avoid gazing eyes.

Often Shakir would stop at a well-built and well-kept two-storey high pucca house in his neighbourhood. There he had heard that scores of people sit upon the floor on straw mats and write the verses from the Holy Gita on sheets of paper, which would later be bounded together into a book, to be delivered to the temples and other places, far and near.

One fine day, the chowkidar allowed him to go inside the building. It was the first time in his life he saw books in Hindi, stacked on rugged wooden shelves and ready to be delivered. Later, his father told him that the Gita is sacred to the Hindus, and it is about the pre-historic battle Mahabharata, where Hindu Lord Krishna gave divine guidance to the Hindu king Arjuna about worldly affairs, when the latter was in a dilemma whether to fight with his own people or not. It may be a pre-historic tale, but Shakir was soon going to realise that it was not simply a tale; it is one of the harsh realities taking place even today, but it seldom gets acknowledged, the way it got identified in the Gita.

Earlier, the only book Shakir ever saw was the Qur'an, which was wrapped in embroidered silk cloth and was kept high up in a taaq or a cornice in his house. He noted that his mother would often touch the book with devotion and reverence. Not every house was fortunate enough to own a copy of the Qur'an in those days. The Qur'an in Shakir's house was brought as dowry by his mother, when she married his father. Shakir's mother kept on telling him that one day he would be able to read it, but for that he first had to go to the nearby madrasa in the mosque to be taught by Maulvi Sahib.

Shakir's house was better than all the other houses in the neighbourhood. It had more than one room with large open spaces in the middle and in the back of the house, a veranda or a corridor, and a small room, the bawarchi khana, which was used for cooking the meals. In most of the other houses in the vicinity, the food was cooked in a corner in the veranda.

At a stone's throw away from Shakir's house lived another weaver family, whose son Anwar was of Shakir's age. Anwar's father used to come to Shakir's house often, and sometimes his clothes had blood stains because for extra income they used to zibah or slaughter animals as per Islamic rituals. It was part of Shakir's daily chores to go to their house and buy meat. Their house was dilapidated and always smelt of urine, maybe because of the live animals which were kept inside. The animals used to roam around the neighbourhood and would often wander to the nearby Lal Diggi which was acres of open land with a big pond in the middle.

Next to the Lal Diggi was a little plot of land, where Shakir's father harvested vegetables. Shakir was not allowed to go to the other side because of the river Rapti that flowed in between. This river brought the early settlers to Gorakhpur, who built their houses near the bank. There was a huge dam or bandha, as the local people used to call it, which ensured that when the river swelled during monsoon the water did not enter the town. Near the plot of land where they harvested vegetables was the famous, or rather infamous, Moti Jail. Shakir often found his father staring at the jail building with sad eyes. Most likely, those were the moments he visualised the atrocities which were committed by the British.

Shakir's mother was ambitious and she wanted her husband to make extra efforts to ease the burden she faced in running the household. She would occasionally say to him, 'Aap Angrezon se mila jula kariye.' (You should meet the English people.) Her husband would simply smile at her request. On the surface, he was happy and content with his simple lifestyle, but in his heart, he was troubled.

This time Shakir's father replied to his wife, 'Tijarat karne aaye, dheere-dheere poora mulk nigal liya.' (They came to do business, gradually swallowed the whole country.) Shakir pretended to sleep because he was curious to find out what went on between his father and mother at night. His friends were always full of 'weird' stories about the nocturnal activities of their parents which ended in a variety of ways, sometimes in sobbing, moaning, and often in screaming. So far, Shakir had nothing unusual to tell his friends.

Often Shakir's father would murmur to his wife his desire to rebel in quiet tones, but would not dare say it to anybody else, because he was afraid that his words could reach 'Angrezon ke pitthuon tak' (cronies of the English people). One night, Shakir overheard his father telling his mother that all the big and rich people of the town were hand in gloves with the British. After the mujra, or the dance parties, they entertained them. Shakir could not hear what else his father said because he heard his mother saying 'lanat lanat'(shame shame) in disbelief.

Shakir's mother would not give up so easily. One time, she forced his father to get out of the house, and find someone who would take him to the Angrez. There were many who had previously boasted about being friends with the British, but when the time for action came, they all slipped away. Finally, he was able to find a distantly related peshkar or a junior clerk named Ghoore, and together they mustered some courage and ventured out on their unclear mission. As they were passing by the Miyan Bazaar on their way to the katchehri or the District Court, they were stopped at the front gate of the kotwali by the sentry.

The sentry looked at them and asked, 'Kahan jaa rahe ho?' (Where are you going?) His voice was friendly but heavy. The men looked at each other and answered sheepishly, 'Katchehri mein kuch kaam tha.' (We had some work at the court.) But before he could complete his sentence, a horse carriage went by and entered the gate. The sentry looked at them, as if to ask whether they knew who was in the carriage.Together they nodded their heads to answer in the negative. The sentry barked at them in disbelief, 'Arey! Miyan Sahib ko nahin jaante?' (Oh, you don't know Miyan Sahib?)

The men were surprised to see Miyan Sahib on a regular day like that because for the general public, Miyan Sahib would only be seen during the first ten days in the month of Muharram, and during that time, the whole city would flock and congregate to the specific routes to get a glimpse of the Miyan Sahib. Ghoore would have loved to see Miyan Sahib, but deep in his heart he resented the fact that during the happenings of 1857, Miyan Sahib's father penned long-winded commendations of the British rulers, and even compiled them in a book titled *Kashful Bhaghavaat Gorakhpur*. Scared to say anything aloud, he murmured to himself, 'Ghaddar' (traitor).

On returning home, when his wife asked him about the meeting, Shakir's father told her with a heavy heart that he was not able to meet any Angrez, because they were praying. She liked the Angrez because they went to church and prayed. Her face brightened up instantaneously. She was right in asking her husband to meet them. She adjusted her dupatta on her head, and said with conviction, 'namaaz padh rahe.' (They were doing namaaz.) 'Dekho kitne achche hain ye log, namaaz bhi padhte hain.'(See, how good they are; they even pray.)

The husband, in spite of being in a difficult situation, could not hold his smile. Suddenly, his laughter boomed in the verandah. He had not laughed in a long time.

SHAKIR WAS growing fast. He was of a medium build, sturdy and was different from the other kids in the neighbourhood. Being the eldest in the family brought many privileges along with plenty of responsibilities to shoulder, and one of them was to run errands to buy things his mother needed to run the household like sugar, milk, thread and needles.

Shakir never liked shopping because often he got lost in the maze of the lanes that would take him to the nearest market in the Urdu Bazaar. The best part of shopping would come to him in the end when he had to add up the amount to pay the shopkeeper for all the things that he bought.

Shakir was good with numbers, and was adept at recognising the coins which were in use those days. He always did the math in his mind, and would state the total cost loudly before the shopkeeper could do it on paper, much to the dislike of the latter. He almost screamed, 'Paanch aana'. (It is five aana.)

Shakir hated the days when he would get lost in the labyrinthine lanes after shopping and would be late for school.

The rule was simple; if you are late to school, you would not get to sit near the teacher. He wanted to sit in the front row, on the rugged and worn out carpet because he disliked the back rows. He wanted to be in the forefront.

The paathshala was right in front of the Lal Diggi. The teacher there was a fat and jovial pundit, who was well respected by all. The respect was not because of the knowledge which he possessed, but it was simply because he was from the highest caste in the Hindu caste hierarchy. He was a Brahmin.

Shakir noticed that there were many kids who were not allowed inside the couple of rooms which essentially formed the school at that time. These urchins were generally in rags, dark in complexion, and would always play among themselves on the street while their parents would go out to do some strange work, which they called 'kamaane gaye' (gone to earn). They were human scavengers and they cleaned human excrement in the latrines, which they collected, and then carried on their heads for disposal. As per the written and unwritten rule, these people were not to be touched. One day, Shakir's classmate Ramu told him that his mother got very upset when she learnt that there were mussalmans studying in the school too.

'Are you a mussalman?' Ramu had asked Shakir almost accusingly. But before he could get a chance to answer, Punditjee had entered the class. Ramu later told Shakir that he was warned by his grandfather not to get close to the mussalmans because they were dirty, quarrelsome and they ate cows. 'Do you eat cows?' He asked Shakir.

The paathshala was a privilege of the rich and affluent while a whole lot of half-naked urchins scampered outside the school walls, only dreaming to cross that boundary and learn what was being taught behind those sacred walls. There were some who rubbed in their status in the faces of others. There was one kid, Jamuna Das, who would come to school in a tam-tam, a horse driven cart. He was the son of Bhagwan Das, a money lender who had a jewelry business in the nearby Urdu Bazaar, next to the grand mosque which was built by Mughal emperor Aurangzeb. Jamuna was lean and thin, and apart from the cart driver, he was always escorted by a servant who waited outside, holding tiffin, which generally resembled a five-course meal, along with ghee in a bottle, mango pickle on the side, and milk separately in a glass.

During those days, the boundary wall at the Lal Diggi was under construction. Shakir's friend Anwar, whose father had some influence with the contractor, occasionally worked there as a labourer. Shakir always envied Anwar; even at that age Anwar was earning half a paisa as a daily wage. To him, Anwar was rich and Shakir wanted to be rich too.

One bright day, Shakir joined the crowd of the daily labourers who would gather at the whole sale market Sahibganj. In the wee hours of the morning, the place would become a joint where all skilled and semi-skilled workers would gather to be hired and escorted by the contractors to the job sites for work. It was getting close to noon, and to Shakir's disbelief, nobody offered him a job that day.

Shakir often found himself on the horns of a dilemma. He was torn between his desire to earn money and to study. He wanted to do it all. In fact, he seemed to be in a great hurry. One night he confessed to his mother his deepest fears when he said, 'Munna was telling me that Muslims get only one life. There is so much to do in such a short time.'

Shakir's mother was astonished to see his ambition, and she simply smiled. The next day, she told Shakir's father admirably about what she had heard their son say. The old man was always busy in making ends meet for his family, and hence like every other time, paid no heed to what was going on inside the house.

Shakir literally burned the midnight oil to go through his books and often was found outside the house under the street light reading whatever he could lay his hands on. People stopped to look at him to say, 'Arey beta, jakar so jao, bare hokar deputy collector banna hai kya jo itni mehnat kar rahe ho?' (Oh son, go and sleep, do you want to be the deputy collector when you grow up, and is that why you are working so hard?)

Shakir did not even know who the deputy collector was, but had often heard this word when the elders talked. It must have been some very important thing to be. One day, no longer having the patience, he asked his father, 'Abba, who is a deputy collector?' His father looked at him, but before he could tell him anything about the Imperial Civil Services which recruited candidates to become a deputy collector, there was a big rumbling outside. There were two well-built men wearing some kind of uniform with a distinct turban on their heads and with staffs in their hands.

One of them seemed arrogant and was in a great rush. He saluted, 'As'SalaamAlaikum'. Shakir's father nodded as if he was not doing it by choice, but by some mechanical means. This was a routine. Every now and then the staff from the zamindar's office would come and they would pay them the lagaan or taxes. His father faithfully kept aside the money that he needed to pay the zamindar. As a matter of fact, he would take great pride when the staff would visit his house for that purpose. His wife would often remind him to go and pay respect to the zamindar sahib, because by not doing so he may be considered rude. She had often seen how people were mistreated by the zamindar's staff or the karinde, as they were called locally. Generally, the local denizens were timid and would shiver on the arrival of these karinde.

Every locality in the town was demarcated, and was put under a zamindar responsible for collecting the taxes from the inhabitants. Besides collecting taxes, they also poked their noses in everything that mattered. Apart from being the ears and the eyes of the higher ups to pass information, they were also responsible for indoctrinating the masses by creating fear to curb any revolt against the system.

With the arrival of the British, modern education was slowly catching the fancy of everybody. The zamindar was skeptical about the awareness that education would bring amongst the populace and was afraid that it could become contagious. He had a firm opinion about education. He was aghast when his munshi told him about Shakir's desire to study.

At that time, education was not for everybody. Though schools were being built, not everyone was welcome in them. One such school was being started by an ambitious Muslim scholar, who had just returned from vilayat, or England. His ambition was to build the 'Oxford of the East', to educate the Indians and consequently, to help the British run the country. He would scoff at the very idea of admitting people of low origins to the school because it was for the nobles only.

Everyone else was encouraged to limit themselves to the study of the religion in the madrasa only. The intelligent ones among them were patronised to memorise the Qur'an and become a hafiz. In fact, a veiled message was put out that rather than getting further education, if Shakir wanted to study, he could 'become a hafiz and ensure that his parents could also go to heaven'. Here, religion was selectively and quickly brought out and factored into worldly affairs, of course for convenience as usual.

Who the nobles were, and who people of low origins were, was not demarcated clearly amongst the Muslims, as it was documented in the Hindu scriptures.

The answer was provided by the Prophet Mohammad in his last sermon, but there were many who ignored it conveniently, to establish their supremacy over their fellow Muslim brethren.

The Prophet was very clear when he stated, 'An Arab has no superiority over a non-Arab and a white man has no superiority over a black man, except by piety and good actions.' But this message of the Prophet got lost in the Indian subcontinent, where some clamoured to be more equal than the others. It was sad but true.

DEVOID OF any land ownership, Shakir's father was an artisan. He was clueless about his roots, almost like everyone else, because his ancestors had not told him much about family history. One of his grand uncles was a Sufi saint and was nicknamed Chini Baksh Baba because of his Mongolian features. His uncle dealt in some business in garments. He would occasionally walk to the nearby hamlet of Basti, a small town near Gorakhpur, to buy cotton durries and would also visit far-flung Bhadohi once a year to buy fancy carpets. He would sell them at Khichri ka Mela, at the local temple, or at the wedding of Baale Miyan, a local festival in Gorakhpur. He would also buy bed sheets, which were made painstakingly on handlooms by the weavers in the old city, and would take them to the nearby village Maghar, and sell them at the shrine of mystic poet Kabir. For Shakir, the business was always good during the month of Muharram, which was a prominent festival in Gorakhpur, celebrated with zeal and fervour under the patronage of Miyan Sahib.

Nawab Zakir Ali Khan was a powerful zamindar of the eastern part of the United Province. In his possession was the handwritten farman or the royal decree from the last Mughal Emperor, Bahadur Shah Zafar, granting him thousand acres of land in this region. His father had the distinction of being the only warrior from this region who reached Delhi, before the failed mutiny. His father had impressed the sulking emperor, who requested him to return back and salvage whatever he could lay his hands on. The emperor could foresee that the worst would soon come, so he wanted to reward his trusted and loyal protégé by letting him escape to avoid the inevitable extinction.

High boundary walls hid the nawab's palatial house. His wife traced her roots to Saudi Arabia, and in social gatherings, she cleverly brought up the topic to prove her relationship to the Prophet Mohammad's daughter. 'We are Syed; our lineage is from Rasool.' She would proclaim proudly that she was very particular about not marrying amongst non-Syeds or others because that, in her opinion, would pollute the future generations. It was sad, but true, that because of her unconventional views, two of her sister-in-laws could not get married.

The sisters had crossed the prime of their youth and were lonely and frustrated. The younger one had started her own school in the back of the compound, whereas, the elder one, who was shrewd and business-minded started looking after the family's farming dealings. She later learnt that she could not claim the farmland, which was in her father's name, as her own. As per the local zamindari laws, daughters, unlike sons, could not inherit the agricultural land. Her control on the land became the cause of disagreement to many; especially her brothers. She failed to understand why could the daughters not inherit agricultural land from their fathers? Her brother made her understand the vast difference between his inheritance and hers and blamed it all on the Islamic laws of inheritance. She did not like what she heard from her brother, but she kept quite because she was always taught that one should not ask questions, especially in the matter of religion.

The zamindar's eldest brother Imtiaz Ali's family was facing difficulties in running the household, because Imtiaz died while his father was still alive, and as per the Muslim laws, if the child passes away in his father's lifetime, the surviving family inherits nothing. Devoid of the inheritance, they lived in a tiny portion of the house that was falling apart because of lack of maintenance. Imtiaz's eldest daughter Sakina was a rebel, and she vocally objected to this part of the Muslim law. One day, Maulvi Sahib explained to her the logic behind this. According to him, the laws were made such to prevent the surviving widow from taking the family property to the other family, in case she remarries. He failed to convince Sakina by this logic.

Not far from the nawab's house lived Qazi Faiz Rahman, who was part of the Islamic jurisdiction. For centuries, his family delivered judgments in compliance with the Islamic Sharia. His word used to be the law, but with the arrival of the British, his role diminished, though he still was the final authority on religious matters.

The Qazi's house was an anomaly. It was in the middle of the mandi or main market, and was impressive with huge courtyards. There were orchards and fountains that surrounded the house. However, the neighbourhood was full of insignificant houses, where petty shopkeepers, hawkers, butchers and people who indulged in menial jobs lived. Apart from being crowded, few other things were common to these houses. To provide for privacy, they all had a taat ka parda or thick jute curtain on the front door, and a few domestic animals like goat and sheep tied outside. Most of the inhabitants had too many children, and because of meagre or often no wages, they all had a tough time raising them. The children were never sure about the afternoon meal. Around noon, they would touch the utensils to determine if they were warm or cold. If the utensils were cold, they would escape outside to hunt for fruits and vegetables in other people's orchards. Having three meals in a day was unheard of in that neighbourhood.

Most men of that neighbourhood had married more than once in their lifetime, which was not unusual those days. The chief reason behind it was because the short lifespan of the child-bearing mothers; child birth made them prone to infections. The birth of a child took place inside the house with the assistance of untrained midwives, often leading to complications. The other thing common in this part of the neighbourhood was the hatred for Qazi Faiz Rahman.

On every first Friday of the month, the Qazi's goons would knock the door of every house in the neighbourhood to collect money. This collection was called ghardawari, or house tax, which the local people had been paying for generations. The goons considered themselves superior or higher in caste hierarchy. This tax business was as old as anybody could remember and the Qazi considered it his 'right' to collect it from the so-called people of low origins. Like Hindus, the Muslims in the Indian subcontinent also practice the caste system, but they practice it clandestinely.

The maximum ghardawari was collected from Ali Miyan's house. Ali Miyan was of short stature, a shrewd businessperson with a pleasing disposition. He often justified these taxes and would tell his son, 'This has been happening for ages, we have to pay this; we cannot be on wrong side with Qazi Sahib. Besides, don't you remember how much Qazi Sahib likes the halwa your Ammi makes?'

However, his son could not be fooled. Qazi Sahib did not care about the halwa that his Ammi cooked; Ali Miyan justified the tax out of fear of stick-wielding goons who always accompanied Qazi Sahib. One of his elder cousins told him that there was an akhada or a wrestling ring inside Qazi's compound, which was often used to thrash those who defied the centuries-old tradition of paying this tax.

The lower strata of the Muslim caste hierarchy kept their heads bent and paid these taxes grudgingly. They generally kept to themselves in matters of marriage and other social contacts and gatherings. They were allowed to pray in the same mosque with nobility, but were conscious of the fact that they could not dare to sit in the front rows. They were never told to find a place in the back row either, but were scorned, if they ever crossed that imaginary line. They were paying this tax simply because they were razeel or inferior, as they were often told.

Islam first came to Saudi Arabia in the town of Mecca in the seventh century. Initially, its influence was localised, but soon it spread to far away places. In India, the first to learn about this new religion and start following its doctrines were the tradesmen, who in search of business, crossed the Arabian Sea, and started settling in the southern tip of the Indian subcontinent. Later, more followers crossed the Khyber Pass in the northern part of Afghanistan, along with the invading armies, and populated the areas around Delhi and other nearby places. Not all Muslims in India came with those armies, but the bulk of Muslims were the local inhabitants, who converted to Islam.

They were the local Hindus, who in quest to escape the rigid caste system, embraced Islam. They had hoped that having embraced Islam, they would find equality, which was lacking in the Hindu religion. However, once in Islam, they found acceptance, but not equality to the extent that they were expecting. This forcible collection of taxes from them was a testimonial to their failed expectations.

'Not everyone came from Arabia; most of the Muslims in India are converts from Hinduism. Even Prophet and his companions got converted to Islam.'One of Ali Miyan's grand uncles had tried to explain this bit of history to him. However, there were many who took pride in their ancestry from foreign lands. They never missed a chance to rub their superiority in the faces of the Muslims in India whose ancestors had originally been Hindus.

The Qazi was taxing them because he thought it to be his legal right but like many others, he had conveniently forgotten the last sermon delivered by the Prophet, which preached equality. 'No Arab is superior to a Non-Arab.' Sadly, this message was lost in this neighbourhood of Gorakhpur, and probably elsewhere too. Qazi was the type of person who would never deter from getting his piece of flesh from the so-called people of low origins. His goons would terrify the people day and night. At night, they would mark the house, where the tax was due the next day, and during the day, about half a dozen of them would go to that marked house for collection. On one such night, they were putting a mark on Ali Miyan's door, when his son was returning from his friend's house. The son, like his father, was lean, thin, bright and studious. The son looked at them with contempt, as if to say 'not my house; not anymore.'

The next morning when the goons knocked his door, he opened the door and yelled at them in a high-pitched voice. 'Go away, we don't give taxes anymore.' The next thing he knew, strong hands caught hold of his shirt and yanked him out of his house. Vicious eyes bore into his. They were more surprised than angry, as they had never expected a rich brat like him to rebel for the kind of money that would be peanuts for his father.

Before leaving, they screamed at him, 'Tell Abba to see Qazi Sahib, or else...' They showed him a clenched fist, making sure that the message was clear but at that time the young boy was so angry that he was shaking with rage, and most likely was not in a position to hear what they said.

Ali Miyan was summoned to the courtyard immediately, where he apologised on behalf of his son, and to avoid further trouble, he happily paid a year's tax in advance.

The son felt betrayed by his father. He could not forgive his father, and one quite night, he along with his family left that neighbourhood and his father's house, to live with his father-in-law. Yes, his father-in-law, Shakir, was living up to the reputation of being on the front row not only of his school, but every where else he went.

EVERYTHING THAT Shakir touched would become gold. Even the dirt he put his hand on became gold. He had the Midas touch. He acquired his wealth the old fashion way. He earned it. Those were the times when opulence travelled to the ones based on their proximity with the establishment, or via the centuries-old golden rule of networking. The ones who did not have contact with the right kind of people placed in high positions were not going to rise beyond a certain threshold. That is how wealth was being distributed. You have to know the right people, even if it implied licking the heels of the rulers, otherwise there was no other way.

In Delhi, if you are standing in the Mughal Durbar, it mattered, whereas in faraway places like Gorakhpur, being in good terms with the zamindar carried weight. Territories were demarcated, and were allotted to zamindars who subdivided it to their favourites. These favourites were responsible for collection of taxes, and passing it to the next in order. In this scheme of things, it was unlikely that an 'out of loop' ordinary person like

Shakir would ever be able to accomplish much. It would take the extraordinary genius in him to break the barrier to stand out and excel, and that is what he did.

Shakir had great business acumen and was swift in working his way up. He was fearless and had the ability to influence people and make friends. He was good in reasoning and in advocating his case. Above all, he was a man of honour. He was kind, honest, soft spoken, scholarly and trustworthy. His ability to pass high school was another feather in his cap. There were not many who managed to pass high school in those days. Education was of not much use either, unless you go beyond the school level and opt for graduation. The high profile posts were not for grabs for everyone; unfortunately, it was the lineage or the family connection that was essential to secure a post. For the public, it was not more than middle school or elementary school education, which was adequate to aspire to a low clerical job. For high profile posts, graduation and shijra or family tree mattered. Someone who did not belong to a noble family had little or no chance of becoming a deputy collector.

By now, it was common knowledge that the British were in India for a long haul. They were very particular about infrastructure and good governance, and India needed it all. The country was on the move. There was a need for everything, everywhere; from railway tracks, roads and bridges to government offices and that was true for Gorakhpur too.

For anybody who was willing to put in hard work, there were many opportunities. Of course, competition was scant, because majority of the people were not enterprising enough to take advantage of situations. They were happy in their own cocoons. The sky became the limit for the one willing to walk the extra mile, and Shakir was determined to walk as far as he could. And he did. He believed in climbing, even after reaching the top.

Shakir, who had once not been able to find a construction worker's job for himself when he was a young boy at the labour market in Sahibganj, was soon building government offices, hospitals and schools. His father's attempt to meet the angrez failed, but he was signing land pattas or leases with the British officers, and soon his children were dressing like the British. One of his sons was on his way to vilayat to get higher education. His house started to resemble the palatial haveli of the zamindar. Since, for most of the time in his life he was swimming against the stream, he knew its ferocity. Experiences in life had taught him how to overcome it.

Now with money in his pocket, Shakir's horizon widened and he ventured out for other things. Inside the country, the call for independence had caught the fancy of all, whereas outside the country, the world was engulfed in a war. The war hastened the decision of the British government to exit from India. Two lean Gujaratis, Gandhi and Jinnah, were calling the shots; one was harping on the division of the country, whereas the other was advocating a united India. The 'Two Nation Theory' of Muslim League was gaining ground amongst the Muslim elites, and the Congress Party was faltering to counter it and to make inroads into the heart and mind of the common Muslims.

The upper echelons in the Muslim society were under the spell of the Muslim League, and were dreaming about their rise to prominence in the new nation, Pakistan that will be created solely for them. For Muslims in India, it was a period of great confusion. The Muslim League was a party of the elites. Shakir could have easily hid himself under the garb of money and influence, which he had earned, and could have joined the club of the elites very easily. However, he could not forget his humble roots. Hence, he decided against joining the bandwagon of the Muslim League, and made a conscious decision to side with a new outfit that was slowly emerging from the east. It was the Momin Conference, which was the result of century's long oppression of the Momin Biradari, his own community.

One of the goals of the Momin Conference was to correct the un-Islamic razeel shareef divide. The razeel were the so-called Muslims of lower status, whereas shareef were the self-appointed noble or higher class Muslims.

In the long struggle for the freedom of India, there are many stories that fell through the cracks, and the saga of the Momin Conference is one amongst them. It represented the voice of the oppressed and the downtrodden amongst the Muslim masses. It was the party of the artisans; people who were in the lower rungs of Muslim society, who were at the receiving end from the British Empire, as well as their fellow Muslims.

The East India Company was in quest to sell its products from Manchester and Liverpool. It had determined to destroy the Indian garment industry; as a result, the weavers or momins who were the backbone of this industry, were facing British ire. They were also the victims of the oppression that was meted to them by the upper caste Muslims. Hence, there was a need for these beleaguered and downtrodden people to unite and fight for their rights, which they did.

Momin Conference was formed in 1925 and participated in

the freedom struggle along with the Congress party. It opposed the Muslim League by proving that 'all' Muslims in India did not subscribe to the Two Nation Theory, which unfortunately resulted in the partition of the country. Probably, Shakir was at the right place, at the right time. His association with the Momin Conference provided him a platform to counter the sinister designs of the Muslim League.

Against this background, the special tax fiasco happened and affected the life of Shakir's son-in-law. Friends advised him to send a warning to Qazi and get it all settled by brute force, of which he now was quite capable. The insult meted out to Shakir's son-in-law was not a laughing matter, and the air was tense with the need to take revenge. There could be a war that, if it happened, could be the first 'class struggle' between the haves and have-nots of Gorakhpur.

That night Shakir's house was teeming with people. Thanks to his hold on the trading community, hundreds of loyalists gathered there to show their solidarity, and were prepared to dic for honour. They kept the markets closed for three straight days.

Those who had assembled were from the lower strata of the Hindu and Muslim societies. They were the atishbaaz (firework makers), bhand (jesters), bhishti (water carriers), gaddi (grazer), mirasi (musician and singers), qasab (butchers), julaha (weavers), darzi (tailors), dhuniya (cotton carders), kunjra (green grocers), manihars (bangle/bracelet makers), saiqalgar(metal sharpeners), rangrez (dyers and cloth printers), kumbhars (potters), nai or hajjam (barbers), teli (oil crushers) and what not? They all had one thing in common; they either were paying taxes, or were discriminated against or looked down upon by the so-called noblemen.

They came to witness what very well could be the greatest event of their lifetime. The roads were getting clogged-up with the number of people who continued to come to Shakir's house. People were coming from everywhere to be a part of this struggle.

Ram Surat Prasad, the leader of the 'untouchables', or the ones who were out of the Hindu caste hierarchy, was quick to find common ground. His fellow people had suffered the worst type of discrimination, compared to what had just happened in Gorakhpur. If people in Gorakhpur could mobilise, then so could they. He had met Shakir a few times but only from a distance, and it took him by surprise when Shakir once asked him to come and sit near him. He had looked at Shakir in disbelief. Nobody had ever asked him to sit next to them. Therefore, when he learnt of the situation Shakir's family was in, he decided to go and support him in his hour of crisis. They gathered outside the village, where dozens of others were waiting for him. They started to march towards the city, but were stopped by the police, who dispersed them with force. The police was conspiring with the zamindar and the nobility. The people were angry and frustrated; but they returned. This was not the first time they had to retreat, but they lacked the courage exhibited by Abdullah and his associates, when they torched the police station in the nearby villages of Chauri-Chaura.

MANY OF the associates of Ram Surat Prasad had heard the story of Chauri-Chaura, the twin villages near Gorakhpur, from their parents. At that time, Chauri-Chaura was the embodiment of all that was going wrong in the countryside. The land was fertile, but it did not help the farmers because they did not own the land. They were tenants and they had to pay hefty taxes to the zamindar, who kept his share and passed the rest to the government's coffers.

It was not only the atrocities of zamindars and moneylenders that were at its peak; there were other calamities like drought and diseases like plague which added to the unease and trepidation among the public. This unrest had not just taken over Chauri-Chaura but everywhere in different regions of the province. It was spreading at a rather fast pace, but was failing to accumulate the critical mass, which was needed to affect the power structure of those days. This turbulence in the environment was ready to be streamlined, and the flow could have been channelised for the desired impact, but there was no leader to take advantage of the opportunity to mobilise the masses. Most of the leaders, who were diminutive in stature, focused on short-term gains such as membership to the legislative councils. Even the Congress party was uncertain about the long-term strategy at that point. They most likely were comfortable in terms of a life side by side with the British, rather than a life without the British at the helm.

The unrest simmering amongst farmers and other marginalised sections of the society finally became the catalyst and as a result, the movement for complete freedom from British finally took off. The incident at Chauri-Chaura added fuel to the fire and there was no turning back. From here, the movement for the freedom of India moved forward with added zeal and full vigour.

During those times, the British were helped by feudal lords and nobility who were getting assistance from nobody else, but the local residents. Unfortunately, these locals chose to forget their Indian origins and were eager to bend backwards to show loyalty to both masters, British as well as the land owners, whose sole aim was to squeeze the maximum from the poor farmers to fill their treasuries. Once they plundered the farmers, they looked for other prey, like artisans and craftsmen, who were making household items to sell in the nearby markets, or which could be exchanged for food or other essentials.

These craftsmen were having a rather hard time. On one hand, their cottage industry was methodically crippled to make way for machine-made products from England that were now finding their way even in villages and small towns, and to add insult to the injury, they were forced to part with their dwindling earnings on the pretext of miscellaneous taxes that were heaped on them. In other words, they were funding the Great War in

Europe in which the British Empire was a major participant.

It was under these circumstances that the inhabitants of Chauri-Chaura had gathered at the village chaupal or meeting place. They all had their own story, which was full of woes, and was not pleasant at all.

Hooligans from the local moneylender, who was looking for his sood or interest, ransacked the gawala or milkman's house. The gawala had taken the money to buy a cow. Unfortunately, he was not able to return the money back because there was no milk left for him to sell at the market after it was routinely taken by force to the thana. To punish him, the ruffians took away the cow as well as his daughter, who was barely in her teens.

There were many other untold stories waiting to be heard. A police constable had burned down poor Razzaq's handloom because he refused to stop making bed sheets, which he was planning to sell at the mela or local fair in Gorakhpur.

Raj dhobi had not been paid by Bare Sahib or his British Master for about an year. His life was worse than bonded labour. His son was thrown in the well because they thought that he was stealing mangoes from their orchards. Luckily, he survived, but since after being rescued from the well, he started walking with a distinct limp in his right leg.

One day, some farmers were summoned to the police station and were beaten by the head constable because it was reported that their wives were secretly 'hoarding' some rice to take to their maika or father's house to help their starving parents.

The kewat or the boatman's boat was also pushed in the well when he refused to give the choicest catch of the day to Rajaji, the local king, for free. Anger simmered in all of them, but they were patient people. They knew that these things, which were there for generations, simply do not just go away. Nevertheless, they were hopeful and it was this hope that had brought them to the chaupal in the wee hour of morning, discussing their anguishes that they had not shared with anybody until now. Their hope came from their belief that times were changing and the country was on the move. Their inspiration came from one man who was responsible for bringing together the entire country in the wake of such trying times, and that man was Gandhi.

It was in 1921 that Gandhi had a very successful meeting in the open field at Bale-ka-Maidan, near Bandha in Gorakhpur. Maulana Mohammad Ali Jauhar, one of the prominent leaders of the Khilafat Movement, also addressed this meeting. The large crowd, which had assembled, were absolutely captivated by them. The meeting was arranged by the local unit of the Congress party, with help from a young Urdu poet, Raghupati Sahay, a scholarly intellectual, who had resigned from the prestigious post of Deputy Collector to serve his country.

Gandhi wanted to re-employ the tools of non-violence in India that had worked for him in South Africa. However, it is debatable whether applying the same tools could have produced the same results as in South Africa because India was a huge country and people were running out of patience.

In Chauri-Chaura, the people were eagerly awaiting for some miracle to take away their pain and fears. One night, in a nearly dilapidated house, a mother could be heard consoling her children. She told them about Bapu or Gandhi. Meena, her little daughter, asked back in anticipation, 'Bapu will fight these people, and they will go back?' Then she hurriedly added, 'Kab aayenge woh?' (When he will come?)

The little girl who looked much older for her age was scared like everybody else. Her nervousness was not misplaced. She had recently witnessed her elder sister's abduction at the hands of hooligans from another village. Her sister had returned home the next day but she was not the same; her condition was beyond imagination, she looked horrified, and her body was betrayed. Each knock on the door made their bones tremble. They lived in perpetual fear that their lives would be disrupted forever with another knock on the door.

The story she narrated was harrowing. The ones who abducted her belonged to a powerful family of landowners, who had no respect for the law. They believed that they were above law. They were two brothers, who took turns in assaulting her sexually, and then left her to the mercy of the servants, who were no saints either and violated the girl repeatedly.

Luckily for her, one of the uncles of these brothers was a gentleman. He reprimanded his brother for the shameful deeds of his sons. It was not for the first time that they had abducted a young girl. The uncle took upon himself the task to rescue the girl and to return her to her parents. The girl was so ashamed that she wanted to die and end her miserable existence, but her mother convinced her to live, by giving her examples of other girls they knew, who had gone through similar experiences, and now were living normal lives. She tried to convince her daughter and said, 'These things do happen to the poor like us, but life goes on.'

Though it pained the mother immensely, this was her way of consoling her daughter. After all, wasn't this endurance a part of their existence? They could only blame their fate. Many were fed up of this mundane existence where they were expected to face all kinds of hardships at the hands of the British and the feudal lords. They desperately awaited freedom and wanted change. They wanted to take control of their destiny, and one amongst them was Abdullah, who had just returned to the village after attending the Congress party's session in Ahmadabad. Abdullah's ancestors were julaha or weavers, but he was a choodihaar, a bangle maker. He was not alone in his quest for freedom. There were others with him including Lal Mohammad, Bhagwan, Vikram, Rudli, Kali Charan and Dudhai. In their belly there was fire, which was fuelled by centuries' old oppression by the feudal lords.

They were the people who were pushed to the corner before, but today they were prepared to defy all logic and were ready to charge like a lion. The reason was simple; most of them were fed up by the oppression of feudal landlords and by the injustice that was meted out to them, because of caste oppression and economic deprivation in that region. They were the Lions of Gorakhpur, and they had a plan.

The volunteers led by Abdullah and others decided to hold a satyagraha, which they had planned to end at the local market. They were moving silently towards their final destination, Mundera market, where they wanted to demonstrate and do dharna against sale of liquor and tobacco. A few enthusiastic ones in the crowd were also eager to ask the daroga or the head constable, Gupteshwar Singh, the reason behind the merciless beating of one of their volunteers, Bhagwan Aheer.

This led to an altercation at the gate of the thana. The daroga hurriedly declared the peaceful march 'illegal'. This was followed by a lathi charge, which dispersed the procession, and in the ensuing confusion, many volunteers ran towards the railway tracks. In this pandemonium, few of them blew the emergency bugle and the volunteers who had reached the market place for the dharna returned.

To resist unprovoked lathi charge, some volunteers started hurling stones from the railway tracks towards the thana. In an attempt to control the situation, bullets were fired in the air. However, this did not deter the volunteers. Shouts could be heard reverberating, 'Gandhiji ke chamatkar se goli paani ban jaa rahi hai' (due to the magical power of Gandhiji, the bullets are turning into water).

These chants encouraged the volunteers and stone throwing got ferocious. Firing in the air ceased, and the police officers started firing the bullets in the direction of the crowd until they ran out of ammunitions. In minutes, there were dead bodies of the volunteers lying all over the place.

In retaliation, by sunset, the volunteers had burned down the thana with the policemen inside. This act was impulsive and was not pre-planned. The police firing had killed twenty-four volunteers on that day and in retaliation, as many as twenty-two police officers along with the daroga were killed by the mob on that fateful day of 4th February in 1922. The army was immediately deployed to crush the disquiet that was building in the region.

The entire village had gone into mourning. Meena was distraught. Her father was amongst the ones who were killed. Her hope for Gandhi to come, rescue them, and show them the way to liberation was shattered. Little did that naïve girl know that Gandhi himself was a diehard supporter of India's Hindu caste system, and unfortunately, Meena belonged to the lowest caste amongst Hindu caste hierarchy.

The village had gone silent. It was not the loss of only a few handful families; both Muslims as well as Hindus had lost someone. However, a larger picture showed that majority of people who were killed were from the lower strata of the society, and why not? They were the ones who were suffering and were protesting against the injustices on that fateful day. There was no reason for the privileged few to join the demonstration when they were enjoying their life, even if it came at the cost of others' sufferings.

The nation woke up to the jolting news the next morning, which left the whole world stunned. There were repercussions that were felt far and near. The lawmakers at Westminster in Britain were furious; and their anger did not come as surprise. After all, the burning down of the thana and the subsequent killing of the police officers was a direct attack at the imperial power which had just had the first bitter taste of the oppressed masses' angst. However, the nation was not prepared to receive the biggest surprise from Gandhi, who was visibly upset by the killing of police officers loyal to the British empire. He punished his fellow Indians by suspending the non cooperation movement, which he had earlier announced to undertake for the freedom of the country.

Some say that Gandhi was negotiating for a generous settlement with the Viceroy, and in a letter to the latter, he gave him seven days to respond, or else he would start the non-cooperation movement. The unfortunate happening at Chauri-Chaura gave him the 'opportunity' which he conveniently used to delay the noncooperation movement while waiting for the response from the Viceroy.

This was going to haunt Meena for the rest of her life.

Gandhi failed to show remorse for her father and other helpless poor who were killed in police firing. Why did he side with the police officers who shot at the innocent volunteers? To add salt on the wounds, there were few in the Congress party who openly blamed the mechanism by which volunteers were selected. They were not happy with the fact that too many people of lower castes were selected as volunteers for the procession. To many, it sounded familiar because they had heard it before. It was not the first time that the lower castes were blamed for the follies of others. In one of his books, great scholar and educationist Sir Syed Ahmad Khan had also blamed 'badzaat julahe' (low caste weavers) for the mutiny that happened in 1857.

The trial of Abdullah versus the Empire was a revelation because along with the British, it also revealed the true nature and character of feudalism in India. Not only the ones who protested against war tax, high prices and oppression, but also the ones with whom they had personal enmity and grouse were rounded up. The verdict was delivered hastily because news of uprisings from Faizabad and Barabanki were giving British officials sleepless nights, and they wanted to stir fear in the hearts and minds of Indians by this verdict to ensure that in future nobody would ever dare to think about doing a thing like this again. The incident at Chauri-Chaura shattered the confidence of the British.

The trial was onesided. As expected, verdicts were quickly delivered by session court of Gorakhpur on 9 January 1923. The verdict was unprecedented, apart from many who got life imprisonment, 172 convicts were given capital punishment, and they were only given seven days to appeal against the verdict. Appeals and mercy petitions were made, and to the dismay of the country, nineteen persons kissed the noose in different jails of the State.

The ones who were hanged were not ordinary men. The likes of Abdullah, Bhagwan, Vikram, Dudhai, Kali Charan, Lal Mohammad, Ram Swaroop, Rudli, Sahdev Kahar and many more like them had given up their lives for the sake of the country. Their sacrifice enabled us to live a free life. Who says there are no lions in this part of the country? These men were the true Lions of Gorakhpur.

They were the martyrs who were not remembered with the honour they deserved. Their names did not even make it in the margins of history books. It was shameful that the country mourned more for the death of police officers on British payrolls, who were burnt inside the police station, than for the ones who were killed in the police firing that led to the entire debacle. The country turned a blind eye to the hangings of the brave men.

Abdullah was hanged and was buried in Barabanki jail. Nobody in his house was able to sip a drop of water that day. Food was brought in by neighbours, as was customary since the deceased's family members are not in a position to cook in the hours of grief.

Abdullah's wife broke her bangles on the hard stone floor and locked herself in the only room that they had in their small house. She braced herself for the colourless life that she was supposed to lead after the death of her husband, unless she remarried. Shakir was her distant cousin, so after she was done with her iddat or the compulsory waiting period for widows, she joined a caravan that was heading to Gorakhpur. She wanted to meet Shakir. Shakir was aghast to hear her tale, but was not surprised because he had attended the meeting that was organised by the Congress party in Gorakhpur. In that meeting, farmers or volunteers who died were not even mentioned, but some funds were collected for families of the police officers who were burnt alive that day.

When Gandhi cancelled the noncooperation movement in 1922 the decision was not well received by many. Shakir knew many students who had already left schools to participate in the freedom movement; a few of his close relatives had also resigned from lowly positions which they held in government. They all felt deceived by Gandhi. Since the noncooperation movement was cancelled, zamindars were happy because now they could start collecting lagaan from farmers again.

Shakir had resolved to avoid a Chauri-Chaura in Gorakhpur, which he could see in the making.

IT WAS past midnight and Shakir's place was bubbling with energy. The latest entrants to the compound were Muslim rickshaw pullers of the town, dozens of them who came along with their Hindu counterparts. They were weary and tired of paying a hefty portion of their daily wage to the bullies who had the patronage of the so-called raees and zamindars of the society.

Along with them came weavers from nearby places like Maghar and Khalilabad, who were indebted to Shakir because he took their woes to the Momin Conference meetings on a regular basis. One of them was fed up with the atrocities meted out to him in his village. Some influential people with money, who did not even belong to the weaving class, had usurped his weaving business, leaving weavers like him to become daily labourers. Their inability to sell the final product had forced them into such submissive state. Here also, like in any other business, it was the middleman who cornered the plump share, leaving the poor weaver with almost nothing for himself. For these influential people there was a fortune to be made even in wartime because now their products, mostly army uniforms were more in demand, and payment was made by the War Chest, which at that time was bubbling with money.

It was getting dark. At Shakir's house, the servants had started cleaning the oil burning lanterns and lamps because they knew that it was going to be a long night. The muezzin from the nearby mosque gave the call for Maghrib or the evening prayer, and everybody started dispersing. The women who had that time of the month shyly withdrew to the inner quarters, while others hurriedly grabbed their prayer mats. Those who did not bother to pray became invisible in the darkness to avoid being spotted.

The mosque was full when the Imam started the prayer by raising his hands, and saying 'Allah hu-Akbar' (Allah is great). The mosque was dimly illuminated, with silver rays of moon streaming in, giving the place a serene and almost heavenly look. Tranquility filled the air once verses from the Holy Qur'an started flowing. For that moment, everyone forgot what was happening outside. For that moment, they were close to their Creator and they forgot their worries.

A small crowd had gathered outside. Among those who had gathered included two men who appeared to be out of place by the way others looked at them. One of them was draped in a blanket, while the other was wearing a long coat. They were coming straight from Miyan Sahib's palatial house, where an important meeting had just ended. The local zamindar and Jamuna Das, who once had studied in the same paathshala with Shakir, also attended this meeting. Since he showed no interest in his father's jewellery shop, Jamuna Das was sent to the prestigious Colvin Taluqdar's College in Lucknow because his parents wanted him to join the civil services, and he was now a part of the city administration. Apart from him there also was a representative from the Gorakhnath Temple, easily recogniseable in his saffron robes.

The words from temple were strict, but were full of humility. The peace and harmony of the town should not be hampered, and if asked for, the temple authority would play the role of peacemaker. Sitting in the corner was Qazi's representative. His face was pale and tired, a visible reminder of the tension brewing in the town. He had seen the agitated crowd outside, and was also getting reports from the old city and from other nearby places. There were people in nearby hamlets, who were eager to come to Gorakhpur and fight.

The kasai or butchers, who were friends to Anwar's father, were sharpening their knives with grim determination. One of them said, 'It is one's duty to die for the honour of the neighbour.' He was right. Islam teaches to help your neighbour when he is in distress. It was for the sake of that honour that those who had never ever lifted a lathi were holding one now. They were in a mood to rebel. It was their moment to be a part of history, and they did not want to miss it. This could be the story that would be carried through word of mouth to the future generations.

The personal message from Miyan Sahib was conveyed by his representative. 'Sahib thinks that fighting will only weaken us. We should settle this amicably.' He further went on and said, 'The division within us should not come out in the public. Nobody is going to benefit from all this. Our weakness will only strengthen the enemies.'

He was not done with the delivery of the message. Just he added, gravely, 'We all are brothers in Islam, and this will put the religion into great danger.' The man sitting next to him nodded his head, as if there was a clear and real danger to the religion itself that only they could look at. It was a closed-door meeting. Everything was decided amicably.

There was a compromise. Qazi will be given a breather, but for that he had to leave the town and live far away. He was willing to spend the rest of his life in Hyderabad. At least, he was given a chance to live. After the night prayer, Shakir made a very unusual decision. He looked at everybody and said, 'We are not going to fight it on the street. We will rather fight it in the court.' Not many people could understand the rationale behind it. They were all expecting passionate words of freedom and retribution from the lion, a thundering roar that would have scared everyone. However, what they heard was not a roar at all. It did disappoint many, but what they all forgot was that lions do not kill for pleasure; they only kill if it is necessary and that too for living. It was the difference in thinking on such grounds that made a king different from the others; for the king looks at a bigger canvas, and that is the reason he is the king.

In Shakir's mind, the events in Chauri-Chaura were vivid. He had not forgotten the atrocities faced by his brothers; the deafening screams of people like him still reverberated in his ears. There were many people who were hanged for burning down the police station and many more who were killed in police firing that preceded the burning of the police station. He knew the events well because Abdullah's wife had told him everything. The same could very well be repeated in Gorakhpur, and at a much larger scale. The Qazi and nobility could manipulate the system, and the poor would end up taking the bullets, as it happened in Chauri-Chaura. One has to learn from the mistakes committed and history is replete with such mistakes, and Shakir was a fast learner.

Around the globe, things were moving at a much faster pace than thought of. The world was at war. Gandhi was getting impatient. The whole country was on the move and the destination for all was complete freedom. Since India was under British Empire, it unwillingly became a party to the war, and that was not cheap either. The expenditure of war was increasing with leaps and bounds and it was up to Indians, along with others, to bear a portion of that burden. Under these circumstances, Gandhi gave a call for Quit India Movement, the purpose of which was to set up a series of non-violent ways, hopefully leading to the long-awaited Independence.

When Gandhi thundered, the nation paid full attention to his call. 'We shall either free India or die in the attempt; we shall not live to see the perpetuation of our slavery.' Everyone was ready for 'Do or Die'. Gandhi's call for 'Quit India' in 1942 woke up the country again and fuelled it one more time. The call for independence had taken a new fervour and soon engulfed every nook and corner of the country, Gorakhpur being no exception.

The concern voiced by the people of Gorakhpur had reached the power corridors. The Congress party now had its focus on this town and as a result, Nehru came to the town to address a meeting in Lal Diggi Park. The meeting went very well. The park was jam-packed. People waited for hours on the ground in the scorching heat of August to hear what the famous leader had to say; some even perched up on treetops and rooftops. Such a large gathering was proof enough that people were uniting to gain independence and this alarmed the British administration.

The District Magistrate, EV Moss, a notorious officer who was well hated in the region because of the atrocities he committed to secure funds from poor Indians to support the war that was now spreading in every part of the world, was sweating in his office. His few trusted colleagues, who were receiving updates from locals after every half an hour, accompanied him. The locals fed them information about the meeting which Nehru was addressing. They were getting conflicting reports about the number of people who were present in the meeting. The most disturbing estimate came from a barber, who claimed the crowd to be more than fifty thousand.

If that was not enough to worry about, there were also unconfirmed reports that thousands of people from the other side of the railway track, which demarcated the town into two distinct halves, were also moving towards the meeting venue. Everyone wanted to catch a glimpse of Nehru.

In the meeting, Shakir was sitting in the front row along with dozens of his friends. His volunteers provided the garlands to welcome Nehru and other dignitaries. The surging crowd gave them the hope that eventually the country will break free from the clutches of the British. The news of the warm welcome given to Nehru with garlands was leaked by mali or the gardener to the District Magistrate, who in his office was fuming every minute as the crowd surged. If he had his way, he would have chewed Shakir and spat him out, even if he had interacted with him a couple of times in the past in a friendly environment.

The list of satyagrahis or volunteers who were going to be in the forefront to oppose the British regime was prepared. The list contained Shakir's name too. The District Magistrate walked to his office with the list in his pocket and it seemed to be burning a hole there. It was high time they crushed the surging movement initiated by Gandhi, and they made a plan to do so brutally and vehemently.

The satyagrahis, clad in hand-spun khaddar, had gathered for a peaceful procession. They were marching towards the Kachehri when the police stopped them. There was no provocation from the marchers, but order from the administration was clear and simple. They have to be stopped at the point of origin.

Obeying orders of their British master, the local police charged the protestors with sticks, but it was all in vain. The satyagrahis were not willing to retreat. They had seen with aghast looks and boiling anger how Nehru was picked from their midst. At that time, they were not able to do anything to prevent it. Because of their inaction, Nehru was in jail and it bothered everybody. Their hands were tied because they were the followers of Gandhi, and they all believed in his doctrine of ahimsa or nonviolence. They would suffer pain but would not retaliate.

Many had the same feeling of guilt which burdened a fruit vendor, one of the satyagrahis, when he sobbed, 'Hum khare dekhte rahe aur Nehru ji giraftar kar liye gaye. Lanat hai hum par.' (We stood and saw and Nehru Ji got arrested. Shame on us.)Their wives chided them for being mere spectators. But Gandhi's words rang loud and clear in everyone's ears. They would not retaliate and give the upper hand to the British. The procession continued in a peaceful manner. Volunteers lined up neatly, and walked with their head held high and their faces beaming with pride. They were ready to sacrifice all they had for the freedom of their country. Loud slogans of 'Inqualab Zindabad' (Long Live Revolution) pierced the sky and the Britishers broke into a sweat.

As soon as the administration gave the order of 'laathi charge', blows from sticks started felling on everybody from all sides. The women volunteers positioned themselves in the sidelines and rushed in to drag the injured volunteers aside to provide them water. Shakir saw one woman got hit on the head while she was rescuing an elderly man.

He ran to help her. He shielded her with his body and started taking unaccounted blows from everywhere. However, he did not falter. Like a lion, he stood and guarded his turf. One of the blows from the lathi hit him directly on the head in a lethal way, and the man who had lived like a lion, died like one. His death was not in vain; it was for a greater cause, and what could be greater than dying for the country. He became a martyr.

The funeral was held behind Lal Diggi Park in the family cemetery. It was the same place where he used to play as a child while his father cultivated vegetables. In an unmarked grave lies yet another Lion of Gorakhpur.

His story may not be in any of the history books, but streets of Gorakhpur were witness to the gallantry of the man; they still recount that there once was a lion who sacrificed his life so that future generations could live in a free country. This is our part of the history and it reminds us every day what men like Shakir lost to ensure we live freely.

AHMAD HAD crossed many time zones, and during that voyage, he would have never thought that after all this, he would end up sitting in front of an old and rugged computer screen, and will be deciphering old history. After going through the crypic notes in the Backroom Diaries, he now turned to audio-visuals. He could see the Tricolour or the Indian Flag, fluttering on the screen. The Union Jack, which fluttered on prominent buildings in India during the British regime, was replaced by the Tricolour. It must have been his Dad's way of defining the moment when India became a free country. Ahmad was appreciative of his Dad's creativity, and he smiled. However, he could not smile for long, because now his eyes were itching badly. He leaned back on the chair and tried closing his eyes. In spite of his best efforts, his eyelids stayed open, and now he was staring at the fluttering Tricolour on the screen.

The hypnotic fluttering was interrupted by some commotion on the screen, as if someone was trying to find the right music that will go with this picture. Moments later after some hesitancy, the speakers strained, 'Janaganamana-adhināyaka jaya hē bhārata bhāgyabidhātā'.

'Oh! That is the National Anthem,' thought Ahmad, and to show his respect for India's National Anthem, he slowly got up from the chair he was sitting on and stood straight, and then put his right hand over his heart, as he had always done throughout his life for the American National Flag. Realisation set in that this was not his Anthem, nor the flag, and he dropped his right hand slowly to his side.

The computer screen was now wavering, and some pictures appeared and quickly disappeared from the screen. When the picture on the screen stabilised, it was a familiar scene. He could see an old house, probably somewhere in the countryside. Next to the house, there was a huge pond, which could be mistaken for a river or a stream.

'Oh! I know this place. I have seen this house in pictures. This is a picture of Dad's house in the early days,' Ahmed murmured as the grainy picture became familiar to him. An old black and white picture flashed in his mind; one of his Dad, when he was a young kid, most likely four years old, ready to go to school, standing in front of his house. The screen fluttered again. Ahmed realised that he was looking at a slideshow of old pictures that belonged to his Dad's young days when he was a skinny young boy dressed impeccably in his high school uniform.

Ahmad's throat choked and tears stung his already itchy and aching eyes. He started missing his Dad. He looked at the picture, and said, 'Dad, say something.'

As if awoken from a deep slumber, the sound that cranked out of the age-old speakers was initially distorted, but later a voice filled the room with a deep bass, a clear treble, and a rich middle range; it was his Dad's. It was a recording from a Kavi Sammelan or a poetry recital, somewhere in Manhattan at a time when Ahmad's mother was carrying him in her womb. He remembered that his mother used to tease his father about his recitation, which she said was so loud that the little baby in her womb got scared and started kicking her in the womb.Today was the first time Ahmad was listening to what his father recited that day:

'Nikat sarita pashanon pe baitha socha karta hoon.
Jeevan ke ghat'te moolyon ko har pal dekha karta hoon.
Kabhi sochta hoon jeevan hai sapna kisi kavi ka.
Tab yaad hai aata jeevan tap hai kisi tapasvi ka.
Matmaila nimnga ka jal prerna deta hai humko
Dhulta rahta hai prithvi se paap ke saare dhabbon ko.
Door kapot ka udta joda bhi shiksha deta rahta hai
Vishwa shanti ke amoolya mantra se
Raag dwesh niwaran karta hai.
Tarangin ke tat pe hain anginat vriksha sookhe se
Aur sarita ke ander bhi hain anek jeev pyase se
Aise hi aatma parmatma mein hai samayi sii.
Phir bhi aatma parmatma milan hai samasya si
Samajh nahi paata rahasya main jalte huye patange ka.
Oopar se phenke paththar ka neer mein waapas gir jaane ka.
Anurag virag ka jeevan har pal badla karta hai,
Manav ka rakt Manav ki pyas bujhaya karta hai.
Sochta hoon karan kya raag dwesh ke vyapaar ka.
Is chanbhangur jeevan mein Manav ke sanhaar ka.
Kya karan hai Manav aaj manavta ka vadh karta hai.
Sochta hoon ki woh aisa kyun karta hai?'

*Tanvir Salim*

Near the river sitting on the boulders, I ponder
I keep on watching the values of life getting diminished
Often I think life is the dream of a poet
Then I remember that life is meditation of a sage
Dull and murky water of the river inspires us
It keeps washing from the earth the spots of the sins
Far, the pair of pigeons also teaches us
By virtue of the mantra of world peace
Eliminates the hatred and animosity
On river banks, there are many trees dried up
And inside the river, there are many thirsty lives
Similarly, the soul is enmeshed in God itself
But still there is a problem in soul and God to meet
I can't comprehend the mystery of insects getting burned
The stone thrown up, why falls back in the water
Love and detachment keeps on changing all the time
Blood of human gives solace to the thirst of human
I ponder what is the reason for the business of hate and enimity
In this mortal life, the reason for the destruction of human
What is the reason that man kills humanity
I ponder why he does that

When Ahmad woke up, the image of that old house still flickered on the computer screen, but there was an aroma of morning freshness in the room.

Ahmad was ready to go deeper into the diaries. He wanted to know everything.

IT WAS in the year 1947 that India became a free country. It was a new beginning. Alam's childhood revolved around his house. He grew up in this house hearing stories of affluence of his great grandfather, Shakir. It was not simply the stories; the old grandeur of yesteryears was still in the air. This house, which his grandfather inherited from his father at one time, was a farmhouse, relatively far from the city, and was spread in a dozen magnificent acres. Every day Alam and his cousins used to discover something new and surprising in the spiraling orchards and unending pathways that lead to lush gardens, wells, stables, kennels, and of course, scores of servant quarters. The place was such a maze that he would find many routes to reach back to the location from where he started. On the far side, there was a huge pond that seemed man made, probably dug to get clay, which was later mixed with dirt to get gaara, or the paste that was needed to glue the bricks together.

The ceiling of the lavishly decorated drawing room was adorned with glass chandeliers, along with a huge panel made up of thin bamboo sheets, from which a rope was dropped. When pulled back and forth, it swung and worked as a fan. On the walls, pictures of leaders like Nehru, Gandhi, Kalam and Patel who played an instrumental role in the freedom struggle were lined up. On special occasions, marigold garlands were put on Gandhi's picture.

Alam's grandfather was a prominent member of the Congress, which was the ruling party. This party was in the forefront during the struggle for the country's independence under the leadership of Gandhi and Nehru, and when the British left, the country generously rewarded the party when elections were held by making it the first party to come to power in free India under the leadership of Nehru as the first Prime Minister.

For about a couple of decades, there was no challenge to the leadership in Congress, but slowly cracks started showing up after the honeymoon period was over. The party went for a split, and it was a devastating blow to Congress when its election symbol 'do bailon ki jodi', or a pair of oxen was confiscated due to internal dispute within the party, and they were given another symbol which was 'gai aur bachchra', or cow and calf. As soon as the initial euphoria faded, deep cracks became visible in the party due to internal power struggle and real politik came into play.

The reasons behind the party's undoing, though no one accepted that there was anything wrong with the party, were ego clashes of party satraps or the old guards, and the ambition of the rising star, Prime Minister Nehru's daughter, Indira Gandhi. The divide in the Congress was not something that happened overnight. The internal power skirmish was not new; there were subtle undertones even before the country gained freedom. Earlier, it was due to ideological differences, but later when the probability of India gaining freedom gained ground, it was most likely over sharing spoils of power. Power has the capability to make people do strange things, but it also acts as an adhesive to make people of conflicting views stick together.

The shift in time was not just evident from the power struggle in the ruling party. Something unimaginable had also taken place, one that shook the country to its core. There was a time when nobody wanted to hear anything against Gandhi; after all, he was the living legend who had captivated the hearts and minds of all, being the main architect behind India's independence struggle. Then one day, the country woke up to the news of their messiah's murder.

Yes, a person adored by millions was murdered in broad daylight on his way to perform his daily prayers. Those were the dark days, and the air was pregnant with anxiety and fear.

Alam remembered how his grandmother had confessed to him about those days, 'We could not sleep out of fear, but were relieved when it turned out that a Hindu had killed Gandhi, not a Muslim otherwise...' She chose not to complete the sentence.

Later one day, she recited to him the Marsia or elegy that was broadcast by Radio Pakistan to mourn the death of Gandhi:

Aiy Qaum Na choote ga daaman se tere dag
Gul toone apne haath se apna kiya chirag.
Bapu ka katl karke toone toda hai woh phool
Tarse ga lahlahane ko ab Asia ka Baagh

O People! The blot will not get washed from you
You have extinguished your fortune by your own hands
By killing Bapu, you have plucked that flower
The garden of Asia will lament blooming again

Alam's grandmother's anxieties were not misplaced. She had heard horrifying stories about the blood bath that had painted the country red after a line was drawn by Sir Cyril Radcliffe, a British civil servant who as chairman of the Border Commissions, dividing the country into India and Pakistan. The partition of the country saw numerous trains reaching their destination with nothing but dead bodies. It was the biggest human tragedy, which most likely saw the largest migration of people in the history of mankind.

To add insult to injury, India's pride took a beating when later it was invaded by China. That was a personal blow to Prime Minister Nehru because the country was found ill prepared for the war, and Nehru's doctrine of Panchsheel was shaken.

Overnight, many became experts on warfare and were eager to elucidate how close the Chinese were to India, and how much of a risk it was to be living in Gorakhpur. The war became instrumental in revealing the strategic importance of Gorakhpur. Suddenly, it became the nerve centre of the Indian Air Force, and soon the deafening drone of airplanes flying over Gorakhpur became a common affair. The residents started getting first-hand experience of the war, with night sirens and blackouts becoming a part of their everyday life. To camouflage, windows were kept closed at all times, and dark shades were put on the glass panels.

One day, Alam heard someone telling his grandfather, 'Can you believe they even covered Taj Mahal with a black cloth to protect it from air raids?' His grandfather nodded his head and said, 'In 1942, government placed scaffolding in anticipation of attack by Germany and Japan, to mislead bomber pilots, and guess what? It appeared as a pile of bamboos from the sky.'

The first major political exposure Gorakhpur got was because of Maniram, which is the neighbouring constituent assembly. It happened when a byelection became essential due to the great churning that was going in the Congress party that time. He found his grandfather very excited one day because the Prime Minister had personally briefed him on how important it was for the party to win this byelection.

This byelection became necessary to accommodate the State's Chief Minister, who belonged to a party that hurriedly sprung up in opposition to the Congress. The Chief Minister, at that time, was neither a member of the Assembly nor of the Council. To keep his job, he was desperate to get elected. However, others were working day and night to see him defeated.

The Mahant of Gorakhnath Temple was fervently supporting the Chief Minister. The Prime Minister put her prestige on stake, and was camping in Gorakhpur for a couple of days, turning Alam's ancestral house into a hotbed of political activities. Alam was too young to understand the complexities of the political situation, but he liked the visitors, especially the one who often visited with her father. She was the daughter of one of Alam's grandfather's friends. A fair-skinned, lean and tall girl with straight hair. There was aggressiveness in her nature. She wanted to put the garland on the Prime Minister, when the latter visited his house to have a cup of tea. She was swift like a jungli billi or wild cat when she snatched the garland from his hand, and before anybody could know what happened, she was there in the front row, putting the garland around the Prime Minister's neck. Everybody clapped and loud chants of 'Indira Gandhi Zindabad' (Long live Indira Gandhi) filled the air.

Alam ran inside his room, refusing to let anyone see the tears that were ready to spill down his cheek. Next day, it was her picture with the Prime Minister which was on the first page of the newspaper *National Herald*. But surprisingly, he was not angry at all. Love sees no age; it can happen to anybody, anytime. To the selected few, it may come early.

Muslim laws became a hurdle for Sakina's father to inherit the riches of his ancestors, but Sakina's prayers did not go in vain. Today, her granddaughter's picture was on the front page of a prominent national newspaper.

The Chief Minister was defeated and was forced to resign. Money power and invocation of religious sentiments was no match for the charisma of a young Prime Minister. The byelection in Maniram became the deciding moment in contemporary Indian politics. India rediscovered a new Durga or Goddess of Power, who brought hopes to many, and who later changed the course of history by playing the role of a mid-wife in creating a new nation in the neighbourhood.

The birth of Bangldesh in 1971 brought India prominently to the world stage, and here in India, sycophants decided to cash-in on this opportunity and shamelessly chanted, 'India is Indira, and Indira is India'. For the Congress party, humility took a back step and was replaced with arrogance, slowly creeping in and strengthening its hold on the very foundations of the party. No wonder, those were the days of great political turmoil.

One day, without knowing the cause, Alam joined everybody who was on the way to the hospital. His eyes widened with disbelief when Alam saw his grandfather on a hospital bed. His face was swollen, and his whole body was blue because of the lathi blows that were delivered to him in the local police station, where he was brought in after a minor skirmish that broke out between the two communities in a predominantly Muslim neighbourhood.

He later learned that his grandfather was requested by the police and government authorities to visit there on a goodwill mission to calm the rioters so that everything could be brought back to normalcy. The police inspector Rahman Khan, known for third degree methods, arrested his grandfather, dragged him to the police station and treated him brutally. To prove that he took no sides, even with members of his own community, he acted like an animal.

That night was reminiscent of the dark night decade's back, when Shakir's house was crowded and the stale and heavy smell of revenge hung in the air. The elders of town from both communities, including his family, decided in favour of 'forget and forgive'. However, Alam was thinking differently. The opinion of a kid, who was on the threshold of his teenage, did not matter much to anybody. But he had other plans. If Gandhi could do it, so could he.

Alam resolved to fast until justice was done. Right outside the hospital room in the corridor, he spread a bed sheet and sat there heralding the arrival of a new Gandhi. In the beginning, nobody from his family cared what he did; there were neither any words of encouragement nor discouragement for him. They thought that it was the whimsical behaviour of a teenager induced by the surge of hormones that would be gone by the morning. After all, the kid was angry. Let him vent his anger this way.

The throng of visitors who entered the hospital everyday made it a point to stop and have a word with him. They all had one request, 'Beta, eat something. Your mother is getting too worried. Your grandfather will get well soon.' But he was curiously waiting for one particular visitor, and that visitor was the father of the girl, whose picture was published in the *National Herald*. As if in answer to his prayers, he came but without his daughter. Alam could not muster courage to ask where she was.

By the time it was evening, everything had changed. The hospital started filling up with large number of people. Security was beefed up. In that pandemonium, nobody seemed to care for a hungry kid sitting on a bed sheet in the hospital's corridor. The Prime Minister, who was on an official trip to Lucknow, flew to Gorakhpur to personally thank the voters of Maniram for standing beside her in the severest test of her lifetime.

Once in Gorakhpur, she also wanted to visit her trusted colleague, who had worked tirelessly to ensure her victory, and was now in the hospital due to police brutality. While coming out from the hospital room, her eyes spotted him. Having not eaten anything for a couple of days now, he looked extremely weak and pale with circles around his eyes. She sat on the bed sheet next to him, while Alam's father proudly explained to her about the 'Gandhian' fast his son had undertaken.

In appreciation, she put her hand on Alam's shoulder. The boy looked at her, his eyes brimming with tears. She took out her handkerchief to wipe his tears, and suddenly the place was illuminated with silver lighting from everywhere. Hundreds of flashlights popped as press photographers started taking pictures, lots of pictures, to mark that monumental event. He smiled at her feebly, looked around in disbelief, but as he turned back, his eyes grew wider incredulously.

There she was, standing with a smile on her face. This was going to be her second picture with the Prime Minister that would be published in almost all the newspapers. The only solace for him was that he would be in the picture too.

Rahman Khan, the inspector, was immediately suspended from his job and was ordered to report to the headquarters. On his way, his vehicle crashed with an oncoming truck, killing him instantly on the spot. The police case registered against him was duly placed inside a file which gathered dust never to see the light of day, otherwise he would have revealed names of people who were behind the plot, smashing the peace of Gorakhpur to smithereens and causing irreparable damage to the place.

It was all about power and money. The skirmish in that locality, where his grandfather was arrested on the wrong pretext of inciting riots, was pre-planned by those who had lost the plot a couple of decades ago when Shakir had decided to take the bull by the horn. They were still nurturing their grudges. And why not? The inbuilt superiority in them, however superficial, did not allow them to accept the changes that the country was going through.

Alam met her again. This time it was under much lighter circumstances since a party was being thrown to celebrate his grandfather's homecoming from the hospital. When he saw her, he approached her with a newfound confidence and asked her, as if by now he had gained some authority over her, 'What is your name?'

She smiled and answered, 'Sadia.' If he had asked her this question on their first meeting, he would have mumbled something barely audible and ran away from there. But not today. He did not want the conversation to end, and so he quickly added, 'My mother's name is Sadia too.' He was awarded with a genuine smile and a twinkle when she replied back, 'I know. Ammi told me about that.'

From there, the conversation picked up. They talked about many things and he told her that he knew which school she went to. They were both going to separate elementary schools, which were run by Christian Missionaries. Even as an infant, he had been surprised to see the spirit of evangelism behind the closed doors in his school. He often wondered why the dark-complexioned folks were engaged in doing menial chores, while others like teachers or administrators were fair complexioned. He was too young to understand that the dark complexioned ones were the local inhabitants, mostly untouchables, who in his great grandfather's paathshala were not even allowed inside the school. Some of them were later on lured into Christianity, most likely for economic considerations.

His conversation with Sadia kept them occupied for hours until it was time for her father to leave. His mother had come to call her, as her father was ready to go. She spotted them together, talking animatedly with each other and she had smiled on seeing her son so cheerful. He was in full spirits and was boasting to impress Sadia. He said, 'We have got a telephone on which you can talk to anybody. You don't have to go anywhere; all you have to know is their phone number.'

But Sadia, being an intelligent girl, thought ahead of the times. She said, 'That must be good, but I think it will be cool if one can also see the person on the other side. Isn't it?' He replied, 'Yes, it may happen someday.'

He looked at his mother, not trying to hide his annoyance. His expression seemed to say to her why had she come to disturb them. His mother noticed that they were holding hands.

Sadia's father, Arman Ali, was a budding politician and an ambitious man. He originally belonged to Lucknow, but after marrying Sadia's mother, he settled in Gorakhpur with his in-laws, and became a part of zamindar sahib's clan. Being an outsider, he was never considered a part of the inner circle, so he was always in search of his identity, and that is what brought him closer to Alam's family, especially to his grandfather, otherwise the divide was very clear. The so-called high statured Muslims were still living within themselves. They had no reason to intermix with other Muslims, whom they still considered razeel or inferior. Probably Arman Ali was different. Many people thought that because of his political ambitions, he was in a haste to spread out far and wide. And now politics was simply a game of numbers; approximately, two-third of the Muslims belonged to the lower strata and if united, they had the potential of becoming a formidable force in electoral politics. Arman Ali had done his mathematics very well.

Arman Ali could not sleep that night. It was no secret that everyone on his wife's side was jealous of the meteoric rise of Shakir's clan in local politics, which was contrary to their expectations. They were expecting that since they were zamindar or higher up in stature, they were the natural choice to be the ones who will be exulted, and would hold prominent positions once the British left India. They were not ready to accept someone from outside their clan taking charge and rising to prominence. Shakir's family, who once fought for the rights of razeel, was still razeel in their eyes. How could they tolerate them being elected to the State Assembly and Council?

And so, they hatched a conspiracy. 'We will encourage Babban to elope with the Hindu girl he is in love with; Hindus will get enraged, and then they will attack their mohalla. Who is their leader? He will come to pacify them, things will go out of control, and here you go; nobody will know what happened.' It all took place as per the plan, except that Rahman Khan failed to do what he was supposed to do.

Arman Ali cursed himself that he had betrayed his friend, and waited for the night to end. In the morning, he was unable to look at his own reflection in the mirror. It seemed to be screaming at him, 'Et tu, Brute?'

And he cursed himself and quietly left for Lucknow, to not come back again.

DEVOID OF any major industry or job opportunities, Gorakhpur saw the biggest outflux of people from the city. In the beginning, they left in hordes to get education and then decided to stay out for a good life, one that they could not have in Gorakhpur. The ones left behind were generally those who managed to have basic or at times no education, and little or no skills. Few daring and adventurous amongst them saw opportunities in neighbouring Nepal. At that time, Indians were crazy about anything that was 'Made in Japan', and hence smuggling things into the country became the latest fad of the unemployed youth of Gorakhpur.

Anwar's son had learned the great art of crossing the Nepal border carrying bounties clandestinely hidden in his bag and body. The craze for foreign goods became so intense that numerous hamlets near Nepal border became shopping hubs for people who were courageous enough to cross the border to put their hands on anything that was not made in India. Sonauli border, near the small town of Nautanwa, became the biggest dry port of eastern Uttar Pradesh, from where hundreds of people entered and exited every day. Majority of them were doing it for monetary gains.

Since Gorakhpur was the headquarter of one of the major branches of the Indian Railways, it became the focal point from where tasks related to construction, operation and maintenance of railways were rewarded. Though the budget allocated to Gorakhpur was not much compared to the total budget of the Indian Railways, but it was adequate to keep the locals busy and occupied. When the opportunity to make money arrived, the desire to control followed. It was not one's ability or competency to work that mattered when tenders or work orders were rewarded, but one's ability to manipulate the system that mattered most. The work was monopolised amongst a cartel of few, who were shrewd and they cornered most of the work for themselves or their cronies.

Sundar Singh was the grandson of a doorman, who had thrashed the son-in-law of Shakir a couple of decades ago. Devoid of any worthwhile education, he became a scrap metal contractor and worked his way up in the syndicate that controlled the lucrative scrap metal contracts for Railways. Initially, he had no rivals, but gradually competition started building thanks to the changing times in Gorakhpur. Organised gangs began to come up in the early 1970s when government initiated developing this backward region, and ample funds were allocated to this region. When money came, so did the gangs. Gorakhpur had become the land of gang wars, and many still remember the title 'Chicago of the East' given to Gorakhpur by the BBC Radio. Ambitious projects like a fertiliser factory and a railway workshop were envisaged for this region and significant amount of money was diverted to Gorakhpur.

There was need for a university in Gorakhpur. In the beginning, there were a couple of degree colleges affiliated with Agra University in town. There were others universities nearby at Lucknow, Allahabad, Varanasi and Aligarh, which catered to the needs of people from Gorakhpur.The University of Gorakhpur was built on great hopes, and it produced great scholars. But more than scholars, it produced many student leaders. The elections of the Student Union proved to be the launching pad for these young leaders. Hence, securing a coveted position in the Union election became essential. Once elected to the Student Union, these student leaders widened their horizons and set their eyes to find a place in local bodies, and the ambitious ones set their eyes on the State Assembly.

Only few were able to make it to the State Assembly or elsewhere, because competition was fierce. All dropouts and good for nothing were the ones who were out there trying their luck. They had seen how quickly a newspaper vendor rose to meteoric heights. However, not everybody was that lucky, so majority of them were left high and dry in the town to fend for themselves by meddling in the town's affairs, and poking their nose in affairs of others.

In Union elections, Sundar Singh was elected with a slender margin. He defeated his nearest rival Rajiv Shukla. Bombs were hurled for the first time, most likely by non-university students. By this time, something unusual had started to happen in Gorakhpur. It was being polarised, not on religious lines, but on caste lines, between Brahmins and the

Thakurs. Although, there was a substantial Muslim population in the city, but they were pushed to the sidelines. Their role was reduced to play second fiddle to the powerful rivalry between Thakur and Brahmin satraps.

It was said that a powerful civil servant, who once was posted in Gorakhpur, played a pivotal role in harbouring this divide. His agenda was Brahmin supremacy, which had to come at the cost of Thakurs. The Thakurs were not going to take it lying low either. Hence, war for the turf began, and as usual, collateral damage was to innocents and bystanders for whom there was nothing to gain in this war for sovereignty. Since Brahmins dominated the Congress party, Alam's house saw more Brahmins, and he liked it that way because there was a superficial sense of arrogance in Thakurs of those days, which he detested.

Since Nepal was not too far from Gorakhpur, people frequented it often. It was his first trip to Nepal, in fact, to any foreign land. The tour was arranged by the university, and they were ferried by a bus arranged by a local Sikh, Sardar Ji. For Indian citizens visiting Nepal, visa was not required, and there were no restrictions to cross the border. The custom and excise officers posted at the border generally did not care to check anybody, unless they suspected a person. In Nepal, people would buy their merchandise and leave it with the shopkeeper, who had 'arrangements' to get it delivered to the customer's house, of course for an extra charge, which may range from twenty to thirty per cent over price of the merchandise.

Alam was strolling in the market when he saw some students flocking to a little shop, or rather a shack that was almost invisible to spot from the main street, and looked suspicious. These students were not very regular in their classes. They were following one Ratan Gupta, who was long past his student age, and was enrolled in the university mainly to help candidates contesting Union elections.

He reluctantly followed them. The pahari doorman smiled at him and pointed him to the corner where they were congregated. Alam walked towards them. They all were peeping inside a rugged View Master, a still projector, which was popular those days. Their sniggering was enough to tell that they were looking at the picture of a full naked oriental woman through the View Master. A man, who looked Indian, had a bored expression on his face and he continued to change the displayed picture to show them the naked woman from different angles. On demand, he obliged and kept a certain pose for longer than other pictures. The woman was plump and petite, and would live in the memories of many for quite some time.The show lasted a few minutes, after which the pahari came to collect money. Ratan was basking in the glory of his newly-achieved celebrity status. He barked, 'Next time, you will see real one; just stick with me.' And with that, he was the new best friend for the boys.

Amongst them, there was a meek and studious boy, Shishir. He approached Ratan and asked him with his eyes fixed on the floor, 'Where can we get those glasses? You know which one?' Ratan knew exactly what Shishir was talking about because in Gorakhpur it was widely rumoured that the Japanese had recently made special see-through sunglasses, and by wearing them, everybody you look at will look naked. Ratan patted Shishir first on his head and then on his bulging crotch, which he was holding by his hands. Then Ratan asked loud enough for everyone to hear, 'Kisko dekhna hai?' (Whom do you want to see?) Shishir flushed a deep red shade, and quickly walked away, leaving behind loud guffaws of laughter echoing. Many in that crowd saw the picture of a naked woman for the first time in their life. This was possible only in Nepal because in India, in the land of Gandhi, such activities were banned.

The return trip was eventful. Police in the town of Maharajganj stopped the bus for a surprise inspection. It was not the 'Made in Japan' merchandise that they were looking for, but a cache of Russian arms that got loaded in the bus in Nepal, the bus which was chartered for a one-day trip for students to learn International Marketing Practices. The arms market was lucrative in Gorakhpur, and here people would pay the premium to own them. Though a permit was required to carry them, but not many cared about permits in those days. Those who could not lay their hands on the imported types were happy with the local stuff that was made in the nearby town Munger, in the adjoining Indian State of Bihar. One fine morning, he woke up early because he had to catch the morning train to Lucknow. From Lucknow, another train would take him up to Kanpur, and finally to another train that would take him to Aligarh, where he was invited to attend a wedding ceremony.

Sundar Singh, the former president of Student's Union of the Gorakhpur University, was now an MLA, from the nearby assembly constituency in neighbouring Maharajganj, which was dominated by Thakurs. Sundar was also on his way to Lucknow by the morning train. He waved his hand at Alam as a sign of acknowledgement and then kept talking to the person, who most likely was going to accompany him in the trip. He was in his usual attire, white dhoti and starched kurta.

Suddenly, there was movement at the entrance gate of the railway station that was generally used by commoners. There were two men plying on a motorcycle, which stopped under cover of a rickshaw, whose driver had quite conveniently gone for a cup of tea in the nearby dhaba. Their planning was meticulous. The first shot was a direct hit on the head, and the second one pierced the chest. Sundar died immediately. This shooting triggered a blood bath between the two groups and it took long for Gorakhpur to recover from its residual effect.

Recovery was not easy. The ones trotting guns became bold and creative. They quickly donned khaddar, a fabric that was popular among politicians, and navigated their way to the corridors of power. It rightly occurred to them that they were ones who did the heavy lifting in the quest to send politicians to the legislatures. If they could do it for others, why not for themselves? They performed this experiment in Gorakhpur. Those who were registered as criminals in local police stations became the flag bearers of some of the major political parties overnight. The most surprising part was that they started winning elections too.

As a result, sincere and honest people gradually phased out from political arena of Gorakhpur, and this, of course, was a big loss to the city. The nexus between politicians and criminals got a new definition, and unfortunately it was there to stay. One wonders if this is what Sir Winston Churchill foresaw when he said why India should not be granted independence. He had said, 'Power will go to the hands of rascals, rogues, freebooters; all Indian leaders will be of low calibre and men of straw.' It was almost midnight, and he was struggling to finish the essay that was assigned to him in class. Alam penned each word slowly and thoughtfully. 'Today Gorakhpur is developing, but at a slow pace. But when I was a child, Gorakhpur was a sleepy town; far away and aloof from the fast-pace life that was threatening the peace and tranquillity of nearby places.'

THERE COMES a time in the life of people from Gorakhpur, when they have to decide whether they want to stay here or migrate elsewhere in search of greener pastures. Everyone goes through this phase. Many will go to nearby places, whereas the daring ones will cross seven seas to venture into different time zones. It is sad but true that there were fewer opportunities in Gorakhpur for a person who wanted to do well in life. 'Gorakhpur rahne ki jagah nahin rah gayi hai.'(Gorakhpur is no longer a place to live anymore.) This statement started echoing in many households and they were not wrong about it either.

The local newspapers were carrying sordid tales of how Gorakhpur was fast becoming the 'Crime City' of the region. The battle for turf became so intense that not only the local press, but also the national media started taking notice. *The Surya*, a monthly magazine published from New Delhi, highlighted this subject by putting it as the cover story and soon it became viral, popularising Gorakhpur all the for wrong reasons.

Many parents were hesitant to send their children to

engineering and medical colleges that were housed in Gorakhpur. It was becoming interesting elsewhere too; many residing outside India started disassociating themselves from Gorakhpur and were often hesitant and shy about accepting the fact that they belonged to that place or have relatives living there. When asked where he was from originally, a professor earning his living in the United States simply answered, 'I am from near Lucknow.' He altogether omitted Gorakhpur.

The Aligarh Muslim University was founded on sound principles to impart quality education to Muslims of the subcontinent, and to great extent, the objectives were met with flying colours. From Aligarh Muslim University came some of the greatest minds of all times, and this place could be a feather in the cap for Muslims of this region, but unfortunately, some odd incidents of the '70s turned that dream sour. It is a hundred year old institution, which was built on high principles by a prominent scholar, who got enlightened during his visit to England and wanted to establish 'Oxford of the East' in India to cater to the needs of the British government, which during that time was tightening its grip on India. The founder, Sir Syed Ahmad Khan, could be considered a great visionary by all means, but not without some reservations. His sole objective was to educate the higher clan in Muslim social hierarchy and unfortunately, he had scoffed at the idea of admitting everybody, especially people of low origins in the university. However, in spite of the founder's bias, the university eventually ended up providing education to all, without discriminating on the ground of caste or religion.

Atul was Alam's childhood friend and was just admitted to Aligarh Muslim University. Atul met Alam during his visit to Gorakhpur and said, 'It is hard to believe that there's a place like this in India. The best part is that when you get bored, you can swing by to Delhi.' Atul was determined to convince his best friend to come to Aligarh for further studies. The university boasted of producing eminent personalities, who later became Presidents of the neighbouring nations.

Atul continued his sales pitch when he added, 'Think of it, Zakir Hussain became the president of India, and Ayub Khan of Pakistan.' But to his dismay, his childhood friend was in no mood to leave Gorakhpur to go to Aligarh.

Atul was not going to let it go that easily. He kept trying, 'All the Chief Ministers, Sheikh Abdullah, Mir Qasim, Abdul Ghafoor, all were from there. Your grandfather must know many of them.' Then, knowing his fancy for movies, like a good salesperson, he pitched that angle too, when he said, 'Filmy log, Khawaja Ahmad Abbas, Begum Para, Renuka Devi, Talat Mahmood, Shakeel Badayuni, Sahir Ludhianvi and Naseeruddin Shah, who is not from Aligarh?'

But Atul was talking to a tough and an aware customer, who rebutted him by saying, 'I don't think Sahir ever went there for anything.' But Atul finally threw the ace and said, 'Even Javed Akhtar, Jadoo Bhai.' He was a diehard fan of movie scriptwriter Javed Akhtar and had watched Zanjeer and Deewar many times. Now it all started to make sense. His admiration of Javed Akhtar intensified when he learnt that the latter also went to the prestigious Colvin Taluqdar's College in Lucknow, as he did. How could he betray the judgement of Jadoo Bhai?

'But this place is in news so often, why is that?' That was a very genuine concern that Alam brought to the table. It seemed that Atul had his lines ready; he snapped back, 'Forget that part. It is all politics. Tum ko isse kya lena dena?' (You have nothing to do with it.)

Yes, Atul was right. Why should he be worried about the issue of minority character of the Aligarh Muslim University, which used to crop up in news every now and then? It must be a sensitive issue, for everyone talked about it; news concentrated more on the political fracas that went on behind the old walls of the university rather than on the more pressing issue related to poor income which Muslims faced.

One day, Alam gathered some courage to ask his grandfather about it, but the old patriarch paid no attention to either the issue or him. He looked at him and smiled as if to say, 'Well, I did not go to Aligarh. I am a product of Lucknow University.'

Alam's grandfather was an ardent follower of the Congress party, and like many others, deep in his heart he believed that Aligarh played a pivotal role in the partition of the country. His grandfather also hated the fact that the British divided India. He used to call Jinnah, Angrez Mussalman (English Muslim), and would often narrate how emissaries of Jinnah from Muslim League were ridiculed when they came to meet his father Shakir in Gorakhpur.

Later, Alam learnt that the Aligarh Muslim University was formally established through 'The Aligarh Muslim University Act, 1920, an Act to establish and incorporate a teaching and residential Muslim University at Aligarh.' It was done after dissolving the Mohammadan Anglo-Oriental College, Aligarh, and the Muslim University Association, which were registered under Societies Registration Act of 1860. He further learnt that since an Act of Parliament established it, amendments could be made only through an Act of Parliament. Even for the so-called Minority Character, such an amendment was required and that was the biggest hurdle for achievement of the Minority Status. However, much like preaching to the choir, the Muslim leadership was not in a mood to accept this reality.

Once in Aligarh, Alam was thrilled as soon as he entered the campus. It was a gorgeous place, beautiful enough to make anybody fall in love with it. The building was a mix of old and new architectural design. The sprawling lawns were meticulously maintained. The residential halls were decent and spacious. At first glance, campus life looked invigorating and full of fun. He found that not all, but some of the departments were world class centres of excellence.

Atul was right. Aligarh Muslim University was indeed dedicated to academic excellence and had thus made a decent name. Its alumni, who were spread all over the world, had positively affected almost every sphere they touched. There was everything to keep the students engaged towards their academic goals, but soon he realised that there were deep schisms within that kept everybody divided on flimsy grounds. The most prominent was the divide based on which region of the country one belonged to. This problem of regionalism was not confined to this university alone, but its ugly presence could be felt all over the place. The situation was worse in the political arena, where political technicians widened the divide between the outsiders and local inhabitants for their own petty gains.

Everything there was going fine, until one day, Alam found that students were planning to mobilise themselves for 'restoration of minority character' of the university. These endeavours were controlled by the student body or 'Union', as it was called, and to some extent the Union was controlled by the so-called Muslim leaders who were stationed in New Delhi. After class hours, he asked one of the student leaders innocently about the issue and was rewarded with the reply, 'If you want to know more, go and study the judgement of Aziz Basha.'

He later learnt that the Aziz Basha judgement was delivered by a five judge Constitution Bench of the Supreme Court in 1968. Thereafter, on pressure from the Union and Muslim intelligentsia, the Congress government in New Delhi brought the AMU Amendment Act in 1981, falsely promising that this Amendment Act will negate the Five Judge Constitution Bench Judgement of 1968. Alam was not interested in these technical details and said to himself, 'To hell with this!', and he started making plans to go home because most likely the university would be closed eventually, as had been the ongoing trend, to avoid disturbances at the campus by students.

Unbelievably, tea shops in Aligarh are notorious for consuming a good amount of students' time. Here you are privy to all information under the sun; everybody is an expert on topics ranging from landing on the Mars to poor harvest in the remote village of Champaran in Bihar. One will be surprised over the confidence they show while discussing the issues, as if they have done doctoral thesis on that subject. It is a general rule that to learn more about any issue, one needs to play dumb, and that is what Alam did, when he asked one of the students, who had probably downed way past a dozen cups of the piping hot tea, 'What will happen if we don't get Minority Character?'

Before he could wait for an answer, he heard chairs being shifted towards him, displeased looks flashing on the many faces that had turned to him to give him the answer. A petite man, who had remained quiet for most of the time, answered with renewed energy, 'Jigar! Jail ko bhar denge hum.' (Dear! we will fill the jails.)

These men seemed damn serious about what they intend to do. But their seriousness had a stale scent of arrogance and stupidity. Alam tried to reason and said, 'But there is a basic flaw in all this. The judgement clearly says that Aligarh Muslim University is not a Minority Institution, because it was established by an act of Parliament, which superseded whatever happened previously via Society Registration Act of 1860, to start Anglo-Oriental College.'

Before he could finish, at least half a dozen students surrounded him, looking menacingly at him. One was almost ready to give him a piece of his mind when another student shouted, 'Saaf saaf bolo tum Minority Character ke khilaaf ho ya favour mein?' (State clearly whether you are in favour of Minority Character or against it?)

His sanity and common sense were intact, and Alam was quick to reply, 'Yes, yes, favour mein Bhai.' (Yes, Yes, I am in favour, brother.)

They looked at each other; made strange gestures to each other, and then they laughed noisily, as if that feeble acceptance was enough to ensure the much-besotted Minority Character. Alam offered them a cup of tea, which they gladly accepted. He looked at the one who now was on his thirteenth cup of tea and sipped it nervously. Probably he had remembered that he had again missed his class in this verbal exchange that had become a daily routine for the youth. Most students were missing their classes daily and were in for a rude awakening when they would later find out that they could not appear in exams because of their low attendance.

Next day, the university was closed sine die. Suddenly, everyone seemed to be heading towards the railway station as they all wanted to go home. The struggle for restoration of Minority Character had brought a God-sent opportunity to many. The budding politicians got an issue; the press got its story to cover. And for Alam, it was everything, for she was there at the railway station.

He was thrilled to see Sadia after such a long time. Like everybody else, she too was heading home. Raptures of unbridled joy gave him a warm glow on his face and his tongue tied in knots as he stood before her, looking at her angelic face. 'What a pleasant surprise!' He finally managed to stumble upon those words, thankful for the deliverance from looking like a complete dumb-founded idiot. Contrary to what he had said, he was not ready for the surprise at all. He was acutely aware of how he looked; his hair scattered, clothes not up to mark. Deprived of shower and shave for many days, he looked distressed. In life, you cannot plan everything. To move forward, you have to take things as they come.

Sadia was very passionate about the issue of Minority Character. She sobbed, 'How can they do this to us?' He tried to reason with her. Much to his relief, she turned an attentive ear towards him and decided to listen to him. He said, 'But this should not be the only concern bothering you. There are other more pressing issues and Muslim leaders are not touching them because they are too hot to handle.'

The train was moving fast. The compartment was packed, and they both were tired. Sitting next to each other, their bodies swayed in harmony with the movement of the bogies. Too tired to care, her head slowly slumped on his shoulders. God knows when their hands met. They were in their own world, away from the tensions and animosity that impregnated the air outside. It was as if they had mutually decided to simply ignore everything that was happening in the real world. They had met as teenagers and had swiftly moved to adulthood, but their understanding of each other was still unchanged even after all these years. Turning their back from here was simply out of the question.

At one time, he had resisted leaving Gorakhpur, but today he realised that it was not a bad decision after all. The other realisation that shook him to his core was that he was irrevocably in love with Sadia; probably had been from the first time he met her as a young boy.

Sadia was all that he ever wanted in a partner. She was passionate, yet simple and grounded. She had a mind of her own and her confidence shone through her aura and left him mesmerised each time he saw her. He accepted with great humility that he loved her wholeheartedly and she may have a liking for him too. Someone had rightly said that when you are in love, the entire universe conspires in helping you to achieve it. There they were travelling together in a train, moving ahead in unknown territories of love with their hands entwined. The train was moving ahead with an unusual gusto, as if it was aware of the presence of two people in there, falling in love with each other with each passing moment. The train took upon itself to travel in its signature meandering way, bringing the young couple closer to each other as much as possible.

Love is a precious gift. It sees no boundaries, and has no barriers. It is seamless. When their eyes met, they both saw what they wanted to see. It was nothing else but love, pure and simple old fashion love. One has to fall in love at least once in his lifetime; otherwise there is no point in walking on the surface of the earth. This train journey awakened the poet in him. With Sadia next to him, he was in his own world, and the words come straight from his heart:

*On a hot summer day in Gorakhpur*

Phoolon ki tarah teri soorat nazar aati hai,
Gulshan mein teri aamad ek naghma sunati hai,
Boondein jo tapki hain barish ki tere rukh pe
Gul pe kisi qatre ka ehsaas dilati hai,
Is tarah tera aana jalwon mein sama jaana,

Mere dil-e-majboor ko rangeen banati hai
Main teri mohabbat ka deewana hoon, deewana
Har ek ada teri chaahat ko jagaati hai,
Jo toone sunayii hai ruddadd mohabbat ki,Ye mere
khwabon ki tabeer batati hai.

Your face has the resemblance of the flowers
With your arrival in the garden one hears sweet melodies
Drops of rain that have fallen on your face
Seems like a drop on the floret
The manner you enter, and blend in the grandeur
Fills my helpless heart with colours
I am madly in love with you
All your actions increase my fascination for you
When you recite the fervour of your love
It tells me about the meanings of my dreams

At Aligarh, the clamour for minority character saw its usual ups and downs. There was a heated debate in the Indian Parliament that raised hope, but in the end, it was hopelessness that reigned. The lawmakers wandered in a maze that was carved in unfamiliar territories, and in the end, they concluded that they were simply running in circles. The movement fizzled out with the hope that it will be taken up by some zealous person in the future.

HIS MARRIAGE with Sadia was simple with family members from both sides attending the ritualistic ceremony. Decades back, many in Sadia's family were not able to marry, because they accepted celibacy rather than marrying someone who belonged to lower strata of the Muslim caste hierarchy. However, with Sadia and Alam, it was entirely different. Love sees no boundaries. Nobody could stop two people madly in love with each other from doing anything. It has been noticed that at this point even Gods do not dare to interfere.

Like any other person with ambition, they moved to the United States of America that was still the land of great opportunities. Their goal was simple, to live happily ever after. In Sadia, Alam found a heart that will never cease loving and a pair of arms that will hold him, when he will be at his feeblest. She provided the shoulders where he could put his head and cry, and eyes looking into which, he would forget all his worries. Who will yearn for heaven when you may catch a glimpse of heaven here on earth in your lover's eyes?

It was a different world out there. New York City treated him well and he made a decent name by his research on stem cells. Sadia had become an investment banker. They had two children, Ahmad and Amna. Though life in the West was difficult and at times monotonous and robotic, it was comfortable. Difficult, because everything had to be done single handedly, unlike back home in India, where they had divided the human race into smaller sets or castes with the fortunate ones dispensing tasks to the lesser fortunate.

Like for many immigrants, America turned out to be the land of opportunity for them too, and they could have lived there happily ever after. In fact, things were happening that way. It was a very normal lifestyle that they had, similar to that of numerous immigrants from India, working hard and living in an effluent neighbourhood. For them, assimilation with the new culture had never been difficult.

However, they still worried about the hometown and would often peep back to the happenings in India. With the advent of Internet and satellite dishes, they caught all the news from India sitting comfortably in their living room. True to human tendency,now that they had done enough for themselves, they thought of the less fortunate who were left behind, and so they occasionally dipped into their savings to take care of them. Yes, charity always begins at home.

The children were hardworking and well-mannered. They were developing a fancy for a different type of career, contrary to the usual career in medicine or engineering that most Asian immigrant's children opted for. The usual immigrant dream of parents were shattered when Amna announced that she was going to cross the barrier and dreamt of becoming a lawyer.

At first he was a little nervous, but then he sheepishly accepted the fact, 'That is good. Your great grandfather was also a lawyer in India.'

He was deliberately smiling because he had read somewhere that an attorney with a briefcase has the potential to make more money than hundreds of goons with arms and political backing. Well, that was mafia's theory of the '60s.

There have been good lawyers like Gandhi and Mandela, whereas for the bad ones, you have those Fidel Castro. But Amna put the final seal of approval when she asked, 'What about your favourite John Grisham, an attorney, hmm? Which book of his is coming next?' Yes, nobody knows a person better than his daughter does. A father loves the moment when a smart daughter manipulates him. He may show annoyance, but warmth spreads around his heart. The daughter knows that anger. She can very well differentiate between a real anger and fake one. That is what a bonding between a father and daughter is all about.

Things were moving rather smoothly until they got stuck by a hurricane which shook them to the core. Watching Sadia's mother die in a New York hospital was a tragic and nerve-wracking experience. But little did they know that another bad news awaited them. It is true that bad news has companions, and it has a tendency to show up one after another. That is the way life is. Nobody had ever said that life would be easy. It is your fault if you think so.

It was a phone call from thousands of mile away. Alam's father had left for his heavenly abode. He was mature enough to understand the nuances of the cycle of life, but the second phone call from India was devastating.

Amna later described that very moment to one of her

friends, 'I put my hand on my father's shoulder and asked him if he needed some water, or a chair to sit down. He stared at me, as if he had not even heard me. We never believed that my grandfather's death in India would turn our lives upside down. In India, we were cheated by our very close relatives.'

Then Amna looked at one of Ahmad's friend and continued, 'At first we were in denial, but later, as we exchanged notes with others, it turned out that every person who leaves their native place for better life faces the same dilemma.'

Amna continued with her characteristic zeal, 'They get cheated by their own relatives, who for some reason believe that this person is not going to return back, and hence they start eying their inheritance.'

Amna was right; odds are heavily loaded against the immigrant because he or she is in no position to fight a civil suit from the comfort of his new abode in an adopted country.

Sadly for Alam, it was his father's ancestral house in India. 'So, why do you care? You have a better house here.' That was Amna's initial reaction.

At that time, Alam was desperately employing the internet search engines to get a glimpse of his ancestral house on the web. Then Amna realised how naïve she was to misunderstand the gravity of the situation. Her father's very 'existence' was at stake. He confirmed it in a depressing voice, 'Somebody out there is trying to trample on my roots and wipe out my footprints.'

'There is a jungle out there.' He would tell everybody after his trips to India. The pain would be distinct, and would often show up on his face marked with helplessness.

'You won't believe how corrupt the system there is.

Everybody can be bought there. And the lawyers out there, they really take money from both sides.' He tried explaining the level of corruption to Sadia. The hate for the system back home was getting intense day by day.

Most of his friends counselled him to forget and move on. Interestingly, they all knew somebody who had faced similar experiences of losing their property because of not residing in their hometown. At end of the day, they simply gave up. According to them, the sooner you make this decision, the better it will be for you.

But, how could Alam give it up? He had fond memories of that house. Today he may not remember, but most likely, somewhere in that house, he had learned how to walk. From its roof, he had watched the moon and stars at night. During daytime he would roam around the neighbourhood in search for birds, reptiles, hares, jackals and monkeys. In the adjoining orchards, he had seen for the first time how cashew is grown, learnt that there are dozens of varieties of mangoes, saw how birds would build their nests, learned how to differentiate between eggs of a snake from the egg of a sparrow. It was simply not a place to give shelter, but in fact was a huge learning laboratory, where every day new lessons would eagerly wait for him.

For him, those memories of childhood and the innocent dreams would haunt him forever, and will definitely stay with him for days. Since his childhood was built around that house, Alam would never forgive himself for not doing anything about it.

Luckily, his prayers were heard and he got help from an unexpected quarter. Someone whom he had not met for ages came to his rescue. Anand, who was one of the great grandchildren of Raees Jamuna Das, was a highly placed official in the government now. They both went to school together just like their great grandfathers Shakir and Jamuna Das went to the paathshala together decades ago.

The power of social media is immense. While surfing on the internet, he found Anand and soon they both started chatting about the bygone days. Anand too was fond of the house, and during school days, he always made a point to stay there during holidays and breaks. Anand could not believe what he heard. A class reunion of selected few was arranged, where many of his classmates were invited to attend, thanks to all the advancements made in technology in terms of video conferencing. Alam was pleased to see that all his classmates were doing well in life.

The plan put forward was simple. The culprits and their immediate relatives were put under microscope, and dossiers were prepared for each of them, to find if they had ever done anything wrong in their lives. Most of them turned out to be law-abiding citizens, who paid their taxes and stayed out of trouble. The scrutiny was so intense that if anybody ever had an affair with any girl on the street, it would show up. Dozens of people were interviewed. The court records and any business dealing ever done by them were closely scrutinised. The efforts were not in vain. One fine morning, intelligence sleuths knocked on a door, and that person was given a simple choice. Use your influence to do what is right, or face the music. That person made the right decision, and next day Anand called his friend in New York with the good news.

The feat he accomplished became the talk of the town in Gorakhpur. Probably Alam's was the first case where a person sitting faraway in New York was able to get back his dwelling, and along with the memories that he had left behind. As a matter of fact, he was not uprooted, and it was a relieving thought for him that there was a shelter for him if ever he ran out of homes.

That night after winning this battle, Alam was in a jovial mood during dinner and told his children, 'I started thinking literally about infinity and my brain started to spin. There are stars out there, and its light has not reached us yet. If we start thinking in those terms, how miniscule we are? How irrelevant we are, and yet we try to grab the extra inch by hook or by crook, thinking that this will make us rich or will catapult us in the next orbit?'

IN THE United States, emphasis is put on helping employees acquire new skills in order to help them grow professionally. That is how top companies retain the employee; otherwise, if they are not learning new skills, the employees will simply leave.

That February morning was like any other wintery day. The sky was overcast and there was chill in the air. The training was getting boring, so lunch break provided Alam a much-needed respite. He had forgotten to bring his lunch to the training class, so he strolled towards his car in the nearby parking lot to fetch it. But he changed his mind, and rather than taking lunch to class, Alam lazily finished it in the car, and then came back to the classroom where the instructor was explaining the essential ingredients required to write a winning proposal.

His steps towards his seat in class were slow, which were a sign of his disdain to get into the training. He looked at the books lying on the desk with disinterest, questioning himself, 'Do I really have to know all this?' Unwillingly, he sat on the chair, without even bothering to look at the instructor, who must have felt insulted because he was returning late from lunch. Suddenly he started feeling strange. 'Wait a minute! There is something wrong. Why I am not feeling well?'A weird queasiness had started forming a bundle of knots in the pit of his stomach. His eyes started to narrow to find an answer to this feeling, which he had never felt before in his life. He was ready to make a judgement, when he said to himself, 'It is not the training class, but something else is going on.' He murmured and looked at one of his colleagues sitting next to him to see if he also felt queer. To his dismay, he seemed to be enjoying the training way too much to even bother looking at him.

This got him more upset.'These hard working guys find interest in strange things.' Having said that, even in his State of confusion, he started smiling. Something funny was going on. A bizarre feeling was making him uneasy and curious at the same time. When he had woken up in the morning, he had not realised that this afternoon was going to change his life forever. Darkness slowly engulfed him around noon time.

This was how Joe, one of his colleagues, had described the episode to him later, 'I was sitting right behind you. After a little while, I realised that you were putting your hands on the desk as if to make sure that it was there, then you removed your hand to touch your face, and then you looked all around as if you were not sure about something.' In that training class, Joe was sitting right behind him, and it turned out that his strange antics forced Joe to watch him for he felt that there was something wrong going on with him.

When he left the room in a rush, Joe followed him. Before leaving the room, he walked to the writing board and tried to touch it, because he was losing the perception of depth. Soon he was walking towards his car, unaware of the fact that Joe was right behind him.

'Are you alright?' Joe asked gently, placing his hand on his shoulder that was drenched with sweat. He shook his head in the affirmative, and replied without even looking at him,'I am heading to my car to get some drink.' He made a reasonable and forceful Statement so that Joe would leave him alone.

Instinct urged him to abandon training and go to the comfort of his house, or somewhere else. Joe later narrated to him, 'I kept following you because something seemed out of place. You went to your car and took out a soda can, but the soda came splashing on your shirt because your hands were trembling, or something was wrong with your motor skills. That was the time I got alarmed and I said to myself that this guy needs help.'

Joe was right because after an unsuccessful attempt to drink, he was walking back out of the parking lot, rather than going to the building that was in the front where the training continued without him and Joe.

After he bumped into the fence, he looked around for help. His hazy gaze focussed at Joe and he was glad that he still followed him. Now, everything was spinning around him and there was a feeling of lightness in his head too.

Next minute, he was lying on a sofa in the lobby, and could hear phone calls being made. Sudden panic surged inside him and he looked around with shock written large on his face, trying to fathom what was happening to him. Minutes later, he had his first ride in an ambulance.

Within minutes, he was in the emergency room at Jordan Hospital in Queens. He remembered talking to Sadia on the phone. He also remembered someone, most likely a doctor, telling him that they had found some blood inside his head. At that time, finding blood in head seemed inconsequential to him. Of course, they would have found blood in the head. Blood is supposed to be everywhere so why would the head be an exception? He was so naïve! Later, he was told that they wanted to shift him immediately to the New York Medical Center by a chopper. However, the chopper could not come due to inclement weather. The doctors decided not to wait, but rather transported him by road. Timing was critical and every minute was important, or so they told him. It was getting blurry and hazy again and then for him everything was dark.

He later found out that he had been born with a rare disorder, which in medical terminology is called Arterial-Venous Malformation or AVM, caused when arteries connect directly to the nearby veins, without having normal vessels, or capillaries between them. If an AVM ruptures, it can cause a stroke, brain damage or death.

That fateful day during that training, one of the veins in his brain had ruptured, and blood had started to discharge, to get collected in the cavity of his skull. That was the blood the doctor had announced about seeing in his skull. He was later told that it was Dr Ogilvy at the New York Medical Center who had performed a complicated, but miraculous surgery, by putting him in serpentine position to remove the blood from his skull. Later when he visited his doctor as an outpatient, his doctor informed him, 'Approximately 120 cc of blood was evacuated from your skull that night.' The doctor failed at hiding his excitement when he said, 'Boy! That was a huge hemorrhage.' He learnt later that in the medical world, they consider anything above 40 cc to be serious. So in a way, that night, he had hit the jackpot.

To perform the surgery, the brain was put in deep freeze by strong anaesthesia, and now since its effect was waning, things were cloudy. Early from childhood, waking up had not been easy for him. He always tried to squeeze in a few extra minutes before getting up from the bed, but for him that night in the ICU was like reliving his worst nightmare. The right side of his injured brain was recuperating from surgery and was struggling to assimilate millions of rewiring to absorb the permanent damage that had occurred due to the rupture of the AVM. Later, he learned that the right brain, which was injured in his case, is dominant for spatial abilities, face recognition and visual imagery. These deficits, he was told, are going to haunt him for the rest of his life.

In ICU, his screams were getting louder. It was not because of any physical pain. In fact, when he thinks of it now, there was no pain at all. The envelope of infinite darkness surrounding him had an aura of uncertainty, like one must feel in the darkness of a grave, where angels embark to ask simple, but very important questions. 'The initial groaning was something addressed to Allah in your language, but after an hour, it was all English.' One of the nurses told him later.

She further elaborated that his mumblings in English were a sign that the surgery was successful. It showed that his brain was responsive enough to tell him that he was in a hospital in the United States, and it would be advantageous to speak in a language that could be easily understood. In a way, he was in control of himself.

The darkness which was initially showing vivid signs of gloom and uncertainty was turning into coarse objects, dull images which were giving cryptic hints as if they wanted him to recognise what they were. Familiar voices, as if coming from faraway places, were struggling to strike a chord with billions of information that were stored in a part of the brain, which was left unscratched.

The images were now settling in known forms and shapes. Patterns that had seemed psychedelic were now showing familiar contours and vistas, as if somebody was pushing the zoom button to put everything in focus and in order. There were neither any angels, nor hell fire, nor beautiful gardens under which rivers flowed with sweet water to quench one's thirst and make one live forever.

No heaven or hell, he was in the ICU. Sadia was looking at him with concern in her eyes. The glow on her face told him that she was getting impatient to announce to the world that there is God, and God had let her win. She also looked relieved, as if she was holding a lottery ticket in her hand and tears from her eyes were screaming to testify that she had the winning combination.

Ahmad in his green jacket, stood quietly, as usual, next to his sister. Amna, who was ten at that time, seemed unwilling to waste a single minute, and was eager to share with her father something interesting that had happened at school during the time he was in ICU. He wished he could have followed what Amna was saying. His soul was willing, but unfortunately his body was not, for it was too tired and weak. He simply looked at Amna for a minute, with a face that lacked any expression and Amna wiped the tears from her eyes when she left ICU.

The ICU is not a place where you may want to stay for too long. The visitors were cautioned not to overstay there. The doctors routinely asked him the same questions every time. His favourite was about the date, along with the name of the President of the United States. Initially, he was not able to move his fingers. The hospital staff always asked him to smile, and to tell them his name. The visitors would come and look at him, and some would even cry, seeing him helplessly lying on the bed. At that point, nobody was even taking any guesses as to what lay ahead of him. He was there, paralysed, and his future life was nothing short of a big question mark.

The visitors came not in dozens, but in scores. When he was transported from Queens to the New York Medical Center, it looked like an Indian carnival. After a while, the visitor's lobby started smelling like Indian curry, because many people who came to see him brought food for his family members, who were camping in the hospital. Even the security guard got so used to it that whenever he would see Indian faces, he would automatically point them towards his room.

The memory of his stay at the ICU was dull and haphazard. After they shifted him to the regular ward, it started to look better. The physicians continued to come every day, and they were still interested in knowing the name of the United States President. One day, before the doctor could ask him, he winked at him and said, 'The name of the President of United States is George Bush, and he is the son of former President Bush.' The doctor gave him a puzzled look, but the nurse who was standing nearby could not help conceal her smile.

Every day doctors would hold his foot and would ask him to push as one pushes the gas paddle. They wanted to evaluate if the left side of his body, which was paralysed, was getting strong or not. At that time, it was everybody's concern whether he would ever walk and get back to normal life or not.

His left side was numb and was devoid of any feeling. He easily got tired and irritated. He silently questioned his Maker why did this happen to him. What wrongs had he done to suffer in such a manner when everybody else around him seemed happy and cheerful? His friends and relatives continued to come and visit him with sad faces, but he was sure that as soon as they steped out of his room, they would get engulfed in their priorities, challenges, joys, schedules, deadlines and other mundane routines of life. That is the way his life is going to be, a sad spectacle. When you are in agony and pain, nobody can feel it the way you do. Most of the people around you can be sympathetic to you, but only to an extent. There is no mechanism by which others may take away your pain; it is your own to endure. Amna tried to comfort him one day. She said, 'Dad, I read that when a good person like you gets sick, then there is a reward. Allah will remove the sins, as a tree sheds its dead leaves, and then comes the green and healthy ones.'

Whittier Rehabilitation Center did for him what play school does for a toddler. This place renewed his hope and gave him a new lease to his life. In the beginning, they made him walk with a four-prong stick, and then it was upgraded to a regular cane.

He was revisiting his childhood days when he learnt to walk. Life had come full circle and like a toddler, yet again, he learnt the basic steps of walking. Initially, he thought that he would be satisfied if he could simply walk with a cane. But gradually, he started thinking about more. His desires started taking new strides and his confidence boosted. His care providers were reluctant to challenge him more, and he rightly guessed that they were more concerned about insurance liabilities. His frustration increased and one day he did the unimaginable. He dropped the cane and walked a few steps without any aid. He was walking on his own. And since then, there was no looking back for Alam.

However, his happiness was short-lived. One night during his sleep, he felt great trembling. Without the doctor's verdict, he knew that it was a seizure. Next day, he was taken for EEG at a hospital in Lexington. His brain was unable to process the signals and the verdict was out. He was epileptic.

A brain angiography told him that he was back to square one because there was one more AVM in his brain, which was like a ticking time bomb. The angiography was repeated after six months and the bad news was confirmed. He had to get it fixed soon. embolisation was the state of the art procedure which could have cured this ailment without undergoing a major surgery. It involves blocking an artery by injecting a blocking material by puncturing an artery and inserting a catheter, which later injects blocking material at the right spot. It was simple to the extent that it could be done by using a local anaesthesia. But as his luck would have it, the procedure failed and the only option that remained was another brain surgery, the second one within an year.

He lay awake and impatient all night. Ahmad had refused to leave him to go to his room, so he was lying next to him on the bed. These days even a kid could search on the internet to infer that brain surgery is a serious business. Surgeons avoid operating on the brain unless it is absolutely necessary. In dire situations, it is a life and death operation. The first surgery on his brain was performed when he had no say in it, but this time the situation was different.

He signed a piece of paper that Stated that he understood

the risks involved in this operation and that include permanent disabilities, and that include death. He started to sweat. What would happen if he were to die?

Brain scans and positioning technology are precise, but there is the old Murphy's Law that proudly proclaims that whatever can go wrong, will go wrong. He felt as if a knife was piercing deep into his head, and his hands went quickly to his head to feel the blood that might be oozing out. But there was no blood on his head. Just then, Amna entered his room. She was scared and she wanted to sleep next to her father. He was staring at the ceiling when she entered the room, probably thinking what would happen to Sadia and their children if the call came from the Almighty.

Ye hawa jo tere gaon se aati hai,
Tera hal-e-gham bata sab ko rulati hai,
Dafn mitti mein mujh ko bhi,
Tere dard ke kisse sunati hai,
Is kabra ke azab ka kya dar,
Teri fikr yahan bhi satati hai,
Pareshan gaon mein sabhain dost,
Is kabra se ek siski kyon aati hai.

The breeze that comes from your village
By telling your woes, makes everybody cry
Buried in the ground, to me, too
Tells the stories of your sorrow
Have no fright of the torture that waits in grave
Here too, your woe makes me restless
Everybody is worried in the village, friends
Why, there are sobs coming from the grave

With both his children next to him, that night Alam was a very scared person. He was in no position to console his kids; he could not form words of comfort, telling them that they should not worry, and everything will be all right. Emotions ran unchecked leaving him sleepless. A feeling of helplessness surrounded him and he felt so vulnerable that he started sobbing, without realising that it has to be done in silence. Sadia was in the other room sitting on a prayer mat, and she prayed all night. God heard her prayers and the surgery went well. Now they were certain that they could live happily ever after.

Getting back to normal life is easy when one has everybody on his side. He felt blessed when everybody went out of his or her way to ensure his quick recovery. He was on the mend, but there were certain areas in his brain that were damaged permanently. But why should he care? The glass is never full to the brim, and all depends on how one looks at it. It is the outlook that matters. Why complain when God has given him much to be thankful for?

However, since he was human, he would often get frustrated. He tried to look for answers and remembered an old film song. *'Kabhi kisi ko mukammal jahan nahi milta, kahi zameen to kahi aasman nahi milta'* (nobody ever gets a flawless world, some don't get their portion of earth and some their place in the sky). What could he do? He could not even cry in front of everybody because that kind of behaviour was not expected from grownups.

At that time Ahmad, who was four years old, realised that he could only beat his father in soccer by kicking the ball towards his left side; otherwise, his father, even after going through all this, was very adept in this game. He was flawless on the right side, but there was something wrong on the left side. He was too young to understand that if the brain is damaged on the right side, its impact is felt on the left side. Strains of stress were evident on his face at times. His walk would be slightly off, but only a keen observer would be able to notice the difference. Ahmad knew that his father was a great actor who behaved as if nothing was wrong. His son knew this, but being a faithful son, he kept his father's secret to himself. For the little four-year-old, these anomalies in his father were enough to make him sad. But he consoled himself by thinking that at least he was alive. Then, out of honest emotions, he would sob in silence.

He knew that on some occasions, his father sobbed in silence too. In spite of the challenges that his father faced, for Ahmad, his father was still his first hero.

NEVER BEFORE in recent history had anybody dared to violate the sanctity of the borders of the United States of America. It was a usual September day when the unthinkable happened, after which, the country never remained the same again.

To the horror and dismay of everybody, security backups that were put in places were breached, and right in the middle of New York City, and in front of everybody's eyes the Twin Towers collapsed. They were targeted and hit by two aeroplanes controlled by terrorists, which acted as missiles. The country was immediately at war. There were enemies out there who did not subscribe to the fundamentals of the country, and they dared to make a statement by killing thousands of innocent Americans who became a victim of their hate. A religion was hijacked by some followers of that religion, and that religion was Islam. The world shook with fear and disbelief. A power giant like the United States was attacked and the equilibrium of the power balance, as they knew it, was disturbed.

The President of United States was forced to draw a line in the sand. There was no ambiguity in his message when he said, 'Every nation, in every region, now has a decision to make. Either you are with us, or you are with the terrorists. From this day forward, any nation that continues to harbour or support terrorism will be regarded by the United States as a hostile regime.'

The President was very forthright to Muslims when he said, 'I also want to speak tonight directly to Muslims throughout the world. We respect your faith. It is practised freely by many millions of Americans and by millions more in countries that America counts as friends. Its teachings are good and peaceful, and those who commit evil in the name of Allah blaspheme the name of Allah. The terrorists are traitors to their own faith, trying, in effect, to hijack Islam itself. The enemy of America is not our many Muslim friends; it is not our many Arab friends. Our enemy is a radical network of terrorists, and every government that supports them.'

Yes, the world was shaken, and more was he, because he lost his one true love in that attack. When Sadia had left home that morning, none of them had realised that was the last time they were seeing her alive for she would not return back home after that terrible day. She perished in the rubbles of the Twin Towers with hundreds of others, who were out there carrying out their normal duties. He watched everything happening right in front of him on a television screen with his children sitting beside him. There was nothing he could do. His sat helplessly with his fists clenched. He looked at the screen when everything went into smoke and his dreams, and his life, ended with Sadia's life. There was nothing left in this world for him to live for. He just kept on repeating, 'Oh God! No!'

That night, he drove endless miles through a town that looked devoid of any life at all. The country was presumably dead. Those alive were afraid and apprehensive about the future. Many families had lost their loved ones and the damage done was much deeper than it looked. All kinds of horrid reports were streaming in through the radio. Amna asked him innocuously, 'Dad, are they going to come after Muslims living here?' He shivered, and without looking in her eyes, replied, 'No, don't worry, we are safe.' He turned the radio of his car off. The AM bands were having a field day as the callers had started getting nasty.

'We will go and kill all Muslims living in this country first.' Another said, 'These Trojan horses should be assembled in a slaughter house and then...'

They reached home and were welcomed by the eerie silence that pervaded in the house. He looked at his children and said quietly, 'You both go to sleep.' Then he realised how could they sleep alone when their mother is dead. He called out to them, 'Wait for me, I am coming.' He went to the bathroom, looked at the mirror, combed his hair as he always did before going to sleep and sobbed in whispers, saying,'Why Sadia?'

After being absent for so many days, he thought it would be a good idea to go to work. There was a message waiting for him at one of the receptionists.

He called back and his call was immediately answered on the first few rings by a male voice, 'Sir, my name is Glenn Brown and I did call you earlier. This is White House. The President may feel obligated if you can accept his call.' Drained of all emotions, all he could ask was, 'Now?'

The reply was friendly, 'No sir, we are planning for some time tomorrow afternoon. Are you going to be available on your home number? Yes, that is an unlisted phone number, we know that.' He said without thinking much, 'Yeah.'

Glenn replied like a robot, 'Thank you sir. We will let the President know.' They plan things with impeccable accuracy, just in time to catch prime time audience on the television. He thought. He found it difficult to concentrate on anything, so he decided to stay home to prepare a good meal for the kids. At about 3 PM, he heard a knock on the door. There was a little commotion outside as a couple of cars stopped and parked in his driveway. He opened the door and saw two men standing at his doorstep.

They introduced themselves as reporters from some local news station which was affiliated to one of the national television. They had a little bouquet for him with a sympathy card stuck in it. The person with Hispanic looks said calmly, 'Sir, we are very sorry to interrupt you, and your privacy. Do you mind if we stay here while you take a call from President?'

After Sadia's death, intrusion of his privacy by media was frequent. He wondered how Sadia would have liked it. He remembered how Sadia kept on looking at him in admiration when he had his debut encounter with a news reporter during a rather eventful visit to the Niagara Falls when his car got into a multiple car accident. He was shy, hesitant, and he stammered a lot. The reporter looked at his son, who was crying in the rear seat, and inquired, 'Is there anything wrong with him?'

He nervously answered, 'No, nothing wrong. Maybe his dentures are hurting, kind of new, you know.' Before he could complete his sentence, Sadia intervened, 'He got his braces yesterday, not used to it.'

The reporter was simply confused, but the cameraman

understood. He mumbled, as they turned away, 'Can't believe, guy drives a BMW but doesn't know difference between braces and dentures.' As soon as they walked away, Sadia took out her camera and took a picture of the son who was still crying, but before taking the picture she giggled and said, 'Alright cry baby, lemme take a picture of your dentures. Hmm.'

That night Sadia gave him nine out of ten points for his performance with the television crew. She was a charmer for sure. Memories came rushing in and left him awash with the feeling of loneliness again.

One of the persons from the television station hesitantly offered him a kit that contained some makeup. 'If you care,' he said with indifference. He looked at it and politely took it, thinking Sadia would have wanted him to look good on the television screen. The other person interrupted his thought by saying, 'Sir, you may want to jot down a few lines. That always helps.' He looked at him in disbelief and could not help thinking again, 'What would have Sadia wanted?'

He wanted to blame it on Sadia. She was living with him every moment of his life. She was his best friend. They were married for good twenty years. Why did she have to go so early?

He suddenly became very tense. Everything was fresh in his memory. He remembered standing at a spot at ground zero, looking at the sky where he could hear planes flying. His head started to spin. His left side was getting numb. An electric spark started running along his left side. His left eye started to blink at a very fast pace. The call from the President was clear. The President was polite, concise and personal in nature. Since he was well prepared, it went well. He was live on national television. The President expressed his deep condolences for his loss. This was the message for him. He also reiterated how he thinks that Islam is a religion of peace. This message was for worldwide audience. He glanced at an old edition of the New York Times, which was neatly folded on the coffee table in which Karen Armstrong had quoted the Qur'an in her article, similar to the message the President had conveyed:

He started to think more and more about Sadia, until sleep made his eyelids heavy and he dozed off on the couch. For him, it was impossible to forget her. He was infatuated by her thoughts every second of the day. She had understood him and made him complete. Their understanding and love made it easy for them to start their life in a new country without any feeling of unease.

It was not easy to adjust in a new world, but because of peace and tranquility at home, they were always happy. They both were willing to go the extra mile for each other. There were compromises to be made at every stage, but they were determined to make the best out of them. Keeping their own identity intact, they were willing to change trivialities that might come every now and then, in married life. After the attack, the country was changing fast. There was so much of uncertainty in the air. As a law-abiding citizen, Alam had nothing to fear. But he couldn't help think that what would happen to his children in these changed scenarios?

News poured in every day about plane loads of Muslims being deported back to Pakistan. He didn't know if those stories were true or not, but thought it better to not let them disturb him or his children. After all, they may be sent back because they were not there legally in the first place. America was slowly closing its doors for many like him who had left their hometowns in search of greener pastures in the great land of opportunity.

He was stunned when one day Amna asked him, 'Do we have to change our names to American names?' The question was enough to tell him that the kids were scared. They were smart kids who were not oblivious to what was happening around them. The turn of events had scared them. One of their ajust relatives with the last name Husain was ridiculed by his classmates, who were asking him if he in any way was related to Saddam Hussein.

One day, he found Amna in deep thought. On inquiring, she just looked at him in confusion. He went near, patted her on the back and said, 'Come on, say something.' Amna looked back at him with eyes, full of tears and said, 'What if 9/11 was an insider's job? Is it true that Jewish people working in the Twin Towers called in sick that day? You may have not seen the crap that floats on the internet.' He had heard rumours that were related to 9/11 but he paid no attention to any of them. For him, images of Sadia kept him occupied every hour of the day.

Someone in the grocery store had asked Amna if she was Arab and someone had asked Ahmad on the social media platform Myspace if they celebrated clandestinely when 9/11 happened? The one who asked that question was unaware of the fact that Ahmad had lost his mother on that day. Being a Muslim was difficult in America, but was not as difficult as it was for thousands of Sikhs in New Delhi in 1984, when then Prime Minister Indira Gandhi was shot dead by her Sikh bodyguards. As retaliation for that action, goons of the party loyal to the dead Prime Minister had systematically massacred hundreds of Sikhs.

Thank God, America was very different; otherwise, Muslims living there would have been sitting ducks. 'This is what makes America great.' He was heard saying that to one of his friends in India, who called him to pay condolences for the loss of his wife.

The person on the other side narrated to him how the Sikhs in New Delhi had shaved their beard, and shortened their long hair to escape the wrath and rampage that went on for days in 1984.

There were stray cases of violence in America after 9/11, but life was put back to normalcy by the government, which was responsible for safety and security of its citizens, and they successfully performed their responsibility. But for him, life was not normal anymore, and it was never going to be any time soon in the future too.

The children were away in college. The house was an empty nest now. He would go up and down the house endlessly, like a person in search of something but only the bare walls stared back at him. He would sit on the stairs of the house for hours gazing at the driveway, as if waiting for someone to come.

However, nothing like that was ever going to happen because the dead never came back. They simply fade away and remain an inseparable part of memories. That is the law of nature. But for Alam, Sadia would never fade away because he kept her alive in his thoughts and searched for her every time he opened his eyes. His brain was not able to process the signals that were generated because he missed her desperately. One night, because of an episode of abnormal electrical activity in the brain, he had a full body seizure and he found himself on the floor when he woke up.

This episode did not surprise anybody because that can happen when you are living with a bruised brain. When all anti-convulsion medications failed to work, doctors advised him to change the surroundings. He was on a plane on his way to India, for an unplanned one-way trip.

He had completed a full circle and was back to from where he started. Mysterious are the ways of life, aren't they?

HE WAS back again where it had all started. He was back to Gorakhpur after spending decades elsewhere, but unfortunately, nothing much had changed there.

One fine afternoon, he was waiting for Nancy Johnston at the Gorakhpur train station. The train was late, so he had no other option but to wait. The place was crowded with people all around, old and young, rich and poor, clean and dirty, many of them in a hurry and others waiting for their train.

Nancy's train was on time. He had seen her picture on Facebook, so he immediately recognised her as she disembarked from one of the coaches. She was young, of medium height and seemed friendly. She recognised him immediately. She must have gone through his profile on Facebook too. They both looked at each other and acknowledged to themselves a mutual trustworthiness. He liked her at the first glance and said to himself, 'Yes, you deserve all the help you need.' She was looking for records of an old court case which was fought in the

Civil Court of Gorakhpur in 1938. The case was 'Razeel verses Shareef' and had caught the attention of many in the past. Yes, it was the same one that was fought between Shakir and Qazi.

'How come a student in the United States got interested in a court case fought in Gorakhpur?' He asked her with a tease in his eyes. She could only smile but he liked her smile. She knew how to converse in Urdu and Hindi, which soon become the talking point of the small community in Gorakhpur. She charmed everyone, including Alam.

'My forefathers were the main architect of the court case you are talking about,' he tried to impress her. Her eyes widened in excitement. All she said was, 'Really?'

She knew all about that case but nothing about class struggle, that was the alternative plan, if Shakir had not decided otherwise. Being with her was a refreshing change for him. They would occasionally go for long drives, during which their discussions often moved from court case to any other topic under the sun. She was well-read and knew a lot about different cultures and civilisations. One day, she astonished him when she asked him about some park near the printing press, where the Bhagwad Gita is published.

'Oh! You mean Lal Diggi Park?' He was quick to reply, showing off his knowledge about that park and its surroundings in order to impress her. Ironically, it should actually have been her knowledge about Gorakhpur that should have impressed him.

While going to bed, he thought, 'Who in America would know Gorakhpur in this detail?' But then he satisfied himself by blaming it on internet search engines. In today's world, everything and every bit of information is available just a click away.

But his inquisitive mind was not at rest. He pondered more

on this topic. Nancy was doing her research on Indian Muslims. There was nothing wrong in doing so. In fact, it made perfect sense since after 9/11, studying Muslims and understanding Islam was the latest fad in the West. His mind wandered to those in America who crowded television stations to give their expert advice about Islam and its followers. Overnight, everyone seemed to be experts on the topic. He himself could have made a living out of it. Universities, as well as local elementary schools, invited him as guest speaker, to talk about this subject, which had rapidly caught the imagination of the whole world.

He hated doing these sessions because in course of the discourse, it was likely that the dormant corner of his heart would suddenly wake up, leaving him with no choice but to think of Sadia and the void she had left in his life with her death. He would get agitated and frustrated and would sulk; as a result, his whole day would be ruined.

After losing Sadia, it was extremely difficult for him to look in the mirror. He would often look at his own face, cherishing the hope in his heart that somehow Sadia's face might appear next to his face. Often, he felt the silky touch of feminine hands on his shoulders, and would turn his head in anticipation to see the love of his life standing behind him. Sadia would stalk him every moment of his life. There was no easy way to stop this. He buried himself with tons and tons of work, often with unnecessary work, keeping himself busy every minute. There was no other option left for him than to be an escapist. Someday when in good mood, he would look at her picture and tease, 'You stalker.' Now these days were not many. Life was getting busier by the day.

There are secret parleys and meetings whose 'minutes' are recorded, but strictly distributed on 'need to know basis' to selected few. If one was lucky enough to be in the list of the selected few, then one would have known that in the high level States department meeting happening at a place which was not too far away from the Capitol Building in Washington DC, the region of interest was the Indian subcontinent.

Nancy felt comfortable in his house in Gorakhpur. The house was a mixture of old and new constructions. Some parts were centuries old while others were remodelled recently. She found Alam reticence and a very private person. He would talk when needed, but once you broke the ice, he will not stop.

Nancy exerted every effort to start the dialogue. After dinner, she said, 'I am surprised to see how Muslim community, especially in North India, is divided on caste lines. Same as it is in Hindus.' He wanted to stay away from this conversation, but soon realised that he could not avoid it for long.

He thought, 'Well, she has come all the way from America to learn about Indian Muslims, so it not fair to brush her off rudely.' She had not stopped, 'I would be upset if someone would think of himself to be superior to me. Don't you think so?'

He replied, 'In India, everybody has felt being discriminated against least once in his lifetime. It is here for ages. Even holy books like the Vedas approve of for Hindus.' She went into deep thought, and rationalised, 'But now times are changing. Look at your State. They are ruling it.'

He replied curtly, 'And yes, sooner or later we will rule. The numbers run in our favour. All we have to do is to bring the marginalised sections of Hindus and Muslims together on a single platform.'

She looked convinced. She had the information ready, 'You belong to the class of Muslims which are in majority, say eighty five percent of Muslims are from Other Backward Classes, and then why is the Muslim leadership in the hands of the the rich, upper caste fifteen per cant?'

She had a point. She looked straight in his eyes and said, 'If democracy is a game of numbers, then you or your people should be Chief Minister of the State. Isn't it?' He said dryly, 'Yeah, we are working on that part.'

Then he looked into her eyes with a mischievous glint and said, 'Why not, someday.' And Nancy smiled.

He went to the refrigerator, took some mangoes out, and started peeling them with a knife. He wanted to continue the dialogue with Nancy. With a plate of sliced mangoes in his hand, he knocked her door gently.

Nancy sat in a well lit room. It was late night. Her thesis was going nowhere. She was putting off the documentation part. She remembered how frustrated she was when she confessed to her parents in California, 'It is too boring to write. I hate that part.' The thought brought a smile and she started typing on her laptop.

'The Western world is convinced that Indian democracy, unlike Pakistan, is going to get stronger day by day. There is only one way to have an influence, and that is by ensuring that democracy is strengthened in India. India cannot be another Pakistan or Afghanistan. Hence, to have an influence in this country, you have to do it the old-fashioned way. Get connected to the leaders who mattered, or who will matter in the days to come.'

She shut her eyes to rest her now aching eyes. She turned her head to look at the person standing in the room with a plate full of mangoes. She smiled and took the plate pleasantly. He found her smile pleasing. He never would have believed how potent a plate of mangoes could be.

On the breakfast table, she was very loquacious, 'At the airport, I met an elderly gentleman who told me his name was Syed Azhar Ali.' He was barely listening; at that time he had no interest in somebody by that name. But she had his full attention when she added, 'That person has direct lineage from the Prophet, that is why he adds Syed to his name, but I wasn't ready to buy it. It can't be true?'

He wanted to end this conversation and rather talk about mangoes. But she was not ready to let go just now, 'In Grad school, there were many students with this title. How can they all be having direct lineage...?'

Before she could finish, he jumped in, and said, 'I don't think it is true. My father knew many who started adding this title; one of them actually chided him for not becoming a Syed by now.'

He felt a faint tug in his heart because he was referring to Arman Ali and suddenly his left side started aching again. Sadia's reminiscences started flashing before him. She seemed to ask him, 'Since when did you start to enjoy mangoes?' He felt as his left side had weakened to an extent that it could not carry the weight of his body. He was under a lot of superficial stress. He knew that today he might limp again after a long time. The brain once injured never heals. All you have to do is to adjust yourself.

Nancy was disappointed to learn that court papers of the lawsuit had been transferred from Gorakhpur court to the High Court in Allahabad. She wanted to get them at any cost. She could not help but notice that he had withdrawn after their Syed-non Syed discussion.

Images of the past jumped in front of his eyes in flashback. Sadia was back again. He remembered teasing her, 'If this was your grandmother's time, then she would have never allowed you to marry me. Isn't it?'

Sadia replied, 'No, she would have crawled to beg you to marry me, after all you were the best thing after the invention of the sliced bread.'

He was ready with his retort, and immediately said, 'Want to try some bread?' Hearing this, she ran and he followed her. The next minute they would be tangled on the bed.

Sadia was very particular about turning the light off and before doing that she would always chuckle, 'Love is like a photographic film and needs darkness to develop.' When it was pitch dark, bare bodies conversed. First in whispers and after a while possibilities knew no bounds. Anything is possible when the barriers are broken and willingness seeks no permission from any God. The naked bodies in birthday suits were engulfed in making love. The flashback was over as abruptly as it had started. He started to shiver. The side of his leg was burning. He could smell flesh; his flesh, Sadia's flesh, smells of cologne, smell of sweat and smell of fluid secreting out? He closed his eyes and took a deep breath.

There was a gentle knock on the door. Nancy was standing with a bowl full of sliced mangoes. She hesitated, and inquired with a look of worry on her face, 'You don't look good, anything wrong?' He simply smiled. There was nothing he could tell her. Nancy did not stop; she put her hand on his forehead to check if he had fever. Sadia would have done the same thing.

Sadia, if alive, would have been forty four years old. Nancy must be half her age or little more. He suddenly felt very weak on his left side, 'What the heck! Am I going crazy?' He felt as if he would die if somebody had shown him a mirror. He simply collapsed on the bed. Nancy panicked and rushed out to get some water for him.

Elsewhere, somewhere in the United States, John Beck had a very boring job. He was a contractor with Homeland Security and one of his qualifications was his knowledge of many languages. He had no designated office and he generally operated from home. He was fed up of reading other people's tweets, YouTube postings and e-mails. He smiled to himself and said, 'This person doesn't make sense at all. Today he is in poetry mode. What are they smoking in Gorakhpur? Look at this, a jumbo facebook post:

Ek haseen see tum baat ho, kal raat ka tum khwaab ho,
Mere dil mein aake bus gayee, har dua ka tum jawab ho,
Tere waste meri har dua, meri zindagi ka karar ho,
Tujhe paake hai mujhe laga, kisi nek kaam ka sawab ho.'

You are beautiful; you are like yesterday's dream,
You came and dwelled in my heart,
you are the answer to my prayers,
All my prayers are for you, you are the solace of my life,
After achieving you, it seemed to me,
you are the prize for some good I did.

This particular person who was assigned to him, seemed to him to be a dry and boring person. He argued with himself, 'Why will he not be? Wife is dead and children are busy in school and college.'

But in his weekly report, he would always identify the number of followers this person added every week. This week, he crossed twenty thousand in a short span of few months. He murmured to himself, 'Must be doing something good.'

He took a swig of his coffee cup and gulped down the lukewarm liquid and waived a bye to his computer screen and said,'I will do it as long as you pay me.' Saying this, he smiled and adjusted his hair with a little comb before stepping out.

John's report was automatically saved on the hard drive of a server, which was located somewhere in the State of Nebraska, and there were personnel who were zealously feeding the data to complex computer programmes,under the tag 'Classified'.

HE WAS unsure whether he should go to Allahabad with Nancy or not. She noticed his dilemma when she found him in deep thought.

'If you are not feeling well, then I can go to Allahabad myself,' Nancy said to him at the breakfast table. He wanted to tell her to go. He wanted to be alone. He was not ready for any intrusion in his private life. Because of the nature of his job he would meet hundreds of people during the daytime, but at the end of the day, he always clamoured for some quite time. His own time, where he could call his children, or if nothing else, would sit down and reflect on the past. The past that was etched deep in his heart, his time spent with Sadia. The memory lanes would never cease to amuse him.

He did not notice Nancy, who was ready to go to Allahabad. A guilty feeling ran over him and he replied without even looking at her, 'Oh! No, wait, I will join you, what time does the train leaves?' He knew when the train was scheduled to leave but pretended to have forgotten.

Money can do wonderful things for you, especially if you are travelling in a first class coupe on an Indian train. As the name suggests, coupes are for two passengers only, with two berths, one below and the other above. She was allotted the bottom berth and his was above. He looked perturbed for a second, and then he slowly climbed the stairs to go upstairs to sleep.

In the middle of the night, Nancy woke up from her sleep. A night lamp dimly lighted the coupe. At first, she saw a foot hanging in the air, next to the steps, from the above berth. She rubbed her eyes and thought that he must be getting down to take a leak and paying no heed, she closed her eyes again. Suddenly, after a few seconds, she heard a little thud. The foot was still in the air, and was swirling in slow motion, as if trying to find something.

Now she was fully awake, and started watching carefully how desperately he was trying to put his foot on the steps to get down. Finally, after much effort, he was able to do so. Slowly, he climbed down few steps, and was standing on the floor.

He looked at her. There was a look of dismay on her face. He felt as if he had been caught doing something wrong and said, 'Why are you awake?' Without even looking at her, he said, 'Getting down using these dumb stairs is quite an ordeal, isn't it?' Saying this, he rolled open the coupe door and walked out. When he returned back, she was still sitting. There was a pleasant silence in the coupe. He sat next to her. She asked, 'Is it difficult to climb down in darkness?'

He smiled and replied, 'No, not exactly. For me, it is more challenging because of my medical condition. My left side is not as skilful as the right side.'

The train was running at normal speed. He was sitting next to her, telling her his story of the darkness which once engulfed him at noon time and since then had impacted his life. Probably, out of sympathy, she gently touched his hand and slowly curled her fingers to hold it. Her silence seemed to say to him to stay there; there was place for both of them. Soon they were half sleep, comfortably sitting close to each other. She was in a pleasant mood and was humming lines about a train journey, written by the 19th Century Scottish poet Robert Louis Stevenson, 'Faster than fairies, faster than witches, …bridges and houses, hedges and ditches,…Each a glimpse and gone forever.' That night for him was like no other night.

The High Court in Allahabad was established long back in 1869 and was one of the first High Courts to be established. The lists of judgements delivered are long, but the one that almost derailed the democratic process in India was delivered against no other than Prime Minister Indira Gandhi by Justice Jag Mohan Lal Sinha. In his judgement, Mr Sinha held the Prime Minister guilty of corrupt practices, and declared her election to the lower house of Parliament commonly called Lok Sabha, void. This judgement was passed in1975, and left the entire judicial system proud, but unfortunately, turned the country upside down.

Indira Gandhi declared a state of Emergency in the country, which restrained the democratic rights guaranteed to the Indian citizens. Most of the members of the opposition were put in jail, and freedom of speech was curtailed. This incident did not go down very well with the country. It was aperiod of which every Indian should always be ashamed. Fortunately, it was short-lived, but still long enough to put a question mark on the integrity of the Prime Minister.

They were walking briskly through the corridors of the High Court when she stopped for a moment, looked at him and said, 'Quite a place. Your favourite Mrs Gandhi was here as a witness, poor lady. Do you remember her election fiasco?' He stopped and reverted, 'Oh! Yes, that was quite some time back. Those were turbulent times.'

He went back to memory lanes and started remembering those days. The crowd at the famous Ram Lila Ground in New Delhi was unprecedented, where a new hero, Jai Prakash Narain, popularly known as JP, had risen. JP roared by reciting Ramdhari Singh Dinkar's evocative poem, 'Singhasan khaali karo/ki janata aati hai (Surrender your throne, for the people are coming)', to thunderous applause. All the tricks of the trade were applied to ensure that response to Total Revolution by JP fizzles out. To divert the attention of the public, Delhi Doordarshan quickly announced screening of the popular movie 'Bobby' on India's only television channel. The electric power supply to unfriendly newspapers was cut off so that they may not publish news about the rally, whose success had sent the government machinery into a tizzy.

'What are you thinking?' Nancy put her hands on one of his shoulders and asked. He almost woke up and smiled, looked deeply in her eyes, and gently reached for her hand, and held it firmly. Human touch is a great healer.

'When you look back at the past, you realise that no matter how significant they seemed at that time, they were inconsequential when the big picture is taken into account…' He was not able to put his thoughts together and was nervous, and Nancy knew that.

He was nervous because he was holding her hands. After Sadia, he was holding someone's hands, especially female hands, in public for the first time. It was different from the handshakes shared by colleagues and friends. His body was getting frail on the left side. Every now and then, his heart fluttered and his left eye twitched. He felt like a careless teenager. Yes, he was nervous. A person of his stature, who was also very conscious of how he would be perceived by others, was defying his own self.

'The heart has its reasons which reason knows nothing of,' echoed from nowhere. He wanted to blame someone else for the feelings that were signalling the start of a new beginning. He wondered what Blaise Pascal, the 17th Century philosopher, was going through when that quote came to surface.

The brain told him that it was forbidden to hold her hands, but his heart had a mind of its own and was overtaking the brain in its own strides.

Nancy gently freed her hand from his. He felt relieved and distressed at the same time. The battle between heart and brain had started the malice, and he was losing control. He wanted to sit down. Soon they were sipping lassi in a nearby restaurant.

As he was about to put the earthen glass of lassi on the table, two teenagers, who were watching him from a table on the far side, approached them. He had noticed them looking at him from their table, and pointing out to each other, but he paid no attention. That must be because of Nancy, because she generally aroused the curiosity of the local population. A good-looking American girl, speaking the local language is a sure sign of admiration and sometimes trouble. These kids are after Nancy, he thought, and why not? He would have done the same, had he been in their shoes. But here he was wrong.

They were curious about him. One of the kids with dark skin, and few books in his hand, said softly, 'I know you sir, I am in your friend's list on Facebook. My name is Raj Sharma. We had a conversation last year.'

The other kid was simply staring at him, as if to convince himself that he was really meeting him in person. Then gathering all his courage, he opened his mouth and said, 'Sir, you write so well, all my friends read your posts regularly.' And before he could say anything further, Raj made a request if he would allow them to take a group picture, which he would post on Facebook.

'So you are popular even in Allahabad,' Nancy teased him while they were scrutinising old court papers. The papers were stuffed into jute sacks and the sacks were numbered in a manner that could not be deciphered by everybody. He could not believe that he was doing all this for a person who few days back was a stranger to him.

A loner like himself was enjoying the company of a girl much younger and was actually looking forward to be with her as much as possible. No wonder they say that heart has strange reasons. He was always tough on himself, was very careful in his moves and seldom got swept by emotions, but today in the evening he was standing next to a kiosk at the fashionable Civil Lines, eating roasted corn with Nancy. Today he was full of energy and was planning to go and watch a movie, if Nancy cared. He could not see his face, but if he did, he would have noticed that lately he was smiling a lot.

The boat ride at Sangam, the confluence where three rivers meet in Allahabad, was memorable. His actions surprised him because he had never done such things before. Sadia used to beg him to go for boat rides, but most of the time he never relented, and thought it to be childish, but today he was telling the manjhi or the boatman to go for an extra trip. He wanted to explore everything, do it all. Like his ancestor Shakir, he was subscribing to the doctrine that since you get life only once, why not do it all. Then he started to sulk, as the portion of his heart where Sadia dwelled, started to ache.

His mind wandered to the lyrics of his favourite Bollywood song. 'Main aur meri tanhai aksar yeh baatein kartein hain, Tum hoti to kaisa hota, Tum yeh kehti, tum vo kehti.' (I and my loneliness usually chat about, how would it have been if you were present, you would say this, and you would have said that.)

He stood there motionless and watched the sun disappearing slowly in the water, as if submerging in the confluence of the three sacred rivers. He did not realise when Nancy came and stood next to him, and when did they held hands, looking at the beauty of the sunset silently. The power of touch is like an elixir that heals like no prescription drug. All along he resisted the healing that he needed badly, but today he felt ready to be healed. His brain was losing, and his heart was taking over. In life, there comes a time when the past slowly phases out and the present clamours to be a part the future.

'Who betrayed Chandra Shekhar Azad?' She posed this question as a teaser after they returned from visiting the Anand Bhawan, which is the ancestral house of the first Indian Prime Minister Jawaharlal Nehru.

He was delighted to find the question easy, and answered curtly, 'An informer.' She hastily shot another volley, 'Like one who informed about Babu Bandhu Singh in Gorakhpur. Remember 1857?'

He quickly added, 'Yes, Yes.'

She was probably picking questions from a list, 'Why do people betray their country?'

He was ready with the answer, 'Greed, money, power…'

Her next one was directed at him, 'What will it take for you to betray your country?'

She was testing his patience. In the usual circumstances, this would have annoyed him, but not this time. He went into a deep thought to articulate a decent answer. Nancy came to his help and said, 'A person like you will never betray the country. I can vouch for your sincerity.' He was not astonished at all. His hold on her hand became tight, very tight. He noticed how his heart was beating fast.

Nancy was a focused person. Her thesis was going well. She was able to find what she was looking for. Her fingers were moving fast on the key board. Everything was being stored on hard drive, as well as on a remote backup from where data would be compressed, encrypted and transmitted to a device stationed in the basement of a building, located somewhere in the State of Idaho in United States.

Her message was simple.

'India is never going to be like Afghanistan or any other Middle Eastern country. The fundamentals of democracy are strong. Muslims here are loyal to the country. Although they are upset with the establishment, and feel being discriminated, they will never be swayed by any kind of fundamentalism from anywhere. The ones who stray away are ones who might have been on the receiving end for no fault of their own.

Yes, there is resentment against America because America is on the side of Israel, and people here do care about Palestine, but they are so busy in their own affairs that they will never take extreme position in support of a country that is too far off.'

One may call it a miracle or just an example of advance

technology that nothing stayed on her hard drive for more than a few minutes. The files would be erased as soon as they were secured on a device in Idaho.

They took the keys of their rooms from the reception, and went on their separate paths. He did not like letting her go because he was getting used to her company.

He was someone who felt at perfect ease when he was alone, but was now scared of being alone. Alam was a loner by choice because he did not want to be disappointed by people who would not meet his expectation. But today, it was very different. Nancy was exceeding all expectations.

The next day, they both were in high spirits. The topic was his favourite one, about Muslim leadership in India.

He was not in a mood to stop when he said, 'Let us ponder about the issues of leadership. One of the casualties of the great migration after Partition was the absence of Muslim leadership on the Indian side. For decades after the Independence, the country was single-handedly ruled by a political party, that is, the Congress party, which thrived on support provided by Muslims and other minority groups.'

She tried to intercept, but he was not listening at all, and continued with full ferocity and said, 'Since Congress party lacked inner party democracy, leadership was entirely based on nomination process, which was at the fancy and mercy of the party high command.'

She grabbed a carrot from the nearby table and put it in her mouth. He did not notice when she grabbed a glass of water and put it on the table, which was between him and her.

He was unstoppable, 'Often, Muslims were selected and groomed based on loyalty factor, and were imposed on populace to gain maximum mileage during elections. In this process, where loyalty was the sole criteria, genuine grass-root leaders were sidelined to give way to sycophants, who were there for their self-interest.'

He paused and lifted the glass of water for a drink, and then continued, 'As a result, the interest of common people became a casualty. The failure of the Congress to protect minorities during communal flare-ups was seen as intentional, because of compulsions of the vote bank politics. Some even say that Congress was working on the British doctrine of 'divide and rule', and believed that by creating a phobia of Hindu resurgent, they will force Muslims to flock to the Congress for protection.'

Then he looked at her to see if she was listening. She was very attentive in fact, she was recording this on her handheld device, which often acted as a phone.

He continued, 'Such was the moral bankruptcy of Muslim leadership that they were scared to raise issues of Muslim security in legislative bodies, because they thought that this act will bring them censure for working against the party line. This honeymoon with the Congress lasted for quite some time and produced leaders, some of them, although were pygmies in stature, but you know what?'

He paused, most likely expecting an answer from Nancy, but finding none he continued, 'These leaders attained high offices and decorated Parliament and other legislative bodies, worked very well, cemented our secular credentials, and caught the imagination of the world. But unfortunately, this did not give full return on the deposit, and the deposit here was Muslim votes.'

Having said that, he was exhausted and surprised. He had not spoken that much in weeks.

He continued, 'There is need for an ebullient Muslim leader, who can perform and negotiate, based on his credibility, without aid of crutches. The crutches in politics generally are patronage of business houses, or a godfather, like Kanshi Ram, who was doing ground work for decades. It may still be not too late for the Kanshi Rams of Muslims to emerge. It will be advantageous to a Muslim leader, if he is capable of provide for himself and his family by his own means. This way, he will not forgo the pledge to his constituents and will not become a participant in the mechanism to generate money by questionable means.'

There was no stopping his train of thought. 'The person has to be educated, widely travelled, and should have vision to look beyond the spoils of power. The person should be able to inspire for change and be able to provide hope. The person should know how to connect with the people of Kashmir to convince them that a powerful and united India is the need of the day. He should be able to comfort victims of communal riots, who struggle to put their lives back in order. He has to be believed by migrant workers working in big cities, that he is aware of their plight and will advocate the case of their unfairly treatment. He should be equally comfortable in the company of rocket scientists, and should be on the same frequency with the not-so-educated constituents. That is the ideal leader we are looking for.'

Nancy was impressed. She was watching a transformed person; a person, whom she thought could not even speak, was at his best performance. She could see a leader in the making.

She was sitting alone in her hotel room. He had gone out to meet a few relatives. She was giving the final touches to her report. She wrote thus:

'It is sad. But in India, votes are cast on basis of caste affiliations. In today's political scenario, some electoral gains made by parties and leaders are based on the numerical strength of the caste they are affiliated with. For the same reason, the person who is vying to be a Muslim leader should be in a position to affiliate himself with birth or with association with a caste that has an advantage over others in the number game. In spite of the fact that Islam prohibits division based on caste and creed, Muslims of the Indian subcontinent to some extent practice caste system, which is adopted from Hindu caste hierarchy. The Muslim community is highly stratified and economically weak and economically weak are placed at the bottom. Although, this section constitutes the bulk of the Muslim population, but they have been marginalised politically. It will play to the advantage of the Muslim leader, if he belonged to one of the marginalised groups, because numerically these groups have tremendous advantage over others, since democracy is the game of numbers.'

Having completed typing, she called her mother to tell her that she liked it in India and thought that she was making progress. Her mother was not amazed at all. She knew her daughter well, and knew that she loved her job because it was for the good of her country. There are many ways you can serve your country, and what better way than getting paid for it too. It does not matter if the country was hit by the tidal wave of recession, for this intelligence-gathering agency, the premier one in the country, is never short of funds. How can they be when they have to take care of almost twenty to thirty thousand employees, and her daughter was one amongst them? Working for the Central Intelligence Agency, commonly called CIA.

THE BEGINNING of the 20th Century saw the rise of a very ambitious man by the name of Shakir, who had slowly but steadily made a niche for himself. He was buying everything that he could put his hands on. However, his love for purchasing land superseded every other fancy. He would say, 'It was the best thing to buy because they are not building it anymore.' Generally, he would buy things solely on his own, but with a few exceptions. He bought the village of Pakri near Nepal border in partnership with his neighbour and assistant Anwar.

The village of Pakri was fertile and was surrounded by thick forests on all sides. It was a hunter's paradise, where an annual festival for hunting was celebrated, which would see gatherings of family members and friends to celebrate, enjoy and feast. This was also an occasion to oblige government officials, who would come and relax. The most-awaited feature of this gathering would be to go for the kill, or tiger hunting, in which kids were not permitted to go.

Gradually, chances of spotting tigers started diminishing due to a change in habitat, resulting from continued land development and poaching activities. With fewer tigers sited, someone in the family bent the rule and gave kids an opportunity to flock with the elders, but only after receiving training for half a day.

The training was extensive, and included a general discussion on the behaviour of the big cat. The elders would narrate accounts based on their past experiences. During those days, the great hunter of Kumaon and Garhwal, Jim Corbett had captured the heart and mind of all. Kids would boast about having read episodes from the books he authored. The guns, each connected with a story behind it, would be displayed to impress everybody.

Generally, a machan, or a raised platform, was made on a tree, and a goat or sheep was tied to the tree as bait. The tree was selected based on the advice of old sages, at a location where tigers frequented.

The last time they spotted a tiger was in the 60s, when Shakir's great grandchildren were out there along with their elders on a Jeep, and one of them had mistaken the tiger for a lion.

Today, one of those grandchildren had just returned from Allahabad along with Nancy, and was catching up on lost time. Work had piled on and he tried his best to get them done expeditiously. There were throngs of visitors outside; some of them were ones who seemed unfamiliar. They bore rustic looks and from their appearance it seemed that they had travelled a long distance to reach there. They all stood up in respect as he entered visitor's lounge. One amongst them came forward and after a salutation said, 'You were a little kid when you used to come to Pakri. I still remember you.'

Memory of Pakri flashed before him. These men were from

the farm, and one of them was in the hunting expedition when the tiger was spotted. At that time, this gentleman was a young lad, but today due to the weathering of time, he looked tired and exhausted. He had come there along with some of his companions to tell him a story; not just a story but a part of the history which Alam was not familiar with. His name was Rahmat.

'The farm is in trouble,' Rahmat said in despair. When he was convinced that he had full attention, he carried on his conversation. His voice had signs of allegiance to the family he had been working for all his life, 'We have learned that they are going to get it transferred in their name, and then will use muscle power to acquire or capture it.'

A look of surprise registered on Alam's face and he gave them a blank look. He had no idea what he they were talking about. Now it was their turn to be surprised. They looked at each other and then Rahmat said, failing to hide the surprise from his voice, 'So you don't know anything? Well, you cannot be blamed. You have lived elsewhere all your life, but you have to do something now.'

The story was simple. The village of Pakri was bought by Shakir and Anwar. Shakir's share in the village was full, with the exception of six paisa, or one anna, which was owned by Anwar at that time. Later in 1916, Shakir bought Anwar's share, and became the sole owner of the village that spread into 750 sprawling acres. As years went by, Anwar's family disintegrated to such an extent that they faded away from the social circles. His descendants became non-entities and some of them got themselves involved in petty criminal activities.

On other hand, Shakir's family used education as a tool, and as a result, they became renowned in the region. They did very well for themselves, spread all over the globe and carried lots of influence. Since most of the intelligent ones left to make a name for themselves in different spheres, the farm was neglected. It was being managed by a couple of Shakir's great grandchildren, who were strictly incompetent, negligent and greedy. Pure greed was displayed by one of Shakir's son when he kept all for himself rather than give share ownership to other rightful owners in the farm. Now, his son Zahid was finding it difficult to manage the farm.

Anwar's descendents saw this opportunity to get a hold of the farm. They knew that the ones in-charge were useless and weak, and would not be able to defend. They forged ownership papers and filed a civil suit claiming Anwar to be the sole owner of the farm.

He listened to them attentively. Rahmat got emotional and started crying,'We have given our whole life to your family. We were treated well by your grandfather and granduncles, we cannot even think of letting it go that easily. They will get it and there is nobody who can protect us.' He continued in hush tones, 'Zahid babu cannot save it. They are timid and will run away as soon as they will arrive. You have to do something.' He raised his head to look at Rahmat and asked, 'What makes you think that I can do anything, when the situation is almost hopeless, as you put it? Besides, they are my relatives. What do you want me to do? To go and tell them that you are no good and you are losing it all?'

Then he raised his hand and said mockingly, 'They will welcome me with open arms, to say that thank you for being the saviour. I understand the gravity of the situation, I also know that Zahid and company cannot play hardball with hardened criminals, but I am also a novice in these affairs. I understand that lately I have done some heroic feat, but that does not mean that I can keep on doing it all the time.'

They were disappointed. Finally, one of them, the youngest among them who was quiet most of the time, spoke, 'There are stories about Shakir Dada that we have heard from our elders. Nobody can be like him, he was a great man.' Then he said in chaste Hindi, 'Woh to Sher the. Aap bhi to unhi ke khoon ho, ek sher aap bhi bano.' (He was a lion. You are his blood. You too become a lion.)

Then they all dispersed. There was an uncanny silence all around after they had departed. Sleep eluded him that night. He could hear the tap-tap sound made by Nancy's frantic typing on her keyboard. Since he figured that sleep would not come easily to him, he decided to set up a video conference. He thought, 'It must be noon time in USA.' He picked up the phone and called his children to tell them the events that unfolded that day.

He wanted to tell them that everyone had their own destiny, and not everyone could make the choice to pursue it. A stranger, whom he had met for first time today, defined his destiny. He could hear the voice echoing manifold. 'Woh to Sher the. Aap bhi to unhi ke khoon ho, ek sher aap bhi bano.' (He was a lion. You are his blood. You too become a lion.)

Nancy laughed upon hearing all this. She came near him and said, 'Well, well, history is in the making. You know what Winston Churchill said?'

He could see the eagerness in her to quote what Churchill said. He wanted to dampen her spirit and quietly said, 'I was not the lion, but it fell to me to give the lion's roar.' He was right because lions would fight when needed.

He gently patted her shoulders and wished her good night, but deep in his heart, he did not want to say good night to her. He wanted to stay with her, and wondered whether she felt the same way about him.

Anwar and Shakir used to live in the same locality and their houses were at a stone's throw away from each other. Shakir used to help Anwar in the beginning, and had him as his assistant, but later Shakir realised that Anwar's destiny was different from his own, so he started to drift away from Anwar. Anwar started losing whatever little he had earned, because he got romantically involved with another woman. Shakir tried to reason with him, but when he paid no heed to his advice, then he did the obvious and he parted ways. He bought back all the properties, which they jointly owned, and became the sole owner and that included the village of Pakri, where now Shakir was the sole owner or zamindar.

It is rightly said that misery has many cousins, who often come after each other. And Anwar was a living example of that. The woman who was his mistress eloped with a younger man, and to aggravate the situation, she took away whatever savings Anwar had managed to hide from his wife. He took to drinking and his children loitered here and there. When interest on capital started accumulating, and Anwar showed his inability to pay, his house was seized by moneylender Bhagwan Das. This brought them to the streets.

Today, the surviving members of Anwar's clan were huddled in a dimly-lit room and were making plans to get back Pakri Farm by hook or by crook. They were desperate, and to them this was the only opportunity that may give them the oxygen they needed badly to survive. They were counting heavily upon the fact that the ones in charge of the farm were incompetent and ineffective people who would not dare to stand up against them. But they were wrong. Not very far, there was somebody who would unexpectedly upset their apple cart.

And that is what happened the next day in court. The judge had to delay the judgement because the night before, he got a very important phone call, a call that literally made the judge shake in his boots. A very high up officer in the government summoned him immediately because a video had gone viral on social media depicting him taking a bundle of cash from some people whose identity was not very clear.

While the judge drove to the headquarter, there was a contingent that followed him; there were six or seven SUVs with unarmed occupants, and half a mile behind them were three or four police vehicles with cops armed to the teeth. They were all going towards Pakri.

Alam thought it to be a waste of time for him to join the caravan, so he utilised his time by planting some trees in his orchard along with Nancy. For him, spending time with Nancy was more fulfilling than going after a piece of ancestral land. Then he did something that left him also surprised.

He called his children and after some casual chatting, he started talking to them about Nancy. He got very excited when his children asked him if they could talk to her. He was nervous as a teenager and was curious to know whether his children would find her as interesting as he did. His heart rammed hard against his ribcage and he felt tingling on his left side, but today he was not annoyed with this tingling any more. He was of the belief that age is no barrier. It is just a limitation you put on your mind. That was him, but what about Nancy?

The next day, he gaped at her when she told him that she wanted him to speak to her mother. He was hesitant for a while and asked, 'Are you sure?' He was not even certain whether Nancy had ever told her parents about him.

He stammered, 'Oh! Hi!' On the other end was Nancy's mother. His voice was carried to a nearby base station, from where it was being relayed to the other end. Nancy's mother, unlike her daughter, seemed laconic because she simply responded by, 'Hi there.' And then she asked him about the weather. He had no clue about the weather because since morning he had not stepped out of the room.

His mind was in great turmoil. The thoughts were haphazard and turbulent with no particular pattern. A kind of mid life crisis was knocking him with a tease. Who says that midlife crisis is boring. He found it more interesting than when he was getting into adulthood.

IN THE other room, Nancy was trying to finish her report, while he sat in the study in a deep thought. How do you define destiny? Something static that was decided for you the day you were born, or is it something that is dynamic in nature and changes every minute, and is being governed by position of the moon, stars, orbits and the sun. Why is he here rather than in New York? Why he is not doing what he is supposed to do? Why? There were no easy answers so he walked to the bedroom. Nancy brought some tea for him in the bed, and he felt blessed because she had made tea the way he always wanted it.

On the television set, news channels blared out about some riots in the western part of the State at a place called Faizpur. Riots are a grim reminder that there are certain differences that can never be ironed out. He felt sad for all the lives that were lost in the riot, the children who were orphaned, women who were widowed and the families that would starve because the sole bread winner had been killed.

A numbing pain slowly began to overpower his entire body,

and he quickly turned the television set off. Elections were round the corner, and polarisation of votes on the lines of caste and religion was necessary for political parties to win the elections. What could work to polarise voters than engineering a riot?

Nancy was curious and she wanted to know more about the riots, so she started flipping the channels on the other television set that sat in a corner in his office. After a little while, she peeped her head out, and said, 'Looks like the administration is not interested in quelling the riots, otherwise they should have stopped it by now.'

She was right because the stakeholders wanted the riots to cross a certain threshold to instil fear in the hearts and minds of the people. In the absence of that fear, they would not come to you looking for help. What a nasty way to do politics! Nancy reminder him by saying, 'Don't forget that transfer of power for India and birth of Pakistan was on piles and piles of dead bodies.' She was right; history is full of instances where religion can be blamed for all the wrongs that had been done for the sake of religion itself.

This riot was like no other riot. Nancy was quick to notice how the pattern of riots was changing in India. Things were not the same as in 1947, when the British left India, or in 1992, when a mosque was demolished in Ayodhya. She stood next to him in the garden, where he was planting a new mango sapling. It was a relatively new variety, gifted to him by his friend from Malihabad, the mango capital of North India. She sat next to him on the ground and said, 'You should read this analysis, looks brilliant to me. Even riots are getting too complicated to understand. Earlier, it was between Hindus and Muslims, but now they are divided at micro levels, alignments are different, too complicated to comprehend.' Without waiting for any response from him, she continued, 'This caste menace is derailing this country; everybody is getting his identity, not only on the basis of religion but also on the basis of caste, and in some cases sub-caste. In this skirmish, there are traces of what would have happened in Gorakhpur in Mr Shakir's era in the '40s. Then she took a long pause and said, 'If I understand correctly, you said that all the have-nots from Hindu, as well as from Muslim community, were united that night to confront Qazi, and everybody else, who considered themselves noble, whether Hindu or Muslim, were united for the cause.' Then she put some stress in her voice and said, 'Same thing is happening in Faizpur; it is no boiler plate type typical Hindu vs Muslim riot. It is a class war like never heard of before.'

She was right. The down trodden, irrespective of religion, were ganging up against the upper echelons of society. Society was getting divided manifold. To be a major stakeholder, you have to have the ability to design a model by incorporating different combinations. The more divided society is, more are the chances of playing the game.

Nancy had done her calculations well, she was of the opinion that certain sections from Muslims and Hindus could be aligned together, based on a common ground and that would be the winning combination. She was of the firm belief that the person planting the sapling had the panacea to get it all bundled together.

Why? Because he belonged to the class which were 'numerically' strong in Muslims and this class had an equivalent class in Hindus. Just add them up and there you have it. If they could fight on this division, then they could also fight together and win elections.

Elsewhere, the scene at the dimly-lit house was of mourning. They had failed to put their hands on the farm, and disappointment was written on their faces. They were backed by no other than the infamous Ratan Gupta, the person who took the credit for showing pictures of a naked girl to most of the students of the university on a projector in the beginning, but later in live shows. He became a pimp, and began supplying pahari girls to brothels in Mumbai. Today his pitch was straight, 'Amreekan ke hote kuch nahin ho sakta hai.' (Nothing could be done because of the American.) Ratan's jab pointed directly to Alam. He had disappointed them all; otherwise, they would have been owners of hundreds of acres of land today.

Javed, who was probably one of Anwar's great grandchildren, and was now middle-aged, spoke with anger and anguish, 'Maar do usko, fifty-fifty baant leinge.' (Kill him, we will divide fifty-fifty.) Ratan had no reason to protest. A sinister plan was verbalised, and all seconded it.

He was unmindful of all that was going on elsewhere. After Sadia's death, he had never got time nor had the urge even to fall in love or get into a relationship. But today, everything looked different to him. The humid weather did not bother him. He was unfazed by the frequent electric power cuts, and above all, he was eager to go to the mosque to pray, because he knew that Nancy would be waiting for him when he returned.

In spite of everything, he could never remove the nagging feeling that Nancy was too young for him. He knew that age should not matter at all; ideally, love should conquer all and there were no set rules about standard age protocol for falling in love. He started subscribing to the belief that age is just a number and, as Mark Twain said, 'Age is an issue of mind over matter'.

Heaven's will not fall if it happens. Besides, it can give you a chance to consider new perspectives and appreciate offerings of a different generation.

She came out from the shower. Her wet hair was spread mischievously over her shoulder and water from her hair had drenched her top, which clung to the upper part of her body. Her body was well sculptured, and only a sage would not want to look at it perpetually. He was not a saint, so he could not remove his gaze from one of the most remarkable creation ever made. His whole body started to burn and it had nothing to do with the injury he had sustained on the right side of his brain. That day, he realised that he was not the type of person to burn with desire and not do anything about it. The voyage of life takes you to terrains that one never thought to be treading upon. Seconds turned to minutes and the minutes into hours. Time is a great healer and it happened on a hot summer day in Gorakhpur.

This eastern part of the State is notorious for mosquito-borne diseases, and it is no fun when you get ill. Nancy had high fever and felt miserable. He cancelled all his appointments and sat by her side all night. It was enough to surprise her and she asked, 'Do you know when was the last time someone sat next to me when I was ill?'

He nodded his head the other way, as if to say, 'How would I know?'

Fatigue and high fever tired her, so she closed her eyes. She could remember vividly those elementary school days, when she was four, and her parents almost lived in her room when she had some viral infection. That was the time someone took care of her the way he did. Her whole body rejoiced at the very thought that there is someone out here, thousands of miles away from her home, who treated her as someone special.

But the next moment her face became pale. What would he think of her when he would learn who she really was? Will he ever know? Suddenly, for the first time in her career, she started hating her job.

Guilt gnawed at her insides and when she could take it no longer, she woke him up in the middle of the night and said, 'Sorry to wake you up, but I want to make a confession.'

He listened to her with patience, and when shc was done, he stood up and hugged her. Then he squeezed her tight and said with his characteristic smile, 'I don't remember a word of what you have just said.'

Then, after kissing her forehead, he looked deep in her eyes and said, 'What confession?' Their eyes met, and they both were again under each other's spell. Silence communicated deeper feelings and they moved on to better things before the sun appeared again.

When dawn broke, the day was very different from any other. The sun's rays did not come in straight lines, but in twists and turns, as if in a playful mood. The birds twittered, as if they were disclosing the secrets of the night to one another. The whole universe celebrated because a good man was cured. The past was no longer going to break him because he had found the love that gave him a new lease of life that he much desired.

Nancy felt like a free person, she knew that she had made the right decision and she felt at peace with herself. Love is the absolute surrender of your destiny to another person, and it makes you do the unthinkable; you do it because an inner voice tells you that your destiny will be in better hands. Without saying a single word, they made a gentle person's agreement that they would go on with their business, and would not cross the invisible line.

The next few days were very busy for both of them. She departed for Lucknow where she had to interview many people, and he stayed back home to give finishing touches to a presentation which he was preparing for national leaders of various political parties.

Everybody focussed on politics of mobilisation, without even bothering to do a root cause analysis of things that had gone wrong in the past few decades. They all wanted to put a Band-Aid on wounds that hurt, rather than doing a full-blown diagnosis of the problem.

Elsewhere, Ratan was on the horns of dilemma. A crafty student in his college days, he was now a hardened criminal and lately he had been involved in contract killing. His latest task was to kill a person who had become an obstacle in a property dispute. He was well aware that this person was no ordinary person. He had been rising steadily in the local political arena, not only due to the clout that he had inherited from his family, but also due to his own abilities. Ratan took one last sip of the desi or local liquor directly from the bottle, and said to himself, 'Well, it is a dirty job, but somebody has to do it.' With a mysterious smile on his face, he blinked his left eye and whispered menacingly, 'Khalas,' meaning end.

CATHY WAS frustrated by the traffic of New Delhi that was moving at snail's pace. She took a breath of relief when her chauffeur-driven car found its way on Shanti Path in the diplomatic enclave of Chanakyapuri, where the traffic was relatively sporadic. She saw some activity at Nehru Park. She pondered at how different this area was from the crowded lanes of Karol bagh from where she was returning. She was glad to be back at the Embassy building. Her office was empty. She rushed to the training that she was supposed to provide to the Consular team in India. She was on a special assignment from the State Department, and was helping the Counsellor for Political Affairs in understanding the subtleties of the Indian political system.

With an advanced degree from one of the Ivy League colleges back home, she was fast becoming an expert on Indian affairs and her colleagues were certain that one day she would head the State Department as Secretary of State, if she played her cards well. India was on the radar screen of the United

States, and anyone with an in-depth knowledge of the Indian political system was without doubt on a fast track to success. She did not bother much about what they speculated about her career, but she was a lot more interested in the career of her protégé and colleague Nancy Johnston. She knew that Nancy would do extremely well because of her impeccable command on Indian languages.

On her way to the Training Room, she glanced at the television set near the coffee area, and the news being flashed on the screen made her stop mid-step. The news of an 'American student shot to death in Eastern Uttar Pradesh' was written in bold letters on the screen.

She screamed, 'Oh God! Tell me that it is not her.'

The live streaming presented the interview of the District Magistrate who had so far not released the name of the deceased. According to him, the shot fired was not for her, but she came in the crossfire. Right next to him was another television crew, who speculated it to be some sort of terrorist activity. By the account of persons who were present at the scene, it was getting clear that she was with a male companion who was also hurt and was immediately rushed to the hospital.

Cathy's worst nightmare came true when a high-level Indian government official called the embassy to convey his deep condolences for the untimely death of Nancy Johnston, an American student who was doing research work on the Indian political system. He also assured that they would leave no stone unturned to bring the culprits to justice. An hour later, the President of the United States made a similar call to Nancy Johnston's parents in Illinois.

Alam was in a deep slumber on a hospital bed, in the same hospital where decades ago his grandfather had once been admitted and where he had got his picture taken with the then Prime Minister of India. His children were advised by the State Department not to come to visit him for safety reasons, until the culprits could be found.

A camera was installed near his bed which was sending live pictures to his children in the United States. The sudden death of the Amreekan, as Nancy was known in the city, had puzzled everybody. They were all waiting for him to wake up, so that he could shed some light on the tragedy that had befallen him. They were all keeping their fingers crossed.

The Chief Minister of the State, who was his classmate in high school, gave strict instructions to the administration regarding his safety, along with an ultimatum that the culprits must be nabbed within the next 24 hours. The rumour mill worked overtime, and all types of stories started floating with great zeal; the most preposterous among them being that the President of United States called the Indian Prime Minister to ensure that he should be given the best possible medical treatment.

Said someone, 'Sach baat hai, Pradhan Mantri jine khud hamse kaha.' (That is true, the Prime Minister himself told me.)

His wife shot back in her customary style, twisted her hands and said, 'Aur koi kaam nahi hai aapke Pradhan Mantri ke paas ki aap ko call karein.'(There is no other work for Prime Minister, than to call you.)Everybody laughed, and that man looked at his wife in disgust. She had scored a point, but it did nothing to lighten up her sour face.

After all this happened, Ratan was a very worried man. And

his worries were not misplaced. After all, the fatal shot was not fired by him or by any of his associates. He was confident that the man lying on the hospital bed would come after him with all his influence.

When he glanced down at the local newspaper that was lying on the table, grainy pictures of him being discharged from the hospital stared back, and he started to sweat profusely. The man in the picture had a weird calmness on his face and his features were set as if in stone, but Ratan could feel the heat of the volcano that was simmering within. His throat was suddenly parched like the desert and he reached for the glass of water kept besides the newspaper, but the vigorous shaking of his hand forbade him from doing so. The next day, he was seen on a bus that would take him to Nepal where one of his pahari mistresses would give him refuge and erotic therapies that he was fond of.

At the same time, someone far away near Pakri was hanging the dead body of Javed from a tree branch. It was a sign that the coming days were going to be tough, and in a situation like these, there was no escape for anybody.

THE PICTURE of a dead man hanging from a tree branch sent shivers down the spine of those who were cognizant of the developments of the last few weeks. For the rest, it was as common as daybreak, and they took the incident with their usual 'chalta hai' (it happens) attitude and paid not much attention.

Rahmat was visibly shaken when he came to see Alam one day. He walked slowly with tired steps and sat down on the floor next to Alam's chair. He got up and brought another chair closer to his chair and kept standing till Rahmat was comfortably seated on the chair. Rahmat rubbed his eyes and said in a very low voice, 'Yeh kaise ho gaya, aap to theek hain?'(How did all this happen? Are you alright?) Then he started sobbing.

There was nothing Alam could say. He looked at Rahmat but remained quiet. He wanted to say something to the frail man sobbing beside him, but since there was so much going on in his mind, he was not able to articulate his thoughts.Rahmat had brought some fresh produce from the farm that he thankfully accepted. During his conversation with Rahmat, his phone beeped to give him a signal that there was a message waiting for him. He looked at the message and deleted it immediately.

A strange smile spread across his lips for the briefest moment after he had deleted the message. The events of the past few years had given him a strange maturity and, with it came a certain amount of shrewdness. A person who had always been content with all he could achieve by his own effort was thrown into the meat grinder again. Destiny had played a cruel hand yet again and had left him hanging in the middle. He felt like a rock in the middle of a stream, where the powerful currents seemed determined to take away everything that would come in their path. But he knew better. He knew that the destiny of the rock is to remain undeterred by whatever is happening around in the near vicinity.

The message he deleted had given him the good news he had been waiting for the entire day. He was happy that on returning, Rahmat would find that the farm was under a new management, his management. By this time, he had strategised everything and his foot soldiers had reached the farm in Pakri with all tactics of the trade. Strategies when carefully collaborated with tactics are a sure way to provide fastest victory. His people had tactfully driven Zahid and company out of the farm.

On the south side of the city, in a very deprived neighbourhood, Javed's widow Nazma waited for him, along with her teenage daughter, Shakila, in their one-room rented quarter. She was sitting on a cot with her legs folded. She looked old for her age, and if he could see her face, he would have noticed that her face was lined with worry. She had recently lost her husband and was observing her mandatory iddat or seclusion period; hence, she was in customary burqa.

Her daughter Shakila had covered her head and bosom's modestly with a dupatta. This meeting was fixed on her request. She spoke in hushed whispers, 'My husband, may Allah give him a high place in heaven, could never kill anyone. He got murdered for no reason.'

Then she screamed out in a wild voice that made her daughter look at her in surprise, 'Why did you have him killed?' After saying that, she adjusted her composure and continued, 'Ratan instigated him to kill you. Ratan is a bad man. He is a loose character.'

He paid her condolence for her loss, and as he was about to leave, Shakila stood up from her place and hesitantly addressed him with a forceful voice, 'Sahib!'

He turned back but by that time, her mother had dragged her inside the house. He waited for a moment, and then hurriedly got out of the house.

Nancy's death was still heavy on his mind. Many questions kept him up all night. Why do people even come in life when they have to go away? Life itself looks like a mystery when people themselves become history. The ones who depart do not even know how difficult it becomes for the ones they leave behind to carry on. Why was this the way of life?

When he looked around, he found people of all ages going about their life, at times with much difficulty, but life moved on. What difference would it have made if many more could have done the same? God has strange ways and nobody knows the pattern that He follows. He was not even sure if there was even a pattern on which God relies upon. Why do bad things happen to good people?

Why does not everybody live to same age? Why ones who are God fearing suffer most in life? Why does God sometimes fail to listen to the prayers? Why did God continue to raise the bar for the few who care to excel? There was no one to give him these answers and the empty recesses of his mind continued to be bogged down with the questions. He slowly closed his eyes.

There she was. Floating on the clouds was the pristine figure of Sadia. She looked sad. She always loathed him when he complained. Slowly, he drifted to the memory lane. It was a room in one of the hospitals he stayed. Sadia was sitting on a chair next to his bed telling him how wonderful Allah is, that He has given him a new life, and urged him to be grateful for his new lease that would make him do things he was meant to. How blessed was he to get another chance? A new life, just the thought of it made him agitated. How good is the new life, if Sadia is not a part of it?

Since there was barely a hint of sleep in his eyes, he went to sit on the rocking chair which was there in his house for generations. The space around him was dimly lit, and a light bulb on the wall directly across his rocking chair cast his shadows into abstract structures, changing form and shape with every passing moment. He sat there for quite some time, until he heard the muezzin's call for morning prayer.

In the morning, there were scores of people who visited Alam. Most of them were people who lived in the surrounding localities, but he never got a chance or had any inclination to know them. Some of them were older in age, but most of them were of his age or younger. They wanted to tell him that they were all with him in his hour of calamity, and he could count on them for support. They were mostly Muslims, who had lived there for generations. In fact, many of them were living on the parcel of land that once belonged to his ancestors. The biggest surprise of the day was the visit of an emissary from the famous Gorakhnath Temple, who conveyed to him the message of sympathy from the High Priest.

A person, who was supposed to do research on stem cells in New York, had completed a full circle and was back from where he started. He sat on his ever-faithful rocking chair and tried to unlock the mysteries of life by reflecting on the span of life that he had lived so far. He remembered having read in numerous books and through the words of his wise ancestors that everything happens for a reason, and every event in life gives you an opportunity, which takes you closer to your destiny. You cannot circumvent the path that is destined for you. If you do, there will be invisible forces that will work against you. This knowledge will not come to you while you are travelling on that path because you are simply too inexperienced to understand these complexities, or too naïve to even get a hint of it. You cannot change your destiny. Nobody can.

The security at his house was augmented. There were extra guards, who were placed at the main entrance and powerful floodlights were installed. He wanted to take things in his own stride. While he would venture into different avenues, his doctoral thesis would gather dust on a book shelf in his study, along with his other collections, notably War and Peace by Leo Tolstoy, which he never completed. However, none of it mattered today because battles of the past were whispering in his ears the need for a war; a war that would restore peace, his very own peace.

The Gorakhpur of the '70s that he had left earlier was not a sleepy place anymore. The city bubbled with energy, which was not getting harnessed properly. There was a need to channelise the flow which slowly gained momentum, and got fiercer by the day. There was restlessness among the youth. They were being empowered by the information that had slowly found its way into their lives and was being etched into their hearts and minds.

They had seen how previous generations had squandered away possible opportunities by subscribing to the ideas that were dictated from temples, mosques and churches. They wanted to be citizens of the global village where opportunities were endless. But somebody had to bear the brunt of the mistakes of others. The role models of yesterdays, people like Sundar Singh and Rajiv Shukla were now part of the folklore, and were slowly phasing out from textbooks. They were being replaced by a desire for change, and this posed a challenge to those who wanted to pursue their agendas of hate to divide the populace.

Unfortunately, the seekers who take their lessons from history are few. The ones clamouring for change chose the easy path, or the path of least resistance and did exactly what their forefathers did. They left the city in search for affluence. The outflow continued because the inertia of ancient politics of religion and caste cannot be overcome by new inventions like internet and other communication gadgets.

He was scheduled to have his first interaction with the local media after Nancy's death. A couple of journalists gathered in a hurriedly erected shamiana or tent outside his ancestral home. Most of the questions were straight and pointed. A smartly dressed young lad asked him, 'Who killed Madam Nancy?'

Before he could form the words in his mind, the next volley came, 'Was that a terrorist act?'

He knew he needed to calm them down if he wanted them to hear him out. But before he could do that, a bulky journalist with dark glasses asked, 'Is it true that you are getting into politics?' A sudden silence descended upon the gathering, and then they started conversing amongst themselves, most likely explaining to those who did not know their history well that he belonged to a family that was involved in politics in the earlier decades.

Now they were more interested in hearing what he had to say. He started in chaste Urdu, and sometimes in the middle jumped to Hindi. His statement was brief and to the point. He showed his unawareness about Nancy's killers. In his opinion, this could not have been an act of terrorism. He skipped the question about him joining politics altogether. The next day, his pictures made it to the newspapers again.

Looking at his picture in the newspapers took him back to the memory lane, to his childhood days when in a hospital, flash lights from cameras blinded him, and he did not know that Sadia was standing there right behind him.The lines from the television show, 'The Wonder Years', started playing in the background, 'Memory is a way of holding on to the things you love, the things you are, the things you never want to lose.' He closed his eyes, and thought of the days gone by.

There was a crowd waiting for him on the other side of the house. They were from neighbouring Mohallas or localities and had come to tell him the stories of how close they were to his family. From them he learnt that Muslim are deeply divided along caste lines within, and are not the monolithic vote bank as they are painted to be by political analysts. They do not provide the critical mass needed to win elections because they always give fractured mandate.Is the division based on caste the only factor? No, it is not that simple. The Muslims have other problems altogether and the most important is the factor of self-importance along with their egos, which may be greater than that of the greatest Mughal kings. They are very emotional people and they have a tendency to escape from the realities.

One of them started to play victim, 'Hum log second class citizen hain yahan.' (We are second-class citizen here.) Then he narrated a list of woes, some of them seemed genuine while others were simply complaints.

He heard them carefully and patiently, and then asked, 'What is stopping you here? If you have issues, go to the councillor of your ward.' One elderly man came forward and said, 'The councillor, since he is Hindu, will not attend to our issues.'

He asked surprisingly, 'But if this is a Muslim-dominated area, how come the councillor is not a Muslim?'

Then someone explained it to him that although it is a Muslim-majority area, too many Muslim candidates contest the elections and hence the votes are divided.Whereas the Hindus put up a single Hindu candidate by forcing all other Hindu candidates to opt out from the race, and that candidate gets all Hindu votes and wins.

He shot back, 'Why don't you apply the same tactics?' Someone who himself was a candidate during last few contests admitted sheepishly, 'Nobody amongst us is willing to opt out because everybody thinks that they are winning, as a result of which nobody wins.' He started laughing and was soon joined by everyone. He remembered that during a conference, which he attended in Boston, he met the Speaker of the House Tip O'Neill whose famous quote: 'All politics is local' was even quoted in India when he participated in the debates. During that meeting, the towering personality of the Speaker had dwarfed him and made him nervous. He wanted to ask him about his quote, but neither of them could understand the other; the Speaker because of his Indian or desi accent, and Alam, because of the Speaker's Boston accent. Politicians and commentators have often quoted this to illustrate that politics demands one to pay attention to sensitivities of local issues because that is what matters when they go out to vote.

After talking to the local men, he got convinced that the famous Speaker was correct when he coined that quote. One has to master local issues, before testing water for any political ambition, in case you have one.

That was the question Sadia had asked him once, after they got married, 'How come you are not in politics; it must be in your blood?' He was ready with his smart answer, 'I will, one day get into it and will keep the seat warm for your father, and then will move out for your father still nourishes that ambition.' On hearing this, Sadia's expression became pensive. Her father Arman Ali had always wanted to be a politician, but luck never favoured him. After leaving Gorakhpur for Lucknow, he tried innumerable times to get into it, but was never successful. Now he was old and sick, but he was still very interested in politics. After Sadia's death, he lost the appetite to live and was on the bed counting his last days.

Alam's decision to contest a local election took everybody by surprise. Nobody was expecting him to plunge into something as meaningless and inconsequential as that. But he was determined to understand the old adage, that all politics is local first. He wanted to know his backyard before plunging in elsewhere.

He, contesting the ward election in the backwaters of eastern Uttar Pradesh, became talk of the town. 'Why after all this education do you want to become a part of a game which has nothing except naali and gaali (drainage and abusive words) to offer?' One of his friends had asked him this question, but he had no answer for it, other than the conviction he had deep inside that now he was on his path towards his destiny.

There were seven Muslim candidates including him, and an equal number of Hindu candidates in the contest. To avoid division of Hindu votes, all Hindu candidates except one, opted out. As it happened in the past few elections, Muslim candidates were not willing to opt out in favour of any one of their own. So in a Muslim-dominated ward, a Hindu candidate would win. There was great frustration amongst Muslims, but there was little that they could do besides being frustrated.

The next morning, a very strange thing happened. As he was getting ready to go for campaigning, he was told that someone from the nearby temple wanted to meet him in private. That representative brought some very unusual news. The temple wanted him to win!

'Why?' That was his first reaction, and rightly so. The answer was as simple as the question, 'We want the best person to win and nobody is better qualified than you. We can't thrive if we keep raising walls of religion amongst ourselves.'

This news spread like a wild fire and everybody began talking about the greatness of the temple, as to how they had walked the extra mile to bring peace and prosperity among Hindus and

Muslims of the city. Not many people really understood the motive behind this extraordinary gesture shown by the temple to ensure his victory.

The story goes back to the days when India had just won freedom. One of the leaders from the temple went to a school in Allahabad for education, along with one of the nobles from Gorakhpur who was a Muslim. The temple head was arrested when Gandhi was murdered and the person who bailed him out was his Muslim class fellow. Therefore, somebody in the temple remembered that incident and was heard saying, 'He was a Muslim who helped that day, so let us reciprocate that gesture and let us help this man for a change.'

This led to the opting out of the Hindu candidate from the race. In the end, it was a direct contest between him and many Muslim candidates. In a scenario like this, victory was sure and easy. The votes were counted and, as expected, he won by a landslide. Not many people in India followed his election closely but there were three people in the United States watched this election with keen interest. Two were his children in New York, and the third one was Cathy Anderson in Washington DC.

After the sweet taste of victory came the bitterness of delivering the promises that were made to the people and this was the hardest part. It was not an easy job because the level of people's expectations bordered on crazy and it was too scary. He told this to Amna on the phone one day, 'It is easy to defend your PhD thesis than to calm the very demanding constituents.' Then he added, 'You should be happy that it is not you but somebody else doing it.' From the other end, he heard a chuckle followed by, 'Enjoy Dad.' He plugged in the battery charger into his the phone mumbling, 'Enjoy what?'

The crowd outside was an impatient one. They were people who were championing the cause of Affirmative Action in India. They were from all sections of the society. Affirmative action or Reservation, as it is called in India, is one of the most effective tools for redressing injustices caused by blunders of the past, where majority of Indians were discriminated against other Indians on one pretext or another.

The Indian Constitution addressed grievances of those who claimed to have been discriminated against and incorporated reservation policy to undo the injustices of the past. Because of which, these have-nots of the society witnessed an upward mobility which otherwise they could have not.

A Few dozen Muslim men, some of them in skullcaps, stood outside. They were hesitant to get inside the house. 'Why are you behaving like untouchables?', He asked.

One of them, Aman in his '50s, kept his eyes lowered and answered, 'Because that's what we are; untouchables.'

Their answer took him by surprise. He requested them to sit near him and tell him their story. The old man said, 'We are Muslims now, but earlier our forefathers were dalits, who, most likely, converted to Islam to escape humiliation that was meted out to dalits.'

He thought for a second and said with a smile, 'So you are Dalit Muslim.' The old man shook his head in a sordid yes. Alam asked, 'Kya hona chahiye?' (What should be done?)

To this, the man replied, 'Samvidhan ka Scheduled Caste Order1950 samapt karna hoga, tabhi Muslim aur Eisayee Dalit ke saath bhed-bhao samapt hoga.' (Scheduled Caste Order 1950 must be deleted in order to abolish religious discrimination against Muslim and Christian Dalits.)

He remembered that his dhobi or washer man in Aligarh, Ismael who was a Muslim, was poor and his sons could not get a job, whereas his dhobi in Gorakhpur, Vippat, who was a Hindu, was doing reasonably well and all his sons had secured government jobs for themselves. The fact is that the Indian Constitution does not recognise anybody who is not Hindu as Dalit, be it is Muslim or Christian. It discriminates on basis of religion, which is ironically contrary to the very spirit of the Constitution. It pained him that the Constitution that was drafted as the holiest of tenets to safeguard the people of the country itself was ridden with a flaw.

There was never a day when he did not learn new things, but faraway across the oceans somewhere in the United States, Cathy was not very happy with the progress. She wanted him to move fast, and learn everything in the shortest period because there were telltale signs of a gathering storm. She picked up her phone and placed a long distance call to India. It was a secure line, which was free even from the ears of National Security Agency which had earned a bad name for itself all around the world recently.

FAR NORTH, away from the Indo-Gangetic plains, there is a different world altogether, and it is beautiful. People from across the globe have visited this place and have fallen in love with it. A poet had rightly written about Kashmir, 'Agar Firdaus bar ru-e-zamin ast, Hami ast o-hami ast o- hami ast.' (If there is heaven on earth, it is here, it is here, it is here.) Nestled in the lap of snow-clad mountains, the valley of Kashmir looks like a gorgeous bride adorned by Mother Nature herself. Its beauty has also given it the title of the stunning jewel in the crown of India. A jewel for which many battles have been fought and too many lives have been lost. Nobody there knows when the serenity of the place would be disturbed by the deafening sound of guns that would tear through the picturesque Shalimar and Nishat Gardens. Tourists at the magnificent Dal Lake on their shikaras would hurriedly complete their shopping from vendors floating on their boats on the lake. Life there is anything but certain.

Sheen had just landed from her flight. Her friends called her the most beautiful girl in Srinagar. But she was not just a pretty face. Her brain matched her beauty and this rare combination gave her an edge against other girls of her age. For her, all the pieces fell in place to make her life comfortable. She had just turned eighteen.

Her trip to Mumbai had been quite a successful one. As per conventional wisdom, an eighteen-year old beautiful girl from Kashmir could easily create a ruckus in Bollywood, but that was not the case with her. She was very different from the crowd that would flock from one agent to another in search of opportunities. One of her uncles, Sayeed, was a successful film producer. Sayeed was her father's younger brother and was totally different from his brother Sami, who considered himself to be a freedom fighter, fighting to get Kashmir liberated from the unholy occupancy of India. During a heated discussion, Sayeed called Sami a terrorist. He wanted his young niece to be away from Kashmir because according to him, 'Kashmir is a very dangerous place to live.'

Sheen kept herself away from the ideology of her father. He would remain absent from home most of the time, but whenever he would come home, he would spend all his time with his daughter. Deep inside, he was a man tormented by the loss of his young son, the son who left for the heavenly abode at a tender age. His death was as cruel as it was untimely. Like all his friends, he had started throwing stones at the men in uniform, whom most of his young friends detested. But he did not expect them to start firing in return. One of the bullets hit the little boy, who succumbed to death immediately.

Sheen was very young at that time. Their mother was not strong enough to be able to cope with this tragedy and she went into solitude. She later became disoriented and did not wake up from her sleep one morning. Her death was a major blow to Sami who had started believing that the occupancy of Kashmir valley by the Indian army was the only reason for his misfortunes.

One day he was heard screaming, 'Why can't we live like any other Indian in any other State? Why is this army here all the time?' Nobody gave him the right answers and darkness pulled him in to make him a rebel.

Nobody had courage to reason with a person who had lost his young son and wife. But he was not alone, there were many like him in Kashmir. They all had a story to tell, a sad story that would haunt you for days. Looking at their beautiful faces, one could never realise that deep down in their beautiful eyes, they were hiding immense pain and suffering. When Nehru was proclaiming his 'Tryst with Destiny' in New Delhi, people in Kashmir were in a mixed State of mind because their fate was in limbo and many thought that they had been betrayed. But much water had flown in the river Jhelum since then.

Like any other evening, Sheen was sitting in her house, feeling bored. She chatted with her friends who wanted her to reveal the nasty stuff about the movie industry in Mumbai. The girls were curious; they simply wanted to have some fun. They wanted to know about the movie stars whom Sheen met during her trip.

Sheen kept telling them that film industry is not what they read in gossip magazines. It is being organised on professional lines and is changing at a very fast pace. Even the subject matter of the films is much more diverse, mature and universal.

'So you will be a model selling what? I think it will be

bra and panties for sure,' asked her best friend Laila. Sheen smiled and said, 'With my uncle watching, all I can do is burqa commercials.' At this, they all laughed vociferously,but stopped when they heard gun shots fired far away. They looked at each other, shook their head in unison, and then one by one they dispersed. This was nothing unusual for them. They were used to situations like this. For them it was the way of life, for they were born amidst these situations.

Once her friends had left, Sheen started surfing the internet. She had many pictures to upload for her Facebook profile, especially the ones where she was standing next to a Bollywood superstar who was wearing tight fitting jeans and was bare-chested. She looked at the picture in awe and then, as if by some strange impulse, she put her lips on his face.

Her eyes closed automatically and she started feeling a pleasing warmth in her body. Her heart started throbbing fast and she could feel her left toe start to clench and her hands getting restless. They were eager for some mischief, which they had never done before, but before she could let the heat of the moment cloud her good judgement she started laughing and said with hilarity in her eyes, 'No wonder they say teenage is a difficult age.' She logged out, and went to perform Isha or the night prayers.

Before ending the prayer, as per ritual, she performed salam by turning her head first to the right and then to her left. On turning to her right, she felt that somebody was on her bed. Quickly, she completed her prayer, and rushed to her father who was sitting on the bed and watching her pray. They embraced each other, and silent tears started flowing from their eyes speaking volumes about how much they had missed each other.

'Sheen, I did not want to disturb you with your friends, so I took a nap,' said Sami while Sheen took out all the pictures she took during her Mumbai trip. They talked until the muezzin made call for Fajr or morning prayers.

In the morning, when she logged in to her computer again, she looked at the post that Laila had forwarded to her on Facebook. The post was composed by a stranger, someone from the United States who was presently doing something in India. 'Who cares?' She shrugged her shoulders without looking at the profile picture of the middle-aged man who would have been handsome in his younger days. Since the post was about Kashmir, she started to read it.

'Kashmir is an integral part of India and so are Kashmiris. I am sympathetic to the cause of our fellow brethren there, and my expectation is that I will be welcomed there with open arms, as we welcome our Kashmiri brothers in New Delhi, Aligarh or in Gorakhpur. It is also my expectation that I will be able to live in Kashmir, like any other Kashmiri brother or sister is able to live in any other part of India. I should be able to own a summer house, grow apricots and enjoy long rides in a shikara.'

Later in the day, while talking to Laila, she brought up the conversation and questioned her, 'Why did you tag that post on Kashmir by an Americano?' Laila was pensive.

Then Laila lifted her face up and said, 'I thought that was funny…An Indian Muslim who is not from Kashmir, wants to have a summer house here.'

Then she said, as if talking to herself, 'So naïve. Doesn't even know about Article 370.' She laughed in a humourless manner.

Sheen was not paying any attention, but suddenly she got up from the stool she was sitting on and said, 'Maybe he doesn't know.

If one removes the biases which have taken a strong hold in us, because of all that is going on here since decades, then he is right.'

Laila nodded in the affirmative, and started looking outside from the window. Her elder sister wanted to marry a Muslim man from Hyderabad, but could not marry him because if she did, she would have lost all her property in Kashmir which was for her to inherit, on marrying a person who was not from the State. At the last minute, she decided to forgo her inheritance and married that Hyderabadi person anyway. While Laila was lost in her thoughts, Sheen forwarded a friendship request to that stranger from the United States.

Her friend request was accepted immediately. Like her, he was also online. She stopped combing her hair and gave a quick glance to the profile of that person. Facebook is an amazing tool because it opens endless possibilities. From the comfort of your chosen location, you open a window, and can see almost everybody who is out there. Now you can interact directly in real time without the interference of a mediatory and get acquainted with challenges that are threatening the existance of the planet, by forming a team of like-minded people with the simple strokes of keys on your keyboard. Technology, on one end, has created weapons of mass destruction, whereas on the other hand, it has also brought possibilities of peace, by talking to each other, to allay dangers which comes along with it.

Her inbox pinged to inform her that an unread message awaited her. It was from him. 'Salaam, how are you?'

She started typing, 'WA Salam… Fine. Thank you. Thanks4 accepting my request.' Either the internet connection on his side was bad or he got busy with something, because she did not get the indication whether her message was seen by him or not.

He, in fact, had got busy because there was a phone call for him from United States. It was Cathy, who informed him that she was coming to India next week and wanted to see if he could meet her in New Delhi.

He looked at the screen of his laptop. There was a message for him from the Kashmiri girl. He pulled his chair close to the table and started chatting with Sheen.

'I thought that you were kidding when you posted about owning a house in valley…Does it really matter to you?'

'I know what eventually you are getting into…I have seen a couple of my Kashmiri friends buying houses in NOIDA…And there they were welcomed…They quickly got assimilated into the neighbourhood…They made friends…V r d same…Then why can't u reciprocate with the same gesture in d valley?…'

'U know y not.'

'Yes…Yes. Yes…da Article…Right?'

'Exactly…Sensitive…Very Sensitive…Can't do much about it…Right?'

'Can't do anything…As long as we leave it up to politicians 2 decide….'

'Should be decided by the people as2 what they want… Generally people and politicians r not on same page… Different agendas…Right....'

'People should interact more &I'm glad that is what v r doin…'

'Nice chat…v'll continue some other time…Have 2 go... Bye….'

Sheen thought about her conversation with him even after she had logged out of Facebook. Yes, Kashmir has always been in the news for wrong reasons, but people tell her that she had not seen anything, for the worst had happened before she was even born. Those were the dark days. The country was partitioned and Muslim-dominated areas became a part of Pakistan with the exception of Kashmir, where although inhabitants of the State were predominantly Muslims, but the Raja was Hindu, who was given the choice to join either State.

Before he could decide, Pakistani forces attacked Kashmir and the Raja looked upon India for help. The help from India came, but with a price, and the Raja hurriedly signed a document which pledged Kashmir's allegiance to India. Had Pakistan not sent its forces, the outcome would have been very different. But today, most Pakistanis have resigned to the fact that Kashmir belongs to India and it is time to move on, but there are some, especially politicians and the military, who dissent with this view.

For politicians, if the issue of Kashmir was resolved once and for all, they would be devoid of an issue that had continued to give them much-needed oxygen to keep their political outfit intact. The military also had its selfish agenda behind keeping this issue alive to ensure that funds continued to flow smoothly for them. Hence, Kashmir is always in the news. The trouble from across the border infiltrates into the valley and skirmishes and conflicts are a part of life there. To maintain law and order in the valley, India has no other option but to keep large military contingents there.

Sheen was not interested in all these things. She simply wanted peace in the valley. She had already forgiven those who were responsible for hir brother's death. Her brother, if alive, would have been a handsome young man by now. Her heart started aching for her brother and mother, and an unspoken pain tugged at her heart.

Not knowing what to do, she logged on to her Facebook account and desperately looked to find if he was online. Sometimes you get comfort in talking with a stranger because with a stranger you can express your emotions in a non judgmental manner, knowing that there would be no condemnation of whatever you say. Also, the stranger will most likely not hold against you, whatever you have said.

He was not online, so she left a message in his inbox, 'Why some suffer more than others? You are suffering because you can't build a house in the valley, and my brother suffered because his house was in the valley.'

She returned back to her computer after a few minutes and was relieved to receive a response back from him, 'We are inconsequential in the grand scheme of things, but way forward someday in future 1 might appreciate the significance of what happened in past…Even that is not guaranteed... Who said that life will b fair2 all?…btw…sorry 2 hear about Ur brother….' She typed back, 'What should 1 do….Feel like crying...' His answer was, 'It is ok 2 cry….v all should do...'

She felt as if a huge burden had been removed from her heart and she started crying. She could not stop the torrent of tears that swept down her cheeks. She cried for her mother, for her brother, as if they had only died yesterday. Once the flood of tears ebbed away, she felt a lot better. Whoever that man was, and wherever he was, he knew how to comfort a person.

She could not remember when was the last time she cried to her heart's content. Like he had said, it is okay to cry and we all should, occasionally. In between her sobs, a small smile crept on her lips and she whispered, as if he was standing somewhere nearby, 'Thank you'. In her mind, that person was no longer a stranger for she felt that she had known this person for a long time.

In the next few days, she became completely dependent on this person. She would confess to him her worst fears, her nightmarish apprehensions, her dilemmas about life, her dreams, her successes and failures. He was the first one she told that her role in a new movie, to be launched by her uncle's friend, has been finalised and she would be leaving for Mumbai soon.

But her next message that was sent to his inbox was not pleasant at all because she informed him that her father was arrested by the police at the time she was at the airport, to catch a flight for Mumbai.

AT THE very last minute, the venue for his meeting with Cathy was changed to Agra, rather than in New Delhi, as was initially suggested by her. When he reached New Delhi, Cathy sent a message to him about change of the location. So he drove to Agra, and met her in a hotel room.

Cathy was in her mid-30s, but looked much older because of the way she was dressed. She reminded him of a vice president at his job in New York, who worked her way up and climbed the corporate ladder at a much faster pace than her colleagues. However, because of her young age, which also matched her looks, the employees refused to take her seriously. Corporate America was not ready for a female vice president of a Fortune 500 company, who was barely in her 30s. So, she started dressing like a person ten years older to her.This wardrobe transformation helped her as everyone, her juniors as well as seniors, started taking her seriously.

He enjoyed these stories fed by rumour mill with others during lunch breaks, where she was often the topic of discussions.

He would envision how Sadia would dress, if she ever got a senior position like that. Often he would call Sadia from work to tell her about the latest fashion Statement that was the talk of the town for today, and Sadia would frown upon him to say, 'Don't you guys have other work to do?'

Cathy's suite window held a clear view of the Taj Mahal, the 17th Century monument built by Mughal Emperor Shah Jahan, in memory of his favourite wife Mumtaz Mahal.

The view from the window reminded him of the description given by a tour guide many years ago, when he was visiting Agra with Sadia and kids. The story goes that a power struggle erupted and his very own son Aurangzeb put the Emperor, who built the monument in prison. From the prison window he stared at the Taj Mahal in remembrance of his wife, whom he loved much. His gazing at the monument cast a spell on it and everybody who visits the Taj Mahal notices that it looks sad, and is not cheerful at all.

After hearing this version, whenever he looked at the Taj Mahal, he noticed that the monument is in mourning; mourning for the Emperor and his wife, who are buried in the basement of the building. For him, it could never again be the monument that epitomises love.

It made perfect sense to him because whenever he saw pictures of the rubble of the Twin Towers in New York, he always felt that he was watching a cemetery, where along with many others, his wife was buried. Later, when the place was cleared up and powerful flashlights were put in, which beamed powerful rays of light to the sky, he felt that those beam of lights were stairs through which Sadia would climb down to earth one day, from the seven skies and the heavens.

He felt a dull pain creeping up on his left side. This happened to him whenever he saw beams of rays emerging out from any source, no matter what. Even rays from a flashlight would make his left side tingle and his mouth go dry.

Cathy took out a picture of Nancy from a diary and put it on the table in front of him, and said, 'You know she was such a brave girl who if she had lived, good things for her country. She held you in high regards.'

He knew she was waiting for him to say something.'Yes, we had a good time together, learned a lot from her, wished she could have lived more.' Cathy nodded her head and said, 'Local authorities were helpful to the Embassy staff, but they could not crack the murder mystery. I wish they could nab the culprits. You were in the hospital, so we were not able to get much from you. But since shots were fired for you, doesn't it bother you?' Guilt reared its ugly head again. Without looking at Cathy, he said, 'It bothers me a lot…But I don't know how to walk the talk.'

His life was moving at such a fast pace, and there were so many unattended balls spinning in the air, that he didn't know which one to grab and which to let go.

Cathy came close to him, put her hands on his shoulders, and said in acommanding voice, 'Watch this.' She held a device in her right hand. At first glance, it could have been taken for a medium-sized portable phone. Soon, the gadget's screen flashed and a slide show of pictures started. The show captivated him and left him speechless.

His left side started to feel bizarre, and his mouth gaped open involuntarily. He felt as if he was losing control of his brain's activities. After a long time, he felt the aura that generally comes before a seizure originates. Fortunately, the prescribed anti-convulsion medication that he routinely took helped, and he was able to absorb the information that he had just witnessed.

His mind was traumatised as if he had lost the capability to think. All he could say was, 'Oh my God!'

Cathy said, 'That is right. There are many satellites out there in sky that are watching all of us, especially activities that are performed in the open. We cannot share everything even with our own agencies; forget the government here in India. By the way, on records, this meeting between you and I never happened. We have arrangements with this hotel, for which they are paid handsomely. There was a reason for not meeting you in New Delhi. RAW has placed some primitive cameras that monitor people who enter the Embassy building through the main gate, but we meet our key assets by letting them stand in the queue, as if they are seeking visa for the United States. We knew that it will be a hardship for you to stand in that queue at 4 A M in the morning.'

He had started pacing the room and now stood at the window, took a deep breath and said, 'Thanks. Yes, I am not an early riser. But since when did you start considering me as an asset? What else do you know about me?'

Cathy stood next to him and said, 'There is nothing we don't know. It is for your own good.' He looked at Cathy and said, 'I am glad we met.'

He started thinking that RAW, the Research and Analysis Wing of Indian government, the Indian counterpart of CIA, was still groping in primitive ages. No wonder United States, the only super power, is light years away from the rest of the world.

He pulled a chair and sunk in it. All this time, Cathy was

watching him very carefully. Finally she said, 'You have started to like Indian politics, isn't it?'

He could not say no because in one of the pictures of the slideshow, there was a picture in which he was laden with garlands of marigold flowers. That photograph was taken when he had won the ward election.

Cathy continued, 'You have a natural flair for politics, and we are counting on you for that. To maintain peace in the world, we need people like you on our side. Unfortunately, we are putting many eggs in one basket, and we do not even have options. India is going to be an ally we are counting on…Even Fareed Zakaria recommends that in one of his books. Have you read his book?'

He quickly said, 'Yes, I think. The title was something like The Post-American World.' Cathy replied, 'I think so, maybe. I am not that much into reading books. I only read briefs that are provided to me.'

Before they parted, she threw the ace and said, 'Nancy thought very highly of you. She, in fact, liked you a lot. In one of the pictures you have seen, the moment just before she was shot was also captured. She took the bullet that had your name on it. Her sacrifice should not go in vain. We will back you. I promise one more thing...Never ever would we ask you to do anything that would go against the country of your birth. I know you love your motherland, as well as the country you adopted to live.'

He drove back from Agra on a four-lane expressway, which was testimony to the progress made by India in the last few years. He saw automobiles zipping past him. He remembered that a quarter century back, there were few choices in terms of cars, but today it is a very different world. His father had an old Morris Minor, which was later swapped for an Ambassador, a product of Hindustan Motors. Those days not many people could own a car. To divert his attention from the conversation he had with Cathy, he started thinking about strange and odd things, but he was unable to manipulate his mind for it reverted back to the dialogue he had with Cathy in that hotel room in Agra.

He was very confused about what would his role be in future, and if this was something that he even fancied. His phone beeped once to tell him that he had a message from Sheen. The message was terse, two simple words that said, 'Dad arrested'. A natural sympathy for Sheen arose but soon it evaporated, and common sense came into play. After all, he knew nothing about the nature of his crime. Not only crime, at this point he knew nothing about her dad. Forget her dad; he did not even know much about Sheen either. A person whom he met on social networking site could be anything. But for some reason, he was not ready to write her off. Not yet. A certain element of sincerity and authenticity made her messages stand out from the usual crowd.

'Oh well! I wonder why?' He said, and looked at the speedometer in his car. It was touching close to 100km per hour. His right eye blinked, and he murmured to himself, 'What the heck? Slow down buddy. What's the rush?'

He was amazed with the speed at which he was driving. He was feeling light headed. He realised that his left toes were twitching, and the pad of his right foot was itching. Suddenly a huge truck was seen overtaking his car, and immediately after that, a white sedan passed next. He started feeling very dizzy and clenched the steering of his car to ensure control.

His left side was tilting or sinking as usual when in stress, which nobody ever acknowledged noticing, but he always felt it. His brain was unable to process the speed with which the cars were moving. His car started to swirl, and slowly started drifting into the next lane.

He tried to turn the steering wheel to keep his car in his lane, but could not do so. He was losing control. The lights from cars moving in the opposite direction, which for some reason were on high beam mode, stared at him threateningly.

After a while, there was darkness on the opposite lane, and he felt relieved but only for a while. He saw the entry point from where cars on the opposite side joined the highway. He slowed down, and watched the cars entering the highway. The high beams of the incoming cars reminded him of stroboscopic stimulation, which he had undergone many times during electroencephalogram tests, commonly called EEG, and are used to measure and record electrical activity of brain. In this stimulation, the brain is aroused and activated to determine the person's vulnerability to epilepsy. He had failed this test many times in the past and was declared epileptic.

Thanks to medications, he was leading a normal life, but today after watching the stroboscopic nature of lights from the incoming cars, he became nervous and a strange sense of uneasiness engulfed his whole body. His throat was parched, and he quickly pulled his car on the curb, and closed his eyes. He started to pray to Allah, the merciful. Initially, it was all in murmurs, but suddenly his prayers became loud, very loud.

Then there was silence, complete silence. First, his hands started shaking and he placed them on the steering wheel, hoping that the shaking would cease, but then his whole body began shaking. He was having a full body seizure. His head came to rest on the steering wheel, and the next moment it was thumping on it slowly. His right foot was pressing the brake paddle with his body weight, as a result of which the car was completely motionless. The vehicles passing by did not even notice anything wrong in the car that was parked on the side of the highway. His prayers were answered, and the Almighty God saved his life one more time.

IT WAS Ahmad's first night in India. The tick-tock of a wall clock brought back some childhood memories. When he was a toddler, he would lie next to his father, asking him to replicate the sound of a clock that would slowly put him to sleep. But today he wanted to be awake.He was sitting at his father's desk, staring at the screen of an outdated computer, which originally belonged to his mother. The screen flickered, as if it felt the sufferings that the man in the car parked on the curb of the highway was going through.

There were loud noises coming from the back of the house and they broke his reverie. Ahmad looked at his clothes, and realised that they were wet with sweat. The air conditioning in the room was not working. The noise coming from outside was from the heavy-duty power generators that had kicked in, when normal power supply went off.

His father once told him that life in the United States had taught them to take many things for granted. How right he was! There he always assumed that flipping the switch would brighten the room, but it may not be so in India. Even the house of an important person like his late father had to face the heat of load shedding.

The butler knocked on the door, and Ahmad knew what he had come to say. The butler was worried because Ahmad had not eaten a morsel since he stepped foot on Indian soil. So far, all he had asked for was water. Ahmad was not hungry at all. He was feeding himself with the snacks that he had bought at the airport in New York. He heard the knock again, and he dragged himself to the door. This time, it was not the butler, but an unfamiliar person. By this time, there were many whom Ahmad had been introduced to, and he was not very keen to exchange pleasantries with the one standing at the door.

That person had a look of concern on his face. Probably, he was informed by the butler about Ahmad's eating habits, or the lack of it, because right behind him, the butler stood with a food tray. The aroma coming from the serving dish told Ahmad that it was one of his favourite dishes. The warm welcoming aroma of home-cooked food enticed his taste buds. The next moment, he was eating biryani, which was savoury but not spicy; it was a kind of pakki biryani, where rice and meat were partially cooked separately, and then layered and re-cooked on slow fire. It was different from the ones sold in the restaurants in United States.

The air conditioning was back, and the room was pleasantly cool again. The loud noise coming from the power generator was gone, but was replaced by another noise, which must be from the power looms that were not too far from the house. He knew it from one of the television interviews that his father had given to a leading news channel. The link of the interview was mailed to him by one of his father's personal assistants.

In that interview, his father had highlighted the plight of the weavers, who were forced to give up their profession because of the changing times. His father also mentioned about the jacquard loom, which according to him 'weaved magic'. This loom had made the weavers of that area famous.

Somewhere in the background, his father's voice echoed, 'We should not forget that modern day computer programming, and designing complex pattern on fabric using jacquard loom has a lot in common. It is sad that the weavers who once made the fabric design by using these looms are committing suicide because of lack of work.' Ahmad remembered this clearly because there was visible anger in his father's voice, which was very unlikely of his father.

Ahmad started feeling lonely again, and not knowing what else to do, he pulled the chair and sat in front of the computer screen once again. This time the screen looked unfamiliar. A distinct DOS command prompt that was simply Greek to him flashed before him on the screen. DOS was a marvel for the previous generation and was not a cup of tea for Ahmad's generation. He looked at the screen in despair. He wanted to know what happened to the person who was having a seizure in the car that was pulled aside on the highway. Was there anything he could do to help that person? What will happen if some fast-moving truck hit that car? Why was that person alone in that car? Where was his family? Why were they not there to help him?

Was he going crazy? These are happenings of the past. But then why did he feel that he was a part of all that had happened in the past? Is that because of the way his father was infused in him and his memories? He looked around. There was nobody in the room other than him, but he could not ignore the uncanny feeling of a presence in the room; he felt that somebody was there, and was watching him closely. It cannot be true, he tried to reason. It is the jet lag. He looked at the computer screen, and felt as if the screen smiled at him in a teasing manner, as if to say, 'Don't you want to know what happened next?'

An overwhelming desire to know more inspired him, and without thinking much, he pressed some key on the keyboard. His eyes widened in surprise because he had somehow pressed the right key and the screen fluttered to life again. His command fetched a cryptic file on the screen, which had a few lines in some obscure programming language. Ahmad's hand reached for some water, and he began decoding what was there on the screen.

Ahmad started to swim upstream in the river of time. He could hear people speaking chaste Urdu. The venue was Lucknow, the city of Nawabs. Ahmad was curious to know what had happened there when a car from Gorakhpur rushed towards Lucknow after the occupant driving the car had a cup of tea from the popular dhaba named Vikram Jyoti.

THE CALL FROM party's headquarters was curt and straight forward. It was a text message that said, 'The Party Chief will appreciate if he can meet her in State capital.' He was on his way to Lucknow, the city of Nawabs.

The reason behind scheduling the meeting was not disclosed. She wanted to consult him for some local party affairs. He was not very excited about meeting her, but had no choice either. After all, in politics, one has limited options and cannot pick and choose.

The meeting was brief. He was instructed to work towards bringing marginalised section of the masses back to the party, and arrange political rallies across the State. Apart from this, he was requested to work on strengthening social media, which was influencing the happenings and was gaining attention of everybody. Recently, policies were being dictated by social media.

He was surprised to see that they had a well-maintained dossier on him at the headquarters. There were newspaper clippings from weekly tabloids, along with a couple of items from *The New York Times*. From all account, it seemed that political parties in India were finally embracing technology.

He looked at one of the high officials scornfully because he was continuously chewing paan, the green betel leaf, a popular condiment in the subcontinent. These leaves, when chewed in combination with slaked lime and betel nuts, produce red-coloured stimulating salivation that can be spotted everywhere, especially in government offices.

There was a pouch of Paan Masala sitting on the table, which the official very graciously offered to him also. He remembered how he had gone as a teenager with his grandfather to the inauguration of a factory, where Paan Masala was produced by trade name of 'Ras-Ranjan' for the first time in Lucknow. Paan Masala had caught the imagination of all, and sold like hot cakes, in spite of severe health warnings printed on the containers. In life, people have choices, and that includes the luxury to pick your poison. During his student days, he was a casual smoker, but he smoked his last puff on the day he brought Amna home from the hospital. By doing so, he wanted to insulate Amna from the perils of second-hand smoking.

Though the meeting went well, he failed to take notice of the clandestine recorder that was hidden in the container, which was supposed to contain that 'weird' Paan Masala. Weird, because once Ahmad, during his infancy, chewed it by mistake, and to his horror, he started throwing up. Amna had reprimanded him for even keeping that 'weird' stuff in the house. The thought of his children brought a smile to his face as he entered the upscale fashionable Hazrat Ganj area of Lucknow.

As he was getting out of the small eatery, which he frequently visited during his school days, he noticed some commotion on the street. Before he could realise what was going on, a low-level government employee, probably a peon, in full regalia along with a heavy turban, jumped out in front of him. After the usual salutation, he bowed down, and spoke with customary humbleness, 'Sir, your car is waiting for you.' He was quick to realise that he had been rewarded a plump position in the government. The trip he made to the State capital was not a waste after all.

He was made a 'Minister without portfolio' in the State government, which meant that he would not be entrusted with any particular department in the government, but would rather be the jack-of-all-trades. It seemed viable that they had done their homework prudently, and were willing to take a big risk on him. He had the essential ingredients that were needed in the trade, except that he was not a member of State assembly nor council; the same situation which necessitated a byelection decades back in Maniram, the constituency next to Gorakhpur.

Thinking of Maniram, he became nostalgic. The Prime Minister's visit to the constituency flashed before his eyes, and then a picture on the front page of the leading newspaper filled his vision—the picture of Sadia with the Prime Minister. Uncontrollable and unstoppable tears started flowing down his cheeks.

These were not tears of joy for the government position he just got, but were for Sadia—the first love of his life. How happy Sadia would have been, had she been alive. Now without Sadia in his life, everything looked meaningless. He lost interest in the red beacon, which flashed on his official car. He let out a strained breath, one he did not know he was holding. One has to live because the other option is not even worth considering. Life is a compromise. If you are lucky, all you can do in your life is to minimise the losses.

A list of assembly constituencies where byelections were due in near future was put in front of him for consideration. He was not surprised to see the he breakdown of voters in terms of religion and caste in almost every ward of the constituency. 'So this is how they have divided the society on micro level,' he murmured. He felt uneasy over how this all happened since inception. 'It is not fair at all.' He remembered discussing this with Venkat, one of his friends in New York, who was a dalit and an activist.

From Venkat he learned that *Manusmriti* is the book that started it all. The scorn in Venkat's eyes was still fresh in his memory, when he discussed and understood how the text promoted caste system. So this book divided Hindus, and later, the same pattern inadvertently filtered in Muslims of Indian subcontinent because most of them were Hindus, who had converted to Islam to escape from the torturous teachings prescribed in *Manu Smriti.*

He called Venkat in New York. After exchanging pleasantries, he confessed, 'You were right buddy, this caste thing sucks. I hate it. It should have no place in our lives.'

He looked down at the list placed before him. One constituency in the list was highlighted by a yellow marker. It was Khairaganj.

So, they had selected Khairaganj for him, and this selection made sense. The caste configuration was in his favour. In that constituency, there was a dense population of Muslims and other marginalised sections. He looked at number charts and prediction charts, and went into deep thought. Everything boils down to caste and religion. One is simply seen as a part of a herd, where all that matters is how you are grouped. Your individuality is inconsequential. Your birth had decided many things, which unfortunately will be the baggage that you have to carry for the rest of your life.

'So you want to play the caste card?' There was an element of surprise in Amna's voice when he explained the situation to her. She was right. Such is the hopelessness that nothing else matters. It is caste, based on which votes will be cast. As if that was the sole criteria or the deciding factor.

Everybody knew he was destined to play this role. The role was perfectly cut out for him. Even Nancy knew of it when she was sending her 'Progress Reports' to her bosses. It was expected of him. This was the first step that would catapult him to high orbit, from where he could escape to be what he wanted. And if he played his cards well, he could be the king. That was how it was all planned for him in the power corridors, across seven seas in the capital city of Washington, DC.

In essence, he was just a pawn on the chessboard, and somebody had made the move. There was nothing in his control. His fate depended on the move made by the opponent. He was frustrated, but there was nobody he could share his agony with. He started playing with his phone, and noticed that there were a couple of calls from Sheen, which he had just missed.

He called Sheen, but his call went unanswered. In the thick of things, it was obvious that Sheen and her phone call got lost from his radar screen. Election campaigning is not easy in India. This is one place where modern technology is not much of a help, and the reason is simple. India lives in villages, and access to these villages is not an easy task. The roads may exist on government records, but the reality is far from it. The funds for these non-existing roads were cornered by corrupt officials, and a major portion of it found its way to the party coffers.

All political parties were hand in gloves with each other, and they faithfully followed the unwritten code of silence, or in other words, you rub my back and I will rub yours.

The government officials were no saints either. They were the ones who indoctrinated politicians about how to mint money by siphoning government funds to their own coffers. Such was the extent of the loot that roads were chronically vanishing, and fortunes of the officials and politicians were soaring to new heights.

The road was bumpy, and half the roads were washed off by the rain at places. The SUV in which they were travelling tilted dangerously, and would have tripped if the driver was not adroit. He noticed an empty bus, which had rolled over because it was not able to keep the balance. What had happened to the passengers? Were they able to survive? He was getting frustrated and angry at the same time. Is there any accountability here? He could not understand why the inhabitants of this place kept on electing the same person for five consecutive terms. Could they not see the condition of the roads? Do they never get the urge to punish him for the lousy job he was doing for them?

He resolved to turn the incumbent's apple cart upside down, and beat him in his own game by crafting permutation and combinations which would load the dice in a different pattern; a pattern that would favour him.

'Loha hi lohe ko kaat taa hai.' (Iron only cuts the iron). That is how a high-level party functionary had explained it to him. Yes, he understood it fully; you could beat them in their game by using similar tools which they used, but your tools have to be sharper than theirs, to make them more effective.

Beating a formidable rival in his own turf was something that caught the attention of everybody.

NAZMA ADJUSTED the flame of the lantern and with sad eyes looked at Shakila, who lay on a mat on the floor and pretended to sleep. There was no electric supply in her neighbourhood for the last couple of hours. These power cuts had become a regular affair because there was acute shortage of power in the State. The power plants in the State were getting obsolete and running on reduced capacity. Attempts by the Central Government to install a nuclear power plant in the State drew a lot of criticism from the residents, who were brainwashed by some outside agencies, which had recently showed up in the region.

Shakila was waiting for her mother to fall asleep because that would give her an opportunity to escape from the house, and meet Raju who was waiting for her near the post office. She was finding it difficult to live without Raju, the love of her life. Her father, when alive, was against this relationship. Raju had all the vices which a man could get into. Shakila knew this, but still was not bothered at all. What right had her father to object to vices which he himself had?

She knew her father well. So any opposition from her father made no sense to her. Now with her father dead, she had to get her mother's approval. She knew that her mother, sooner or later, would relent. But little did she know that her mother had more pressing concerns to worry about. She was worried about Nancy's murder. She knew that the bullet did not have the American girl's name on it. It was for the person who was with Nancy. From reports printed in newspapers daily, she had learnt that he was now a very powerful man who held a pull in the government. With Javed dead, he would come after the family of the man who wanted him dead in the first place. Her meeting with him had given her no assurance as to how to perceive things. Shakila found Raju standing near the post office, but his body language was tense and alert. He seemed to be in a hurry.

'Is Ammi sleeping?' He asked with a voice which was taut with worry. Shakila nodded her head, and looked around to see if anyone was around. There were a few stray dogs, and surprisingly too many stray cows around. 'From where do all these cows and buffaloes come during night and fill the whole street?' She often wondered about this. During daytime, these animals mingled with people, and hence their presence went unnoticed, but at night with commuters and others gone, they spread out and filled the street.

Raju did not answer her. He had not even heard her. He had some other plans. He came closer to Shakila and asked something in her ears. Shakila nodded in the affirmative. A cunning smile crept on Raju's face, and his demeanour changed drastically. He held her hand, and started pulling her towards her house. His confidence came from the fact that Shakila had put the drug given by him in her mother's food. It was to ensure that Nazma would not be awake for the next few hours. Like thieves, they entered the house, and with Nazma sleeping in the veranda, he pushed Shakila in the only room the house had.

Shakila was not ready for this. She was puzzled. What would happen if Ammi woke up? She was not sure whether she should stop Raju or let him continue what he was up to. She started feeling uncomfortable.

Suddenly, a lantern flame flickered and there was total darkness in the house. Darkness serves as a guide to many things, which could not be envisaged in light. Little did she know that Raju was not after her body, but was more interested in the cash that Javed used to keep in the room, the cash that he planned to take and flee.

Javed was right; Raju was a man of many vices. When he violated Shakila, it was painful for her both physically and emotionally. She tried to wipe away the telltale signs of what had construed behind those closed doors and fell into the depths of renewed worries.

At the crack of dawn the next day, the mother-daughter duo were worried for different reasons. Shakila was worried because she had been deflowered by a man who she thought loved her, but was only after her father's money. Nazma was baffled with worry because she had lost whatever savings her husband had left for her. They both looked for Raju, but could not find him because he had crossed the border to escape to Nepal, only to return once things were long forgotten.

Yes, misery has a company. For Nazma and Shakila, the worst was yet to come. A loud tap on the door heralded the advent of another misery. Policemen stood at the door to arrest

Nazma for helping Raju kill Javed.

Before Shakila could recover from the shock, they had taken her mother away. Nazma could not look straight in the eyes of her daughter. Raju had done to her what he did to Shakila that night, when he lured her to the house from the post office.

Shakila knew about how her father had died, but she could never imagine that her mother was unfaithful to her father. That day when 'Sahib' had visited her house to pay condolence, she wanted to tell him whatever she knew because he looked like somebody who was utterly trustworthy. Now with her mother gone, out of sheer impulse, she left her house, and knocked at Sahib's house for favour.

When Shakila knocked at his door, he was in his study, and was intensely working on secret connections he had with the intelligence agencies through a computer, that did not have an IP address. These were the privileges one could have when a powerful friendly nation put faith in you. The satellites hovering the space with the high-end cameras are ready to capture moments which might be overlooked by the naked eye.

He vividly remembered how a couple of days back he was able to see moments, exclusive videos captured by high magnification optic lens before dead Javed was brought to the tree from which his body was found hanging. They wanted to make it look as if he had committed suicide. However, they, being novice, did a lousy job. From the recording, he could see how the body was brought and hanged to the tree by a person who looked ill at ease. From his movements, it seemed that he was young because of the swiftness in his moves.

Next what he saw surprised him enough to leave him gaping

at the monitor. There was a silhouette of a woman, who was assisting this person in tying the rope around Javed's neck. The woman walked with a limp. Everything flashed back. He started recollecting his meeting with Javed's wife, Nazma. Most of the time Nazma sat on cot during the meeting, but when he stood up from the chair to leave, he remembered how she had also stood up to bid him farewell, but she did it with great effort. Now he could put a name to the silhouette he had watched on his screen.

Nazma may not have been the one who killed Javed, but was a conspirator in the act. He started feeling sick in the stomach, and rushed to the sink. His phone rang and the guard informed him that a young girl was outside, and she wanted to see him. He had no interest to meet anybody at this odd hour because he was working overtime to crack the mystery of Nancy's death. There had to be some data somewhere that could show him moments before Nancy was shot.

The lack of privacy in today's world disturbed him. The disturbing and nagging feeling that someone somewhere would be watching your every step is the burden of technology suffered by the world population.

'Gee, I am living in a glass house,' he would say to himself, and would look up at the sky before poking his nose, as if somebody watching him through those satellite cameras would feel disgusted to see him pick his nose.

His office was State of the art. Without any outside support, he was able to put everything together. His computer was equipped with every facility available that made it absolutely hack-free. He had done the Microsoft Certification course in New York because his company was paying for it. He utilised those tricks he had learnt to make his connections fail-safe.

He was getting smarter day by day. He often worried about the depth of penetration these intelligence agencies, particularly this agency, had on happenings around the world. He would get very frustrated when 'Access Denied' would flash on his screen. A man of impeccable integrity, he would always mind his own business, without getting into forbidden zones because he knew that eventually one has to pay the price of knowing too much. Often, knowing too much becomes a curse, especially when you start relating it with mysteries you are trying to decode.

One winter night he received a cryptic phone message from Cathy. All it said was to come online. He left the session in a huff, and was soon staring at the screen waiting for Cathy to show up. Cathy looked sombre. He flipped a few buttons on his phone-like device, and brought the phone camera to his left eye, as if he was going to take a picture. The device on the other end did some calculations that confirmed his identity. Now Cathy's voice echoed in his ears.

She said, 'I know that you were awake last night. There was tremendous data downloaded from a server which you think had stored the location where Nancy was shot.' He started feeling uneasy, and swallowed loudly. Cathy continued, 'Nancy's fatal shot was fired by somebody you know very well. You thought that people around you were trustworthy. Guess what.' He blinked, while Cathy said slowly, 'Your own relatives killed her. It was Zahid's work.'

Disbelief and guilt turned him to stone. A young and pretty girl drenched with water after a shower came in front of him. Cathy continued, 'The farm which your great grandfather bought has taken the first blood, and that blood would have been your own, if it was not for Nancy, who became the collateral damage.'

After this conversation, he had no desire to meet the young girl who was waiting outside. He sent her the message to come some other day. But his message was not delivered because he was told that the girl was so traumatised that she simply fainted, and collapsed on the front door.

So now, he was stuck with her, and there was nothing he could do about it. He said patiently, 'Well, she can be an addition to the staff, if she can do the dishes.' Yes, she was ready to do the dishes in exchange of food, shelter and security.

IN MUMBAI, Sheen stood in a red dress ready for the next shoot. It was a commercial for an airline, which certainly was on the verge of bankruptcy. The commercial was a fairly simple one which depicted an occasion in the past when the Queen of England travelled in that airline. When the crew started packing up, Sheen came in the dressing room. She sat on an old sofa which had seen many years in that room. She felt a discomfort of sorts. She was confident that she was a good actor. In spite of whatever was going on in her life, with her father's arrest and the charge of being a terrorist levied on him, she was able to camouflage her feelings and look cheerful and happy. Her insides seemed to scream at her, taunt her for being two-faced, and not the least concerned about the well-being of her father.

Her head started spinning, as it had started doing quite frequently lately. She squeezed her eyes shut for a few seconds, urging the ground to stop its incessant spinning. She started feeling light headed again. She put her hand in her purse, and all she could get was her phone. She looked at the phone and saw an unread message from her father's attorney asking her to call him immediately.

She tapped into some invisible source of force and punched in the attorney's number. Mr Garg, her father's attorney, picked the call in the third bell.

Mr Garg was hired by her uncle. He may not be the best in the trade, but was still influential. Although she had considered hiring another lawyer who had a better record of winning cases, she was unable to retain him because of some conflict of interest. Mr Garg said very slowly, 'All politics, Beta. You know election time...You know.' He tried to convey the message to Sheen as cryptically as he could but since Sheen was not in the right frame of mind, she could not comprehend all that was being conveyed to her.

With her thoughts completely muddled, she wondered what her father had to do with elections. And as far as elections were considered, she had never paid any interest to them. She hated politics; politics was the real killer of her brother. How she wished that there could be a world without politics. Why could not everybody live the way they wanted to? Why was there a need for someone to rule?

She remembered a quote by John Lennon, 'Imagine all the people, living life in peace, you may say I'm a dreamer, But I'm not the only one, I hope someday you'll join us, and the world will be as one.'

The thought of elections reminded her of her new friend on Facebook. She had read in a magazine a few days back that he was contesting some election in his home State. All her messages to him remained unanswered, except one, where he said that he felt sorry to hear about her father's arrest.

The way her father was arrested on false claims infuriated her.

And the fact that she was unable to help him added to that stress. As per the officials, her father was a part of the group of terrorists who had raided the Arms Depot. In the crossfire that ensued, a few Indian soldiers were killed. Recollection of that day brought a renewed fury in her and her conviction of her father' innocence grew stronger. She remembered that night vividly because she herself was witness to the fact that her father was in her room at the alleged time of raid. She had noticed his presence when she had performed salam in her namaz. So the charges were pure fabrication. But how could she prove otherwise?

To make matters worse, there were people who had testified under oath that they saw her father entering the Arms Depot with other unidentified men. 'They all are lying.' Her insides screamed and she clenched her fist. Anger seethed in her and she started breathing heavily.

There was nothing to prove them wrong. It was his word against the rest. Her uncle Sayeed told her that since her father was the sole sane voice, a kind of moderate, extremists despised him for his philosophical attitude. Hence, for hardliners in the group, he was always the odd man, whom they wanted out. At this juncture in his life, there were not many who would help him. Even his close associates were not willing to take phone calls.

In normal circumstances, this would be enough to hinder the carrier of a budding actress, who had just entered the cruel and unforgiving world of filmmaking, where competition and jealously rules. But today, Bollywood probably is the only place in India, which may be notorious for all the wrong reasons, except for being communal. The film fraternity has never been known to discriminate on the basis of religion. It has embraced people of all faiths and ethnicity. Actors from Punjab, Bengal and the far-flung North East have managed to carve a niche for themselves and are in the forefront in every aspect of film making there. After some initial hesitance and reluctance, everybody was accepted as an insider. For Sheen, it was no different. Why should the deeds of the father be considered to judge the daughter?

Said a producer when asked, 'They are two different individuals.'

She started receiving fan mails. The youngsters from far places would be sympathetic to her. The hardliners in industry were also willing to not judge her by what her father was. A prominent politician of Mumbai, who made his career by preaching hate and creating schism between those who came to Mumbai from outside and Marathi-speaking locals, greeted her with folded hands when they met at another film star's birthday party.

He later confided to an aide, 'Yes, her father may be at fault, but she is ours, an Indian, who is working her way in the industry. By avoiding her, she will go defensive, and don't forget, by our actions we have to prove that we don't treat Kashmiris differently, and why should we?'

Another hardliner said, 'Bitiya, we respect you for your talent; you are an Indian, like me. You are like my daughter. India has to move forward from these petty squabbles.'

Sheen was surprised by the love and affection people were giving her. They were the same whom she had seen spewing venom on television programmes, where they would raise their voices to such high levels that nothing that they said would make sense. There, on television, they were against everything that they were not. They would scream at others, and chastise them as outsiders. They would make notorious claims against the ones who did not speak their language. They would make threatening gesture at those who would put signposts in languages different from the local language. Their local militia would do all sorts of evil to spread the language of hate. They would pretend to be someone they were not, and with gusto.

But contrary to all this, there were many who were not pretenders. Their intentions were evil. They wanted to prey on society widening the chasm. They were the people who had not yet benefitted from the politics of hatred. They revelled in making fortunes from others' miseries. One of them was in Gorakhpur; late Sundar Singh's son, Shakti Singh. Sundar Singh had died decades back. He had been killed by an unidentified man who had pummeled many bullets into his body at the railway station, when he was on his way to catch a train to Lucknow. Those days Gorakhpur made it in the news solely for murder, exhortation, land grabbing and smuggling.

Despite his death a long time back, Sundar Singh's relevance in politics in this part of the State had not diminished. Today, his house was packed with people who had come to take blessings from his son Shakti.

Shakti had dropped out of school because of his hatred for going to school. He had become a folk hero overnight when some religious zealots demolished a disputed structure in a town not very far from Gorakhpur. The news that Shakti was the first person who climbed the structure's minaret, with an axe in hand, travelled fast and far. His mother was so upset by his action that she had refused to talk to him for many months. After her husband's death, she became detached with affairs of the land, became reclusive initially, and then went into a shell. But later, she found enlightenment in the teachings of Sufi saint Kabir, whose shrine was stones' throw away from Gorakhpur in a sleepy town called Maghar.

Kabir was a mystic poet of the 17thCentury, and was a weaver by profession. He migrated to Maghar from Varanasi to defy religious doctrines, which claimed that anybody dying in the holy land of Varanasi would go straight to heaven. He chided the followers of Hinduism and Islam for social ills, and many other superficial practices.

In the early days, many, including Shakir, made it a point to send a chador to Kabir's tomb every year. Some even say that one of Shakir's uncles migrated to Maghar and joined the cult, whose followers were called Kabirpanthi.

Today, Shakir's great grandson was visiting Kabir's shrine for the very first time in his life. He also had a chador, which he wanted to spread on the tomb of the great saint who preached unity and brotherhood.

It was a quite morning. Many people did not visit the place on a regular day. Lately, to promote tourism, the State government had identified this place as National Heritage, and held yearly conventions, which saw this sleepy town, burst into activity.

He started to look at the dohas or verses which were depicted on the walls of the tomb. He remembered having read many of them in his textbooks. Since there were not too many people around, he started reading them loudly:

'Bura Jo Dekhan Main Chala, Bura Naa Milya Koye,

Jo Munn Khoja Apnaa, To Mujhse Bura Naa Koye.'

He resolved to explain this to his children later, and hence translated it in English: 'When in search for the evil or bad, I could not find the bad; when looked inside myself, no one else was as bad as me.'

Suddenly, he looked at his left and noticed a young man in a heated argument with a lady, whose face he could not see because she was leaning against a pillar. He walked around the pillar to make sure that nothing untoward was going on there. The lady seemed calm and pacific, but the young man was not pleased. Seeing him, the lady raised her hand towards him and said in a voice which was full of authority and affection, 'Bhaiyya, isko samjhaiye kuch.' (Brother, give some advice to him.).

He was astonished and asked, 'Who, me?'

She moved closer to him, and so did the young man, who looked carefully at his face, as if he was trying to recognise him. After thinking for a few seconds, the young man said, 'I think I have seen you somewhere.'

He thought it to be another Facebook moment. But, actually it was not. He did not know him through social media, but had met him earlier at a party meeting in Lucknow. He was the one who had escorted him to the meeting, where a recording device was hidden in a seemingly innocent can of Pan Masala. Recognition dawned, and the very next moment they were shaking hands.

Before they could exchange another word of pleasantry, his phone started vibrating. He put his hand in his pocket to retrieve his phone, looked at Shakti and said, 'Well, we should meet soon. Why don't you visit my place?'

He looked at his phone. It was Sheen. He answered her saying that he was in a meeting, and told her that he would call back later. That night, he talked to his children about Kabir. The saint was forgotten by India, his country hardly paying any attention to his words of wisdom, but in his view Kabir's message still mattered in India.

'So do you think I should do the term paper on Gandhi?' Amna queried.

He was about to nod his head to agree with her, but suddenly words came straight from his heart, 'No, this time, on Kabir.'

From the other end, Ahmad exclaimed, 'What? You mean, Kabir Khan, Bollywood actor.'

He sighed and said in a low voice, 'Kabir, the Sufi saint, whose shrine is near Gorakhpur.'

His computer screen flashed the prompt that he had an unread new message in his Facebook account.

The message was from Sheen. But for some reason, today his heart was still in Maghar, and Kabir's verses were heavy in his mind. He started reciting, 'Sayeen Itna Deejiye, Ja Mein Kutumb Samaye, Main Bhi Bhookha Na Rahun, Sadhu Na Bhookha Jaye.'(O Lord, give me so much, which is sufficient to fulfil my clan; I should not suffer hunger, nor may the visitor go unfed.) This was Kabir's idea about economic equality, which was forgotten by the world conveniently.

SHEEN WAS online. It had been long since he interacted with anyone on any social networking sites. His life was completely devoted to political activities. His gradual rise in the power corridors was phenomenon. The country was in a State of confusion. At one end, they wanted to get out of the shackles of religion and caste, but these factors were so etched in the DNA of electorates, that often at the last minute they succumbed. The new generations of voters were looking for credible people in the political landscape, and that is where he was becoming a hit. In fact, for most of the time he was double dipping because of caste factor that was in his favour too.

He answered Sheen sending her a 'smiley'. She was so excited to finally get a response from him that she immediately dialled his phone in desperation.

'Where are you?' She shot a question. He was surprised with her informality because in her past interactions with him, she would always start with pleasantries first. This was probably the second time she had called him.

'Yes, I was getting your messages…Sorry…I could not get back to you earlier…' Before he could finish, she almost yelled, 'I want to meet you.' He heard the unmistakable sniffle and the next minute, Sheen was crying like a little child.

'It will be alright. Truth will come out. Nothing will happen to your father.' He kept on repeating consoling words like these, but Sheen's crying on the other end did not cease. Probably, today she remembered how once he had told her that it was all right to cry. She continued crying, and he listened to it all very patiently. He wished that he too could have the luxury to cry the way she was crying. He wanted to cry for Sadia and for Nancy too. But how could he? He was a man and men don't cry. He gave a mocking smirk at this thought. Men should cry too. Even Prophet Mohammad cried when his only son passed away. If you do not cry, then there is no difference between you and a machine.

He looked up at the sky. Sadia was there sitting on the clouds, and she was looking down at him with a smile on her lips. Tears welled in his eyes and before he could compose himself, he started crying. He cried a lot that day. Sheen on the other end quietly listened to him while he cried. Empty and strangely relieved, they both felt better. This strange act of crying had bonded them together. Now he was ready to meet her.

'Yes, I can meet,' he said in a voice that was sniveling. 'You will?' There were hints of excitement and disbelief in Sheen's voice. Had she been alone, Sheen probably would have kissed her phone. Desperate people do strange things when they see a ray of light. The next day, he anxiously waited for Sheen to walk out of the arrival gate at the domestic airport in New Delhi. He was going to meet a person whom he had just met on facebook before.

There she was. He could recognise her from the colour of her skin. She was very fair. Her complexion gave her away as a Kashmiri for her cheeks had a natural red tint to them. Almost all the bystanders at the gate turned their heads to catch a glimpse of her. They were curious to see whom she was going to meet.

She was wearing dull blue jeans with a modest shirt. She also had put on dark glasses, and her hair was neatly spread on her shoulders. She was of medium height. She was very pretty. The great English poet Byron would definitely have written volumes on her, especially on the way she walked. Her walk was graceful and light, captivating so, like a pure and calm river flowing gently with twists and turns.

She was not carrying much luggage. Her presence was so noticeable that everybody around, whether old or young, could not stop themselves from watching her.

He noticed that the curiosity level of quite a few in the waiting gallery was heightened in anticipation. They were from local hotels, waiting for guests to be ferried away to hotels. They kept on guessing if she was the one whom they had come to ferry away to the hotel. They were watching a very beautiful girl, who was looking all around, as if she was searching for somebody. For many, simply watching this pretty girl was worth the trip to the airport.

A tall and lanky fellow, carrying a placard of a prestigious hotel, simply quipped, 'Foreign ka maal hai.' (She is a foreigner.) He smiled. Sheen's father was branded by government as someone in cahoots with the wrong elements from a foreign country, and now this guy had the nerve to find a foreign connection in her too.

He raised his hand, and Sheen saw him. He looked tired and weary, and old for the age, which she had thought he might be. She was happy that he was there. There was relief and gratitude in her eyes when she looked at him. He turned her smile sheepishly, mildly aware of the bystanders looking at them shamelessly. Somebody in the crowd suddenly recognised her, and in a fit yelled, 'Arey! Sheen!' If there was anyone who had not yet noticed her, the shout made them snap their heads in that direction. For them, spotting an actor from Bollywood meant boasting about the same to their friends and family. Had it been Mumbai, people would not have cared that much, but New Delhi is different. People would often go back home telling every living soul who was in the same flight as them.

He tried to lift her bag, but she prevented him from doing so. They both smiled. Sheen seemed in the least frazzled by the buzz that she had created at the airport. There were people frantically making calls to tell whom they spotted at the airport, while others were busy taking photos from their phones. They both looked calm, as if they knew each other for ages.

Not far away, there was another woman, most likely in her mid-thirties watching them closely. She took out her phone and dialled a number, but her call was not answered. She tried calling again. Most likely, her role was simply limited to raise an alarm on spotting the girl from Kashmir.

On their way to the hotel, Sheen kept quiet. He politely asked her about the trip, but she looked at the driver of the car, and then looked at him, as if to say that it may not be a good idea to talk in the presence of company.

After completing formalities at the reception, she came to

the lounge, where he was waiting and said, 'Sorry it took so long. The scanner was faulty.' He nodded absent-mindedly as if he knew everything about the scanner that she was talking about. Then she continued, 'If you don't mind, I will go to the room to freshen up. It will hardly take five minutes, and then we can have dinner. You must be hungry. I am.' She spoke without waiting to take a breath and gave him a sweet yet embarrassed smile. He had no other option but to say, 'Why not?' When she left for her room, he dropped himself on the sofa, and closed his eyes in thoughts. Here he was, in an upscale fashionable hotel of New Delhi, waiting for a girl who was younger than his daughter was, and who was going through a very turbulent period of her life. And the worst part was that she thought that he had panacea that would end her worries.

In the past few years, he had gone places and had made some friends who possessed great influence, but her situation was simply beyond his comprehension. Most likely, it was an issue related to national security.

His left side tried to warn him that he was under deep stress. His brain was very active, but the body was tired. At this time, his brain must be crunching lots of data; numerous images floating by inside the grey matter. His eyes were hurting, and his eyelids were getting heavy. His left hand was resting on the side rest of the sofa, and the aura was building. He did not even realise when they started shaking. First his hands, then legs, and finally his whole body. He was having a full body seizure after a very long time.

When he woke up, he found himself in a beautifully decorated hotel room. The bed was comfortable. He turned his head and saw Sheen resting on a sofa nearby. He was in Sheen's hotel room. He started to sulk. How ironic! He was supposed to help this girl who had flown in especially to meet him and take his advice, and here he lay on her bed after his seizure. And he had not even begun helping her!

Sheen saw him open his eyes. She stood up gently. She walked closer to him and looked at him as a mother looks at a child. He wanted to say something, but he could not find the right words. He lifted his left hand, and put it on his chest. He wanted to sleep. He wanted to rest. He felt very comfortable in the presence of a stranger; a stranger, who had taken care of him for the last two hours.

Sheen said softly, 'You had a seizure and fortunately the person sitting next to you noticed it. There was a guest in the lobby, who was also a physician. They put you on the floor, and by the time I returned back, you were calm. But I insisted on bringing you to my room. You have been sleeping since then. You must be hungry.'

Without waiting for his reply, probably because she knew he was incapable of giving one right now, she continued, 'I have ordered some food from room service.' He looked at her in appreciation and spoke gently, 'Sorry that you had to go through all this. I would rather leave. I think I am all right now. Looks like my medication level dropped. Don't worry, I keep extra dose. Can I get some water please?'

She brought him a glass of water from the table. He took out a pill from the inside of his wallet, and placed it under his tongue. He looked at her. Worry was written all over her face. He stood up slowly from the bed and said, 'Amidst all this going on with me, we forgot the real crisis before us, your father.'

The mere mention of her father broke Sheen's floodgates and could not hold back her tears anymore. He moved near her, and put his hand on her shoulder protectively. She took a deep breath and placed her hand on top of his. He whispered, 'Don't worry, things will be fine.' She removed her hand from his hand, and shot back, 'How?' She had heard people saying this too many times now that she refused to believe it anymore herself. He was caught off guard. He had no answer. So far, he had not even understood the entire situation.

He put his hands on Sheen's shoulders and pushed her to a nearby chair to make her sit. He said in slow voice, 'Now, please tell me all about it.'

While Sheen was narrating her story, there was a lady, the one from the airport, inquiring about her at the hotel's front desk. The hotel, as a part of its policy, refused to divulge any information about the guests who were staying there. On her insistent enquiry, all they said was that there were a few female guests, but they did not tell her about the man, who by sheer accident found his way to a room, which was registered to Sheen, from Mumbai.

But that lady was not one to give up so soon. She made a few calls from her car, and then adjusted the rear view mirror to look at her reflection. The smile on her lips would tell anybody that her mission was accomplished.

Sheen was speaking slowly. The words were manifestation of the pain that was inside her. He had no reason not to believe anything what she told him. Her face was wet with tears. She told him that her father was present in the house when the Arms Depot was raided. She kept going on and on, unburdening herself by narrating everything she had in her mind. It looked as if a volcano had erupted, a volcano which was dormant for ages. She told him about her brother, and about many more who had become victims of the circumstances. She told him about her best friend's father, who was picked by the army in the dark hours of night never to return. She also told him about the many Kashmiris, who prayed day and night for situation to normalise.

According to her, there were many who might wage a war one day against India, Pakistan, or whoever would come in their way of achieving total independence. She had not spoken that much for years. While speaking she continued to look at him and wondered whether he believed what she said or not. In the end, she asked him a very simple question, 'Can you please tell me why all this happened to me? Why to me?'

The question had seemed a simple one, but the answer was not so simple. He himself was struggling to find out why certain things happened to him. Why did he suffer from his ailment? Why did Sadia die? Why was Nancy killed for no fault of her? Why did he sit here with this girl whom he had never met before, listening to her story? Why? Why? There were just too many whys, but no answer. He could have said to her what many had told him, that if things do not work the way you want, then God has something better in mind for you. But in life, things are not that simple. Only one who suffers truly knows the pain.

He left her room in the wee hours of the morning. The attendant at the reception eyed him suspiciously, but the person sitting next to him whispered something in his ears. Most likely, he was telling his colleague about the commotion that had happened in the lobby because of his medical condition. He saw the attendant pointing towards him, so he stopped.

The attendant came near him and inquired if he needed any help to go wherever he was headed for. He politely thanked him, and headed towards Western Court, the place where he was staying in Central Delhi.

It had been a long day for him. He wanted to rest but his brain refused to comply. There was no point in lying down since he knew sleep would not visit him, no matter how hard he tried. Even if he closed his eyes, he could see Sheen's face. The girl expected so much from him. And he knew that he could not meet those expectations. Her father had been convicted in a fast trial court. The only option left for him was a mercy petition to the President of India. It was strange that in India, where cases linger for decades, verdict for her father was punishingly swift.

To aggravate the situation, there had been so many killing of Indian soldiers on the other side of the border recently. The Indian public was restive and was clamouring for retaliation. The government was under too much pressure. If they refused to act fast, the Opposition would be out on the streets. They were demanding blood.

The government cancelled the visit of a high-level delegation to Pakistan, when shutterbugs posted a picture of Pakistan's high commissioner with leaders of separatist movements in Kashmir. The opposition was demanding stern action against the high commissioner. It was rumoured that to avoid spoiling relations, Pakistan would replace the high commissioner in a day or two.

Sami's face started showing up on billboards. He saw one right across the place where he was staying. It simply said 'Hang the Traitor'. This billboard was put up not by any hard-line party, but by a so-called secular outfit.

Sayeed's latest movie saw lukewarm response at the box office. There were volunteers from a right-wing outfit, who stood at theatres to dissuade moviegoers from watching the movie. Some of them even carried flowers for the guests, who would subscribe to their call, and would leave the premises without watching the movie.

He was tired, but he had no choice other than going to the party's meeting immediately. The agenda of the meeting was about the possibility of a snap poll. Everybody was put on standby. He was personally asked by the party chief to take additional responsibilities, which he gladly accepted. He was delegated to play an important role in State politics, and if all went well then he could be projected for the highest office there.

It was all very tempting, but he was not ready for that. He was well aware of his limitations. To conquer the world, one has to adopt new techniques of warfare. He knew well that courage, chivalry, and determination could only take him that far, but for the voyage beyond that, he needed cunningness, resourcefulness and ambition, qualities that he knew he lacked. The bar was being raised for him, and he had no other option but to flow with the flow. It was the first time in his life that he was willing to change.

He considered these challenges to be Godsend opportunities. The logic was simple; he would take whatever he could to keep busy. He had to be busy, to forget the happenings of the past. His life with Sadia was ideal. It was meant to be forever. Alas! That ideal life was short-lived and it crumbled down with the mighty towers when the borders were breached and the world super power looked vulnerable. In the rubbles, there lay loved ones, ones who were supposed to come back home, to be with their family and friends, and there lay his ideal life. The one thing that he learnt from that incident was that there were no guarantees in life, and anything that may seem unimaginable at a certain point may actually happen.

Sheen left for Mumbai by the evening flight because she had an important meeting with a producer. In the flight, she kept thinking about him. She realised that she had burdened an already overburdened person by sharing her ordeal with him. She was unsure whether he would be able to help her. How could he? He was not the President of India, who at this stage held was the only one with the power to release her father by approving the mercy petition.

She could not help but think what he would have thought of her. In spite of all these thoughts, she did not regret coming over to meet him, although, she was unsure whether she should tell Sayeed about this meeting or not.Sayeed was already showing sign of cracks because his movie was not doing as he had expected. He was under a lot of stress, but who isn't in Kashmir. She sighed at this thought and waited for the flight to reach Mumbai.

When she landed, it was raining. She quickly slipped inside the taxi that she had reserved by calling her travel agent from the hotel room in New Delhi. She failed to notice that there was a dark and plump man, who nodded to someone hidden in the sea of people when her cab moved away from the road curb.

When she was about to enter the shower, her phone rang. It was him. He was very excited, and in spite of being a taciturn and a very private person, he wanted to tell her to watch the television because there was news was about him, and his recent promotion within party ranks.

It was after a long time that Alam was sharing his emotions with someone other than a family member. After disconnecting the line, he dialled Amna's number in New York to tell her to read about him in some desi newspaper. Amna chuckled and asked, 'You mean *India Abroad*?' He smiled because he remembered how restless he would get in New York, when Amna would hide *India Abroad*, the only weekly newspaper, which was available those days.

Throughout the shower, Sheen could not stop herself from thinking about her father. She quickly dressed up to go to the meeting, where Sayeed may also be present.

Sayeed was in a bad mood when Sheen entered his house. He simply pointed her towards the inner entrance of the house, an indication that he did not have anything to say to her, and she may go inside and spend time with her aunt and cousins.

Sayeed was not this way before, but recent incidents had affected his life quite a bit, especially when his livelihood was threatened. The collection from his movie was not much. The bleakness of the future made him agitated and snippy. Trolling on the social media about his movie was already giving him sleepless nights.

On the way to the meeting, there was an unnerving silence in the car. Sheen hesitantly broke the silence, 'How was your BP in the morning?' Sayeed replied curtly, 'Fine'. He kept his focus on the road. Sheen took her phone out, and looked at the message that she had just received.

It was from him. It simply said, 'Take it easy. By worrying you can't solve anything.' Those simple words gave her some courage and she replied 'ok' and started looking outside the window.

THERE WERE not too many people who attended that meeting in Maine. The President was vacationing there for a couple of days, and for some strange reason, he wanted to mix some business with pleasure. The pulling out of troops from Afghanistan was getting bumpier day by day.The internal turbulence in Pakistan was not making things easier either. There was quiet on the Indian front, except for sporadic turbulence in the neighbouring countries. There was a political hanging in Bangladesh, which had brought people on the streets. In Sri Lanka, a sting operation carried out by few reporters from neighbouring India had revealed massive corruption in the recently concluded arms deal. In Nepal, intelligence reports had identified at least five training camps under the tutelage of the Chinese. But worst was the intrusion of Chinese army personnel into Nepal in disguise of relief workers, to help the survivors from the earthquake that had devaStated the tiny nation.

Cathy briefed the Secretary of State via video conferencing

about all the challenges in her plate so that he could pass it on to the President. Before Cathy could repeat the secret code signalling the end of conversation, the Secretary asked, 'How's your mole doing in India?'

Cathy was stunned. All she could say was 'Excuse me'. As per the protocol of the State Department, a direct question like this was definitely out of question. The Secretary realised his mistake. He blushed, and immediately rectified his slipup by saying, Taj Mahal. Even that reference, which was so direct, was against the protocol. But what can you do about some of people in high places? Even in a country like the United States, where merit is the sole criteria for ascend, many in prominent positions are there by virtue of the families they were born in. There are strong and influential political families in all countries, where real power actually resides.

Cathy started feeling sour in her mouth. For some reason, she felt very uncomfortable the way the Secretary had spoken of Alam. A 'mole'. By following him for the last couple of years, she had attained respect for him. He was different from the rest. He was certainly a gentleman. He was not born in one of the elite families, nor was his ancestors from royalties that dominated the Indian landscape, but yet he was the type who attained greatness by his own doing. He had no vices, and she was not sure what his stand would be if he was ever called to pick between the two countries. That is why she wanted that answer in black and white before it got too late.

In Cathy's profession, people were more interested in weaknesses or fragilities of a person, which actually could be the point of strength for her. She was privy to information about people in high places, which, if revealed, would turn many continents upside down. The recent turmoil in a country where rebels were regrouping after a brief calm was because of the systematic release of classified data by the so-called whistleblower, who had attained the status of a celebrity overnight. What if the whistleblower was not a standalone adventurer, but a mole planted by a rogue nation?

So far, this person had disappointed Cathy. Often she ended up admiring him, but the next moment this admiration would frustrate her. 'Well, there has to be something.' She would murmur in despair. She knew that 'Honey Trap' would not work for this particular one. But today she saw some hope, when she was informed about his interactions with Sheen. She almost fell off the chair. 'No. It can't be true. Give me some juice.' This was all she said to the woman, who had insisted that the photo she took at the airport was factual and not doctored.

'The girl is exceptionally pretty,' she said to herself. 'But the guy is a saint. And I hate this part.'

In her career, she had seen middle-aged men do strange things, and the possibilities were endless. Why was he an exception? He was single, reasonably good looking, and for him, the stars were in his favour. Nancy always spoke highly of him. But that was a long time back. Men get crazy when they enter adulthood, but they get crazier when they are at the tail end of middle age.

It was a dirty job, but someone had to do it. In Sheen, she saw some hope. Maybe she could dig out something. There had to be a raw nerve that could be pinched at the right time to guarantee that the person would follow the dictate. 'Oh! Pretty girl, please give me something.' She raised her hands, as if asking for alms.

On her flight to India, she kept on wondering about him.

She started having a strong urge to see what he would have done if left alone in a room with a pretty girl. Would he make the first move or would he let his companion do all for him? How would he look with no clothes on his body? She had watched few head of States in compromising positions, not knowing that they were being recorded. She had to know those things. She had a job to do. She made up her mind to see him as soon as she reached India.

Luckily, he was in New Delhi when Cathy called him. Their meeting was arranged in a safe house in Noida. Cathy took a cab from an upscale shopping arcade of Connaught Place, where she left her official car because it could be easily recognised with the unique registration number allotted to Embassy vehicles.

'Why is there not much of precaution as was during the Agra meeting?' He asked her immediately. Cathy continued looking into her handheld device and said, 'That time we were simply unsure about how far we would be going with you, so we did not want to take any chances. Now things are different.' He wanted to ask her what made that sudden change, but on second thoughts, he avoided that question altogether.

She was still looking at the device in her hand when she asked him, 'You are becoming very popular. I hear they like you in the party.'

He felt troubled over this question, and started rubbing his hands. There was an uneasiness that started creeping on the left side of his body. What business did anybody have to peep into his affairs?

He did not like Cathy violating his privacy. From the very beginning, he was a private person who hated when people started poking their nose in his affairs. That might have been the reason why he had few friends.

It would have upset him a lot more if somehow he would have known what he was called by the Secretary of the United States, for whom he was simply a 'mole'.

He, whose ancestors were of impeccable character, and were highly respected by all, was nothing more than a puppet and his strings lay in some very strong and powerful hands. His forefathers had sacrificed their lives and resources for the sake of their country, and today he was sitting with an emissary of a foreign country, for whom he might be nothing more than an asset or a member of their 'Sleeper Cell', who could be activated when the need arises.

It was all meticulously planned. And that is exactly what Nancy had confessed to him. But then, why was he not smart enough to cut the cord? What was he waiting for?

Cathy sensed the anxiety on his face, and she cleverly changed the topic. Now they were discussing about the expansion of the city. He recounted how this part of Noida used to be a barren land when he had visited this area during his college days. These petty conversations only acted as fillers. Neither was paying any attention to what was being said. They looked at each other, and realised that they both were wearing the mask of fake smiles. They were both playing the mind game.

Frustration was spelt clearly on both their features. From the sprawling window of the safe house, he could see how India had progressed in geometrical progression in the last decade. There were six or seven towers that housed hundreds of high-end apartments, very similar to the one in which he was sitting uncomfortably with a very smart person. At the far end, he could see darkness, with contours of life in them. Most likely, they were villages where life still moved at snail's pace. Soon those villages would vanish and would be replaced by enormous monuments, which will shout the saga of progress to the world. The inhabitants of these villages would never be able to afford those indicators of progress because progress is a term that may not apply to everybody with the same fervour.

He spotted a raspberry muffin in the tray, on the table, and stopped looking out of the window. How many people in the world could resist a raspberry muffin? He grabbed the muffin, took a scrumptious bite and looked at Cathy, who was still waiting for an answer. He said, 'Yeah, things are great. Aren't they?' They both looked at each other, leaving a lot unspoken.

Cathy was not the type of person who would beat around the bush. She hesitated, and said, 'We are getting a flood of information from across the border; neighbours are getting belligerent.' Now she had his full attention. He slowly said, 'War is not the solution.'

Cathy realised that she had hit on some raw nerve. She stared outside the window and said, 'For some reason, I think that the political situation is dicey, I wonder what they will do.'

'In situations like this, extreme steps are taken out of sheer desperation,' he said cautiously, and looked at Cathy, trying to fathom what was going on in her mind.

Cathy paused, and without looking at him said, 'Everything used to be possible in war and love, but now you never know.'

She sat back in the chair and reached for a glass of water from the table. Then she turned to him and asked, 'Will you care for a glass of water?' But he did not hear her question. His eyes were focussed on the latest edition of a weekly news magazine. On the cover page, a picture of Sheen's father stared back at him, with the caption 'Should he be hanged?'

His throat was suddenly dry like the desert, and he looked at her and said, 'Yes, I need some water.' The itchy feeling was slowly creeping up on the left side of his body.

Cathy lifted the magazine, looked at the cover page, said, 'I will feel sad if this guy is hanged.'Before he could check his emotions, he reacted instantaneously and asked, 'Why?'

Cathy paused for a moment, adjusted her voice and said, 'Because he is innocent. My assets tell me that he was not there when the depot was ambushed.' Then she looked around, as if to make certain that nobody else was in the room.

In his eagerness, he stood up, but immediately realised that in situations like these, one need not reveal the State of the mind. He unfastened his reaction and said in a slow but measured tone, 'That is what she says.'

Bull's eye, Cathy thought. She knew the answer, but still she asked, 'She? Who is she?'

'Sheen, his daughter. I met her recently.' Cathy looked intensely at his face and said, 'I know. You waited for quite some time at the airport.' There was a sadistic pleasure in her voice.

She chose not to say anything more and started looking sideways. There was a definite change of colour on his face. He said, 'You know a lot about me, Isn't it?' Cathy replied coolly, 'Yes, not only a lot, but almost everything.'

He did not like the answer. He felt as if someone had punched him. His face got red, his fists started to clench. He looked at Cathy with despise on his face and Cathy was quick to sense his disapproval. She did not like that look.

For the first time in her life, a shroud of guilt had engulfed Cathy. She looked at him, and then quickly started gazing at the floor. For some reason, she felt like a dwarf by the stature of the man standing in front of her. Cathy, who was trained not to be swept away by emotions, was finding it very difficult to control herself. She moved forward, and came very close to him.

Then she did something she had never done before. She put her hands on both sides of his shoulders and sobbingly said, 'I'm sorry, I'm sorry.'

Now it was his turn to feel sorry. He gently tapped her head and whispered, 'It is alright. It happens.' He glanced at the open window. In his subconscious, he could see a satellite, far away in the darkness of the realm.

His left side had not ceased its itching, and too many signals travelled from his brain to different parts of his body in quick succession. These signals, which initially were cryptic, later became bold enough to convey messages that even an imaginary camera, somewhere high in the sky, was also not able to prevent. God knows who made the first move, but in a matter of seconds, their lips were sealed.

Before they could go too far, he heard a feeble but distinct bleep, as if some electronic equipment nearby, most likely somewhere in the room, had changed gears. He understood that they were being recorded. However, he did not stop, and continued what he was doing.

Cathy was a no nonsense kind of person, not the type who would mix pleasure with business. For her, pleasure and business were two parallel things, and she was always very careful in keeping them separated. But this assignment in India was full of hard challenges that she had ever faced in her career, and hence she was not willing to take any chance. India was an important country, and if she could deliver India, it would jump start her career, and she would be the de-facto Czarina in the power struggle that was going on back home in the State Department.

Being unsure of how far Sheen would go with him, she devised the Honey Trap, and for the first time in her life, she scripted the role of Honey for herself. Loaded with looks along with brains, she was confident that she possessed the right ingredients to lure even the most hesitant and reluctant one.

In all sense, it was not that simple. Cathy loved challenges and adventures, and this time, she wanted to test herself at a different level. She believed that she could do anything she wanted to do, even if that meant luring a middle-aged person. She was putting all types of justifications to herself, but she was in simple denial of the fact that her admiration for that person was coming from somewhere deep in her heart.

Being cognizant of the fact that a camera was concealed somewhere in the room, he did not stop. Stopping after coming this far would not have been easy either. Above all, Cathy was hard to resist too. He slowly but firmly walked towards the bed, with Cathy coming along with him, without putting any resistance. But just before he was about to put her on the bed, he turned around, and she automatically turned around with him too. Soon they were away from the bed and were on the couch, which was positioned opposite the bed.

Cathy could not believe what he had just done. Now the camera she had installed would capture the lifeless bed with no activity on it, whereas the action on the couch would remain unrecorded. But even with this last minute change, she was more pleased than surprised, because a person whom she knew as possessing saintly characteristics was all hers. Her plan misfired, but still for some reason, it was a proud moment for her.

He was staring at the ceiling from the bed. This was not the first time in his life that he had surprised himself, but this time it was for an entirely different reason. He wanted to beat Cathy in her own game. If for her, he was simply a tool, then for him, she too could be a step towards saving the life of an innocent person. A triumphant smile played at his lips. It was the same smile which he had a long time back when he had received the message that Pakri farm had been conquered.

He wondered how much one needed to suffer, or be deprived to prove to be different from others. You get life only once, so enjoy it as much as you can, because tomorrow never comes. You are only here for a short time, so make every moment count. Life dwells in today; everything else is just a check, or an 'I Owe You' that is waiting to be cashed. You never know whether you will be able to reach the destination to get it cashed or not. Note of caution is provided in the scriptures, but often there are occasions when the spirit indeed is willing, but the flesh is weak. Today he was in a similar situation. After all, he was a human, not a Prophet.

They both sat near the window, and watched the stars for hours. They did not say much to each other. There was a lot that could have been said, but they wanted to leave it unsaid, at least for that night.

Elsewhere, Sheen was scrolling his Timeline back and forth, because she was curious to find the real meaning behind one of his latest Tweet:

Swinging to Slytherin from Gryffindor…Sorting Hat, do u care?

Sheen wished she had her collection of Harry Potter books nearby, so that she could go over the books again, brush her memory and decode his Tweet.

The transformation in him had begun. He was wondering if Sadia saw all this from heavens. He was no longer going to be Mr Nice Guy anymore.

SAMI WAS in a good mood today, Sheen had come to see him in jail during visiting hours. In Sheen, he could see the face of his deceased wife and son, whom he would never see again. Sheen noticed the emptiness in her father's eyes. For as long as she remembered, she had seldom seen her father cheerful. He was a sad soul, who wanted to live like everybody else, but it was not destined. Maybe all his miseries were because of being a denizen of a State of India, considered to be a disputed land by many in the world.

This land of his was a jewel in the crown of India. He always admired the idea of India—a land so diverse and yet united. A country where people of different religions and castes, speak different languages, follow different cultures, worship different gods but still live together in harmony and in peace.

Where in the world will you find a country like India, which has unparalleled resilience, not found elsewhere on the globe? There have been moments in the past, when many had predicted the end of the story for this diverse nation. But, guess what?

India has always bounced back making its critics wonder what fuels this engine, never slowing it down even in the most trying times. The fuel is blood and sweat of its inhabitants. No matter when and from where they come from, they never hesitate to adopt this land as their own, and are always in the forefront to give blood or sweat, whatever the land demanded.

In the jail cell, Sami generally kept to himself, but yesterday he had a scuffle with a fellow prisoner who had recently started calling him Jihadi. He must have caught wind of the news from the outside world, where this sobriquet was being used for him on television talk shows. In ordinary situations, he would have not cared much, but recently everything had started bothering him. He found himself in a constant struggle with himself, his inner jihad.

Sheen was thinking about her father and the fond memories she had with him. She remembered how they had walked along the lake, where she would pick flowers from the meadows, would pull him to go wherever she wanted. Like any other daughter, her father actually was her first love. She would remember how her father would dress her up every day, take her to school, and wash her school uniform in the evening, so that in the morning they would not fall upon each other to find things. Before, when her mother was in sound mind, they had their tasks demarcated, but after her mother withdrew herself from worldly affairs, Sami immediately put on two hats, that of father as well as of mother. Truly said, to a father growing old, nothing is dearer than a daughter is.

Today, after meeting Sheen, Sami started thinking about what was in store for him. Probably, he would end up at one end of the noose of a hangman. Then it would all end, like it ended for his son and wife. He may not live long enough to watch the success story of the only prized possession he had, his daughter. He felt blessed to have her as his daughter, his Sheen. He became restless, and for the first time after many years, he started crying. People nearby heard him say, 'Ya Allah! Help me.'

He remembered the court hearings, which were taken rather lightly by him in the beginning. The nuisance which lawyers were capable of creating irritated him. He started finding lawyers tricky, but still he kept his cool. In fact, he always had a lawyer joke ready to be shared with Sheen, whenever she came to visit him. Last time, when she had complained about his attorney, he had calmed her down, and asked with a glee in his eyes, 'How can you tell when a lawyer is lying?' Since Sheen knew the answer, she could have replied, 'When his lips are moving.' But rather than replying, she stared at her father's face. She was in no mood for any joke, not when print and electronic media was blaming her father's lawyer for not doing enough to get him convicted.

He remembered how his so called friends or comrades lied in court about his involvement in the attack. Two of them confessed receiving the extra ammunition from Sami while they were shooting at the guards, who were protecting the depot. One amongst them was Shareef.

Shareef was feeble at heart, and after making damaging confessions in court, he slipped away from the security cordon and simply vanished to an undisclosed location. Last he was seen by a US drone, which was on a routine surveillance on the other side of the border in Pakistan, but judging by consecutive surveillance videos, his mental condition seemed beyond repair. All day long, he would curse Sami, and one day after watching

Sheen on the news, he yelled, 'If not father, then get me daughter. They all are traitors.'

All these people who once were with Sami now wanted him to be convicted. For some of them, it was no longer a secret that Sami was planted amongst them by the intelligence wing of the Indian Army. On the other end, the Indian Army was on the horns of a dilemma to acknowledge this because it would put lives of two other high value informers in serious jeopardy, at a time when they were about to deliver a key information which would politically turn the valley upside down.

So they were willing to sacrifice Sami. It was like a game of chess, to save the King, you sacrifice the pawn. It is rightly said that you cannot play chess if you are kind-hearted. Sami, for some reason, had never played chess in his whole life for he never had a normal life. There were not many people of his age in Kashmir who had a normal life. For most part of his life, he saw apprehension, restlessness, anxiety, and worst of all, no hope for the future.

But by remaining silent, he saw hope; hope for the valley. Very soon, the Indian Army would make a major breakthrough and people would realise how wrong they were in believing what they had believed for so long. But the question remained, how soon? With the hysteria on the street and the mood of the nation, add to that the looming elections, there was a possibility that things would get out of control and he would be made the scapegoat. Earlier, he did not care much, but now he wanted to live.He wanted to live because Sheen's success story gave him hope. His empty eyes were learning to dream again. It was for the first time in his life that he saw the glass as half full and not half empty.

The result from data crunched from the Opinion Polls, was

keeping everybody on edge of the seat. The possibilities were bothersome because too many unknowns were factored into the equation, and everything looked uncertain. The elections were around the corner and punters were shying away from giving any clue about where to put the money. India had never seen this kind of election before. Everybody was apprehensive about the direction to which swing voters would sway. It was simply a matter of few points, and they all knew that these points are up for grabs. The situation was so precarious that a silly gaffe or a chink in the armour may ruin all calculations. The political parties were desperate to find the panacea what would put them on the saddle. Desperate times call for desperate measures.

A delivery vehicle dashed off the magnificent South Block in New Delhi. This vehicle carried in it many files that were kept in a leather box in a very particular order. The trip of this delivery vehicle at Raisina Hills has been a normal routine, which these Mughal and Rajputana style buildings, made up of rose pink and pale yellow sandstone, have been watching for decades. This was the in-house mail distribution system, probably invented by the British. A very important file was being delivered to the President of India for consideration.

The needed signatures for approval on this file were taken in the meeting that had just ended. The National Security Advisor, who was hurriedly brought in from his foreign junket, and was given this important assignment, recently, chaired it. He had a very important meeting last night at Bukhara at Maurya Sheraton, where some important emissaries from the embassy of a neighbouring country feasted on famous Chicken Tikka. Everybody was full to the stomach, including separatist leaders from Kashmir, who were being provided delicious food from the most expensive restaurant of the city, but their demands were outright rejected and they returned home empty handed.

Elsewhere, a crowd was surging at Ram Lila Ground, where an important public meeting called by opposition parties was about to commence. The mood of the crowd was belligerent. Nobody wanted to take chances, especially when it concerned the security of the country.

Elsewhere, at the party headquarters, there were scores of journalists who were especially invited to cover a very important announcement. The planning was impeccable. After the announcement, messages would be relayed on social media applications by thousands of volunteers across the nation. They were eagerly waiting to dump the chatter to their followers and friends in social media.

The press conference went as planned. The Opposition's plan was nipped in the bud by a senior emissary of the ruling coalition, who said, 'We will never take chances with the security of the country, and to anybody who endangers security of the country, we will be there in the forefront to deliver justice in accordance with the law of land.'

The media got the message. Yes, he would be hanged.

The volunteers on social media started pushing buttons on their laptops and smart phones as fast as they could. Phones started ringing, and television screens came alive. The crowd that was headed to Ram Lila Maidan retreated, and the meeting venue started to look deserted. They were now more interested in debates that ensued on television news channels, shouting away at each other, refusing to listen to what the other was saying.

This election was going to be like no other election of the past because now the stakeholders or voters were loaded with new tools of trade that were very different from what their fathers or grandfathers had used.

The torch was passed to a new generation eager to break the old way of operation. There was no denying that GenerationX was in command now.

The rally planned by the Opposition was cancelled at the last minute. They had learned it the hard way that an hour is a long time in politics. Volunteers of social media exchanged notes and relayed data with lightning speed, and along with them, there were people in high positions who were making tough decisions, and one such person was the jailer of the prison where Sami was kept.

FOR THE first time in her life, Cathy was looking forward to the vacation that she had planned. She wanted to have a quiet week with him at an off-track place, where nobody could recognise them. It was not hard to find a place like that. First, they would fly to Gorakhpur take a road trip to nearby Kushinagar from there, and easily mix with the tourists who had flocked that town to catch a glimpse of the Sleeping Buddha. The government had just opened a five star hotel in Kushinagar, where they had booked a suite for themselves.

They arrived at the airport by the only flight that catered to the needs of Gorakhpur. As they walked to the one-room building that housed the airport, his phone vibrated in his pocket. He looked at the tractor trolley next to the aeroplane, where the passenger's luggage was being loaded. Cathy watched it all with amusement in her eyes. Yes, Gorakhpur Airport was still in a primitive stage.

The phone call was from Sheen, and she sounded frantic, to say the least. It was hard to understand what she was trying to say. All he could hear was, 'Aap ko Allah ka waasta. Mere paas aaiye.Fauran.' (For Allah's sake, please come to me. Now.)

He looked at Cathy. There were only a few passengers around them. Most of them were away looking for their luggage. None of the people paid much attention to Cathy because of the recent influx of foreigners in this area, thanks to the efforts of the State government that wanted to develop Kushinagar as a major tourist hub.

He grasped Cathy's hand and said, 'We are going back.' He looked down at the ground, and for some reason, was unable to look into the eyes of Cathy. He rushed to the one-room airport terminal and asked one of the staff members about a return flight. He was informed that the same flight which had brought them to Gorakhpur would go back in an hour, and they had seats to accommodate him and Cathy.

Cathy knew immediately that her vacation plans had been ruined but she did not say a word about it. For some reason, she enjoyed someone else telling her what to do. Most of her life, she dictated her terms, and made sure that they were followed. This change was refreshing and she did not want anything to dampen her spirits. The back-to-back journey took its toll on them, and they both dozed off in flight. Cathy gently tilted towards him and put her head on his shoulder. He was sleeping like a baby.

At the New Delhi Airport, restless Sheen paced up and down. She was getting more and more impatient with each passing moment. She looked around and found a chair to sit. She took her phone out from her pocket and started searching for something on the panel. Suddenly, she found what she was looking for. It was his Facebook account, and she started looking at the pictures that he had posted on his timeline.

She kept thinking after every few minutes what was taking him so long to come. A twenty-year old was infatuated by a forty-year old man. She put her fingers on the panel of her phone. Touching his picture had a soothing effect on her, as if she was getting healed by the touch.

Elsewhere, in a flight bound for New Delhi from Gorakhpur, Cathy found comfort on the shoulder of a man, with whom she definitely was falling in love with.

At the airport, Sheen did not know what else to do, so she started walking in the waiting area, but her eyes were glued at the gate. Relief washed over her when her eyes sought him out from the passengers who were exiting.

He had put on black corduroy pants along with a matching Armani shirt, and was coming out with tired and heavy steps. Sheen looked at him for a while and ran towards him. Before he knew it, she had embraced him tightly. Few bystanders looked at her, but they did not find anything odd.

Cathy was stunned. He was embarrassed by Sheen's act, and started looking sideways to see how many people had witnessed what she had just done. Sheen was crying without stop.

She released him from her grasp, took a small step away from him and said, 'Achcha kiya aap aa gaye.' (It is good that you have come.)

He patted on her shoulder, and then turned to Cathy, who was not standing too far away, watching all that had ensued with bewilderment. With a dry throat, he said to Cathy, 'I would like you to meet Sheen.'

Cathy smiled and extended her hand towards her. Sheen looked at her extended hands, then looked at him, and then started crying again.

Cathy moved towards Sheen and said, 'Looks like you are having a bad day dear, and you need some rest.' Before Sheen could say anything, he said to her, 'You asked me to come. Here I am.' By this time, Sheen had collected her composure, and felt embarrassed for the impulsive act.

It was clear to Cathy that much could not be achieved by standing there, and hence she became herself, authoritative and in control. She said, 'Ok, I think we should be moving.'

Then she looked at Sheen and said, 'It was nice meeting you. Take care, dear.' He looked at Cathy and said sheepishly, 'I will call you back once I figure out why Sheen wanted to see me.'

Now it was Cathy's turn to take things in her own hands, rather than beating about the bush. She said, 'Correct me if I am wrong. Sheen wants to discuss the latest development about her father.' This confession by Cathy shocked Sheen, who did not even know who Cathy was.

He whispered, 'I think before dispersing, we need to put our heads together to see what is going on.'

All three sat in three different vehicles, and left the airport separately to converge at his suite in Central Delhi.

On reaching there, Sheen sat on the leather sofa with her eyes fixed on the floor. She had worry written over her face. Too many things had happened in the last few days, and the latest fiasco at airport was embarrassing at a whole new level.

Why had she done that? What would he think about it? What right she had on him? Why had she started depending on him too much recently? Why was he on her mind all the time? He was simply trying to be nice to her.

Cathy kept looking at Sheen, who was wearing a long skirt with a perfectly stitched blouse, and thought to herself, 'She is beautiful. Deep down to her soul, she is beautiful.' For the first time in her life, Cathy envied a beautiful face.

He came close to Sheen and said to her, 'Cathy and I are good friends. She is aware of the troubles you are facing…' Before he could finish, Sheen said, 'Sorry to interrupt, but I am extremely sorry to impose myself on you like this…' Then she took a paper wipe from her purse and cleaned her eyes.

Cathy thought that now was the time to take command of the situation. She got up from her chair and walked a few steps to be closer to the wall. She divulged some information to them. She told them how his own colleagues had duped Sami. She told them in detail how the Indian intelligence had recruited him, and since how long he was in the watch list of many, including her own department. She promised to show them the surveillance data that was available for Sami, which could prove his innocence. It showed that Sami entered his house at the time the depot was blasted, and he never left his house until morning.

But what she did not tell them was that how an extremist group in a neighbouring country would love to help Sami because his wife was the first cousin of their leader, who was allegedly blamed to have caused ruckus in the financial capital of India a few years ago. She also did not tell them that her government would have loved to have Sami on their side, because he was privy to so much information that could be valuable for planning the future.

Like obedient students, they listened to Cathy. She was brilliant. She had explicit details on the tips of her fingers. During the discourse, Sheen looked at him a few times, and found him listening to Cathy with rapt attention. His presence in the room was comforting to Sheen, and for a moment, she forgot the miseries that had entered and had found a place in her life.

She started to feel better, much better just by looking at him. She looked at him in awe. He was looking at Cathy with admiration. The euphoria, which had lifted Sheen's spirits moments ago, subsided. She felt trivial in comparison to Cathy. She looked at the woman before her who was bubbling with energy, a combination of beauty and brains, all in one.

Sheen wanted to cry again. Everything seemed hazy and blurred and slowly she leaned back on the sofa, before darkness engulfed her. All this was too much for her to absorb, and with her tumutous feelings, she could not take it anymore and became unconscious. She was too young, and too many challenges were staring at her.

It was past midnight when Sheen woke up. She was in his suite and in his bed. There was a nurse who was sitting on a chair next to the bed. She told her that he had to go with Cathy because of an emergency, and she and the physician on call attended on her, while he was out. Sheen was tired, exhausted and hungry. She looked at food on the tray, and without saying a word, began to woolf it down.

With food in her stomach, she started feeling better. She slowly lay down on his bed, drew the comforter on her body and closed her eyes. Everything from near past started coming back to her. She could see herself getting overwhelmed when she saw him at the airport. It was all fresh in her memory. She cuddled herself in his bed, and put her hands around her chest and started taking deep breaths. She was inhaling the environment that she was in. Nobody could even understand what she was going through, but she was certain her body and her soul were getting healed in this process. She felt that her worries that dwelled in her were escaping away. She was feeling better after a long time and she wanted to go to a place where everyone could see and hear her.

She wanted to scream loudly, 'Don't scare me. I am ready to face anything.' She was right because when you are deeply in love with someone, you are blindfolded in a way that all threats and challenges look trivial to you.

Sheen wanted him to come soon, but how could he? There was a lot going on everywhere.

AFTER DROPPING Cathy off, he wanted to go straight back to his suite to see whether Sheen had woken up or not. He was also invited by one of the major television channels to participate in a debate about the impact of the caste factor in a byelection, which had just concluded in his State. He had data ready to prove that in spite of living in the 21st Century, people here still cast their votes based on their caste affiliation.

He was sitting in the rear seat of his limousine, which passed through the part of Lutyens' Delhi where high-ranking government officials and parliamentarians live. Generally, there is no commercial activity in this part of the city, except for lazy dhabas selling tea and refreshments, and little kiosks where they sell flowers and bouquets.

He asked his driver to stop at one of the kiosks and went to look at the flowers. He wanted to buy some for Sheen. He tried to remember the last time when he had bought flowers in his life, but drew a blank. He realised that he had never bought flowers in his life. Well, there is always a first time, so now could be that first time for him to buy flowers.

He looked at the flowers. They were of many types, but he thought that none of them had the elegance and sophistication that Sheen possessed. He simply told the flower vendor, 'Kuch bhi de do.'(Just give me something.)Hearing this, the vendor, who was in his teens, laughed loudly and said, 'Biwi ke liye le jaane mein log adhik nahin sochte.' (People when buying for wife don't pay much attention.) Then he looked at him, grinned mischievously, and asked, 'Kiske liye hai?'(For whom is it?) He thought it best to not bother answering that question.

He returned back to his limousine with a rose bouquet for Sheen, and that was when he saw a message from Cathy flashing on his phone. Cathy wanted to see him immediately, so he told his driver to turn the car back.

Cathy was anxiously waiting for him when he reached her place. He gave the flowers that he had bought for Sheen to Cathy, who looked at them with surprise and said, 'Knowing you, I was not expecting these. Looks like some transformation going on, isn't it?'

He moved closer to her, looked into her eyes and said, 'These flowers would feel lucky if you would touch them.' Cathy definitely was pleased and said, 'I can't believe this, person buys flowers for the first time in his life, and that is for me. I am honoured.'

'So Cathy was right; she knows almost everything about me.' He thought and the realisation changed the colour of his face and he shifted his weight from one foot to another. Cathy noticed the change in colour and as well in his demeanour. He put his hands on her shoulder and asked, 'So you know everything about me. Tell me what colour underwear I am wearing?'

Cathy bent her head towards him and said, 'Oh really! That should be easy. But you may want to know something else, if you are ready?' Of course he was. So, like an obedient pupil, he sat on the chair to let Cathy take charge and to do what she does best, that is, fill the room with her presence and impress her attendees with her knowledge and personality. She started by saying, 'I am really impressed. How many people will say no to money? Not too many. Am I right?'

He smiled. He knew exactly what she was up to. He was offered money by the crony of a prominent business person, who was known for his dubious dealings in Ukraine and other countries. To the crony's surprise, he had politely refused the money. He looked at Cathy who was scripting something on a piece of paper.

She was doing some calculation on that scrap of paper. She raised her head and passed him the paper and said, 'In Indian rupees, this is what I get. Converting these currencies is not my cup of tea. But somebody has to do it. Am I right?'

He looked at the number she had calculated and smiled. It was close to what was being offered to him. Now he had reached the point in his life when any action of Cathy ceased to surprise him. To him, Cathy was omnipresent and in the true sense of the word, a pantomath. He was lost in deep thought, and did not hear Cathy telling him, 'That was quite a chunk of dough you left on the table. Isn't it?'

He stared at her with a blank face. Money was the last thing that would impress him. In her previous assignment to a neighbouring country, Cathy was dismayed and distraught by the sight of people falling over money like vultures. She could not conceal her joy when she thought, 'Well, people like him are rare in today's world, and may soon be found in the list of extinct species.'

She was happy that she was sitting with a person who was different from all the others she had known so far. At least, in the land of Gandhi, they were still making honest souls and she had the privilege of knowing one of them very well.

She walked towards him and brought herself very close to the sofa he was sitting on. For some reason, she wanted to be closer to him, so close that she could hear him breath. She wanted to put her ears on his chest, to see if his heart would beat loudly by her being so close to him. She wanted to hold his hand, and feel his pulse rate to see if it ran fast, which could be indicative of emotions, if he had any. For some reason, Cathy was desperate to know whether he also had the same feelings for her that she had for him. She wished she had the ability to tap on his heart and directly ask about herself. But matters of hearts are not that simple. They were never so simple and are never going to be.

Now, rather than facing each other, they were sitting next to each other. He moved to hold her hand. Cathy's hand moved towards him and their hands touched.

He squeezed her hand and without looking at her asked, 'Can I ask you a question?' Cathy replied immediately, 'Sure, why not?'He hesitated and asked, 'Do you trust me?'

Cathy was not ready for a direct volley like this. Her heart started to beat fast. She replied, 'In my profession, we trust, but verify.' His grip on her hand tightened and he asked cautiously, 'So how did the verifying portion go?'

Cathy was looking down at the floor when she said, 'You are all set.' Hearing this, his grip on her hand tightened. Cathy looked at the flowers and asked, 'How is Sheen doing? Poor girl, I hope she is alright.'

He looked down at his shoes and simply nodded. Cathy was enjoying his nervousness. There was a lot going on in his mind. He was thinking about the injustices being done in the world, and the trials and tribulations that innocent people had to go through. His mind was thinking about all the collateral damage and innocent people being caught in crossfire only because they were simply at the wrong place.

He had seen how Sadia and Nancy became victims of circumstances, and now Sami awaited the same fate. How could it happen again under his watch?

He looked at Cathy and said, 'What is that you asked me to come for?' Cathy replied, 'I heard that jail authorities have been instructed to do a mock hanging. The hangman would use a sandbag of the same weight as Sami's.' He was not surprised to hear this. He had already seen it in the news. But what had surprised him was the fact that Cathy had called him for information that by now was in public domain and was being screamed out loudly from every form of media. While he was with Cathy, there was a lot going on elsewhere, and Cathy knew about it, but she chose not to disclose it to him. In fact, that was the reason she wanted him to be away from Sheen.

There was a jailbreak, a quite daring task when it is carried out during daytime. They were highly trained commandoes, supposedly from an enemy nation, who most likely sneaked inside the country from the northern side and got Sami out of the jail. Even the Great Wall of China was not able to stop them from entering the neighbouring country from where they crossed the porous border from Nepal side into Gorakhpur.

Their movements were precise. There was hardly any bloodshed. Nobody, including the media, knew anything about it. The government did a great job by keeping it secret. Cathy got this information in bits and pieces from cryptic intercepts decoded at a naval base station in the vicinity of a tiny but very powerful country near the Red Sea. They were monitoring the chatter to keep a check on rebels who were regrouping in a country, which broke away from Soviet Russia after end of the Cold War. This information along with other resourceful data was routinely recorded on powerful servers that were residing in different friendly countries throughout the world.

Cathy wanted him to be away from Sheen as now, after the jailbreak, heightened surveillance by intelligence agencies was expected around Sheen. At that point, Cathy was also not sure about the motive of the people who were behind that jailbreak. Most likely, they were not doing it to save Sami from dying. What if they took Sami for further interrogation, and in that case might use Sheen as sacrificial lamb to make Sami speak? What if they had plans to kidnap Sheen as well, and if they did, what would happen if they found him with Sheen? What if he tries to save Sheen? What if he comes in the crossfire and gets hurt?

There were so many possibilities and Cathy did not want to take a chance at this stage in the game. So, she took a very conservative decision, and rather than letting him go to Sheen, asked him to return back to her.

Waiting for him was not easy for Sheen. She had no idea

what was happening with her father at that moment, but a phone call from Mumbai gave her the news about what had happened to her uncle Sayeed.

The call was from Sayeed's sister-in-law, who had called to inform her that sometime during last night, Sayeed had committed suicide. Nothing much was known at that time, except that Sayeed had received a couple of phone calls from abroad just after dinner, and they had disturbed him so much that he took a heavy dose of some medication. The doctors were yet to figure out which medicine had he consumed. In the morning, he was found dead in his bedroom. During the last few days, he was very depressed because his movie was pulled from many theatres in India, and it turned out to be a damp squib in the overseas market also. The phone calls he had received were from one of the financiers, who insisted on getting his money back, or else he would send somebody for 'collection'. Sayeed had understood that it meant that he would be killed.

Sheen caught the next available flight for Mumbai. She tried calling Alam repeatedly but all her calls to him were in vain, as his phone was out of coverage area.

It was raining when Sheen's flight landed in Mumbai, and she hurried towards her uncle's house. As expected, the house was full of mourners, and not many people noticed her when she entered.

AFTER THAT brief encounter with him at Kabir's shrine in Maghar, Shakti had become a frequent visitor to his house. Most of the time, he sat in the waiting area, from where some of the important visitors, after a preliminary screening by a member of his staff, would be ushered into the exclusive area reserved for dignitaries. He liked this side of the house because Shakila was given a living quarter nearby. He was sympathetic to her for all the miseries that she had faced this early in her life. In her, Shakti often saw his little sister who could not survive the epidemic of encephalitis, which had claimed the lives of many in the early '80s in this region.

In Shakti, Shakila found someone whom she could trust, but for Shakti Singh, his interest was more in her employer than in her. Because of local political rivalries, he was assigned to keep an eye on the political activities going on in this house, which had recently become the hub centre of politics for this region. Shakti was on a voyage, trying to sail by keeping his feet on two different boats at the same time. In fact, everybody was eager to jump off the sinking ships, and was ready to board the one sailing smoothly with plenty of promises to take you to the Treasure Island. Such was the politics of these times. The road to power is paved with hypocrisy and casualties, and like many successful politicians of those days, Shakti was ready to tread on that road.

Today, Shakti was waving a new political flag. The flag that symbolised opposition to all wrongs that were done in the past and politics of religion was one amongst them. Shakti knew that one could fool some people all of the time, and all of the people sometimes, but you cannot fool all of the people all the time. And that made politics unpredictable. Men can change their party for sake of their principles, or can change their principles for the sake of the party.

Shakila smiled when she saw Shakti entering the premises. She knew that he would repeat the same question, 'Tumhare Sahib abhi tak nahin aaye?' (Is your Master not back yet?) But today, for some reason, Shakti did not ask that question. In fact, he was on a different mission today.

He asked Shakila to come closer and said something to her in a hushed tone, to which she simply nodded her head for a definite no. Shakti wanted to get inside the study, on the pretext of checking whether an invitation card for the marriage at his village had arrived or not. If not, then he would inform the host to send another one. However, it was far from the truth. It was not about the invitation card.

Actually, he wanted to confirm whether the information he got from one of his associates about a secret database about party's candidates being stored here, was correct or not. He wanted to know who was the party fielding from the constituency from where he himself wanted to contest. If the grapevine was correct, then he might opt out of the race or would change party.

Shakila never allowed anybody to enter his private quarters, especially bedroom and the study. She had taken the task of cleaning and maintaining these areas for herself. In Sahib, she had found a true well-wisher, a father-like figure, who treated her more like a family member rather than an ordinary housemaid. But, what if Shakti was right? It would not be a big deal to look for the invitation card. So she invited Shakti to hurriedly look at the pile of mail which was gathering dust on one of the side tables in the office.

Shakti entered his office, and the first thing he noticed was a picture frame on the wall, a kind of a collage depicting an old structure that he remembered at once. It was the Babri Mosque, which was demolished by religious zealots decades back. To Shakti, it all looked as if it had happened yesterday. Another corner of the collage illustrated fluttering white doves, symbolising peace, and in the centre, there were a few lines that were penned by Alam:

Mandir Masjid ki baat kal ki thi,
Chale aao aaj koi nayi baat karein.
Pareshaniyan apni ek see, aey dost,
Unhein door karne ki koi baat karein,
Bah chuka hai khoon yoon hii bahut ab,
Aao koi pyar ki nayee baat karein,

The issue of mosque, temple was of yesterday
Come, let's talk about something new today
Our worries are similar, O Friend!

*On a hot summer day in Gorakhpur*

Let's talk about how to eradicate them
Unnecessarily much blood has flown
Come on, let's talk something new about love

Shakti wanted to ignore the collage but he could not. He hurriedly threw a cursory look at the pile of mail sitting on the table, but his eyes searched for something else. He carefully glanced at the shelves, where numerous binders were stacked next to each other. He could not resist himself, and pulled out three or four binders and stacked them on the table. Seeing the true intentions of Shakti, Shakila's eyes widened in disbelief, and she immediately crossed the room and stood in front of him, and asked, 'Kya kar rahe ho tum?' (What are you doing?) Without even looking at, her, Shakti ignored her, and then pushed her aside.

Shakila looked at Shakti and said in a voice that sounded alien to her too, 'Hat jao Bhaiyya, Main kahti hoon ki bahar niklo.'(Move out Brother, I am telling you to get out.) But Shakti paid her no heed, and continued turning the binders swiftly. Shakila came near to stop him again, but he pushed her with greater force on the ground.

Shakila was not ready for this assault, and instantaneously she screamed loudly, 'Sahib dekho, ye chori kar raha hai.' (Look Sahib, he is stealing.)

To Shakila's surprise, her SOS was answered. The lights of the office turned bright and his voice echoed from one of the speakers, which was hidden somewhere in the room. He said, 'Shakila tum pareshaan na ho. Sab record ho raha hai. Police aa rahi hai.'(Shakila, you should not get worried. Everything is being recorded. The cops are on their way.)

God knows where he was, but even from a faraway place,

he was keeping an eye on his assets. This is the new world order, and today's rules of engagement are very different from those of the past. Today, even in politics, only the fittest are the ones who deserve to survive.

Shakti quickly understood everything. He knew that he had been watched and recorded. He looked up at the ceiling to figure out where the hidden speaker, camera and other electronic gadgets were, and he started crying like a child, 'Maaf kar do. Please maaf kar do.'(Forgive me. Please forgive me.) He kept on repeating it like a mantra, until the cops came and arrested him.

Shakila cried the whole day. Even in her sleep, she kept on repeating, 'Sahib maaf kar do.'(Sahib, forgive me.)

AFTER LEAVING Cathy's place, he reached his suite and threw himself on the nearest sofa he could find. His staff told him that due to some emergency in Mumbai, Sheen had left. He missed all the phone calls that Sheen had tried to make, as his phone was on 'surveillance mode' due to some unusual activities that were going on in his office in Gorakhpur. He was worried about what had happened at his house and could not grasp the motive behind what Shakti was up to. He was also troubled about Shakila. In Shakila, he had found an honest and a faithful soul, whom he had started trusting more than any of his relatives and acquaintances in Gorakhpur.

He woke up as soon as sunlight started creeping into his room. It was late morning, and he noticed that breakfast was waiting on the table in the other room. Next to the breakfast, he also saw a couple of daily newspapers that were neatly stacked on top of each other. He dragged himself to the table, and lazily moved his right hand towards the glass containing orange juice.

But, before he touched the glass he gave a cursory look at the pile of newspapers, and his hand stopped mid-air. His eyes could not believe what he saw in the newspaper that was on the top. He immediately pulled his hand away from the glass of orange juice, as if he had touched fire, and started rubbing his eyes in disbelief. Sami's picture stared back at him from the front page of the newspaper with the headline 'Justice Delivered'.

Sami was hanged early in the morning, just after completing fajr. After reading the article, he felt his whole body had become numb and motionless, and darkness swamped him from all around. First, it was his left side, and then his whole body started shaking. His head spun, and slowly he collapsed on the floor.

It seemed that the hanging was done in a great hurry. The media was having a field day, and speculations were rife whether family members were informed soon enough to come and meet the deceased before he was hanged. The government spokesperson curtly said, 'It was done as per procedures, and we followed the protocol. Yes, the family was informed by the courier mail service. To avoid the situation getting out of control in the valley and to protect lives there, the body was buried inside the jail premises as per Islamic rituals. It is the government's responsibility to maintain law and order in the country.'

Today was like no other day; he did not even have the luxury of staying too long on the floor. The electronic control panel on the wall of that room flashed to inform him about the guests who were waiting for him outside. There were visitors from party headquarters, who insisted on seeing him immediately. He was being summoned by the working committee to give final touches to the party's election manifesto. The poll bugles were blaring loudly from everywhere. The political parties were ready for polls.

He had never met Sami in his entire life, but somehow, he had this strange feeling that he knew him very well. An innocent man had become the victim of circumstances yet again. He sat with his head in his hands. He knew that somewhere there was evidence to prove Sami's innocence, but that evidence could never be produced in the court of law. If done, it would have seriously jeopardised many other clandestine activities that might be of more significance than Sami's life.

Who would have believed that there are devices in places that recorded the actions of many, day in and out? How would have people reacted if they were told that there are cameras up in the sky looking at them, recording their every movement. Such disclosures would have created bedlam, which could have rocked not only the country, but could have impacted international relations also.

All these countries were playing the game for their advantage, and were using people like Sami as pawns in their great design of things. Why only Sami? He himself was a pawn in the big picture, and he was not even sure what his role exactly was in the great design. People like him and Sami are privy to certain information on 'need to know' basis. Then, they are used and are thrown away to the wolves. This is what might have happened to Sami. It was rightly said by someone that countries have no permanent friends or enemies, only interests. They are with you as long as their interests are served.

He looked around in vain, but there was nobody around. He said to himself, 'Right. To be alone has its own blessings, but sometimes this blessing looks like a curse. Why, only he?' Like always, there was no easy answer to his question. Tears rolled from his eyes. He noticed a couple of calls from Sheen, but they were from yesterday. Today he felt so helpless that he could not gather courage to call Sheen. Calling Cathy was out of the question. Why would he share his helplessness with someone for whom he was just a pawn in the great order of things? Not knowing what to do, he called Shakila. Most likely, this was the first time he had ever called her.

He adjusted his voice, and asked, 'Kaisi ho?' (How are you?) Shakila was surprised to get a call from Sahib. She stood up obediently from the bed she was on, put her dupatta respectfully on her head, and replied, 'Sahib main theek hoon, aur aap?' (Sahib, I am all right, and you?)

He wanted to talk to Shakila, and to tell her how lousy he was feeling at the moment, but he simply said, 'Main theek hoon. Tum apna khyal rakhna.' (I am all right. You take care of yourself.) After talking to Shakila, he felt somewhat relieved. He thought of calling Amna in New York, but then he dropped that idea.

His thought process was racing at a very fast pace. Multiple images were randomly floating all around him. The images from past were hissing in his ears, and were challenging him for all decisions he had made in his life so far, as if, they were mocking at him, asking him to acknowledge all the happenings where he had failed. There are millions of people out there counting their blessings and enjoying life. And here he was, lonely, frustrated and feeling helpless. Where did he go wrong?

He realised that it had been long since he had paid no

attention to his phone, and there were numerous messages that needed his attention. He wanted to ignore them all, especially the one that was from Cathy. He deleted Cathy's message, and once again, the peculiar smile crept on his face. He felt like a free man. History of free men is never really written by chance but by choice; their choice. He exercised that option, and had made that choice just now.

Then he called the party chief to tell him that he was on his way to plunge himself into the just-announced elections. It was high time that he took charge of himself. He rushed to the shower and started soaking himself generously. All the pain and suffering that was residing in him, started coming to surface through the pores of his skin and found a way to escape with the water. He stepped out feeling fresh, and ready to face the world. A new resolve and renewed energy had given him new mission. After dressing up quickly, he sat in the rear seat of his limousine and headed for an important meeting in the party headquarter.

HE WAS attending the hurriedly called meeting of the Working Committee, which was the highest authority in party hierarchy, to consider final selection of candidates for the elections that had just been announced.

He was seated in the midst of the male-dominated gathering looking at the credentials of one candidate, Anju Kumari, who was a schoolteacher. According to the feedback, she had exceptional skills as a teacher and most of the students she mentored in the last five years had done remarkably well in their life. Along with that, she was honest and a high achiever. Without any outside support, she had successfully developed her school from one room to twenty rooms in a short span of five years. Everybody in her locality adored her because irrespective of their economic and social status, she had stood for them in their hours of need. Although she was very capable, her candidature was dicey because of her caste. There were not many voters belonging to her caste in that particular constituency, and if votes were polled based on the caste factor, as they generally do, then she had no chance.

Anju's name was put up before the committee and her picture was flashed on the screen along with a video, which was prepared by her team to highlight her candidature. She spoke with conviction and was persuasive. She explained how she took everybody along and had worked tirelessly to curtail student dropout rate in nearby slums. Her constituents depicted her as bold, honest, and identified her achievements to prove her record of accomplishment, of being a fighter who always stood up for the values she subscribed to. The video narrated how she broke the tradition and was the first female from her village to get higher education, for which she was even shunned by village elders.

Then party observers gave a detailed presentation about that particular constituency from where Anju was interested in contesting. They were against her candidature because the caste factor did not work in her favour. All her other qualities and achievements were sidelined.

The team leader's concluding remarks were, 'Inki jati ki jansankhya kam hai. Doosri jatiyaan unko vote dene kotay yar nahin hogi.' (Her caste population is less. Other castes will not agree to vote for her.) Another member of the Working Committee who was promoting one of his friends, a business tycoon, thumped his hands on the table and said, 'Maafi chahta hoon, Zamanat zabt ho jayegi.'(I beg your pardon, but we will lose her deposit). Hearing this uproar of laughter reverberated in the room.

When the time for decision came, ones in favour were asked to raise their hands. No one raised their hands except Alam. His lone voice had no meaning in situations where numerical strength mattered. He felt dejected and asked, 'For how long are we going to play this caste and religion game? When are we going to vote as an Indian? Please stop this divide and rule game and let the best candidate win.' He looked at everybody in their eyes and delivered the punch line, 'If we will not learn, then the voters will never forgive us.'

There was sudden silence in the room from where guffaws were heard a while back. Not many people liked what he had said. It was like talking to a brick wall. Although, no recording devices were allowed inside the meeting, somehow some of the proceedings of this meeting were captured on a hidden camera. One of the members, Akhilesh, in his quest to settle score with the party chief had made arrangements with a spy agency to record, and arrangements were made to selectively pass some information to the press. That agency did a last minute gaffe, and after passing parts of footage for which they were hired, they also made public the part where he voted for Anju and spoke in her favour, and chided everybody for subscribing to politics of caste and religion. This part was broadcasted live by media and soon it became viral. The public fell in love with him. In him, they saw somebody who had spoken what they had wanted to hear for long. Soon, #goingtovoteasIndian started trending on Twitter and on other social media platforms with a ferocity never seen before. On Twitter, it was retweeted 100K times in an hour, which was a record in itself.

While driving through the crowded Sadar Bazaar, he was spotted by few in the huge crowd that had assembled there for the party's public meeting. He was requested, rather forced, to get out of the vehicle and was ushered up on stage to say something. Though unprepared, he delivered a speech and it was received very well.

He said in a commandering forceful voice, 'We want to see a future where every child goes to school, and later gets a job. There should be no more street urchins doing menial jobs or begging on the streets. The law of the land should be followed. There should be no need for the public to come on the streets to remind the elected representatives of their duty. The representatives should know their duty.

'People should wake up in the morning to go to their jobs and work to the best of their ability. They should know that they would be rewarded for the hard work they put in. They should also be aware that consequences would have to be faced, if their performance was not up to the mark.

'Turning the light switch should mean that the room would be lightened. No more erratic power supply would be tolerated. The factories should hum and should manufacture products to be proudly sold in other countries. Electricity should be generated by non-polluting means.

'The power should be with the people. The thugs and rascals should find a place in jails, and then politics would become a harbinger of change and a way to serve the people. 'The infrastructure should be robust and no 'chalta hai' attitude would be tolerated. There should be health care available to all. Senior citizens should be loved and respected by all. The fire fighters and policemen should be looked upon as real heroes by all.

'These are some of the things I am looking to change. These are not impossible. We have to bring the change. I know we can do it. Thank you.'

He spoke with his heart and everyone heard him. People had simply stopped doing whatever they were doing and clustered around their television screens with rapt attention. They liked what they had heard. For the first time it seemed that somebody was telling them things which they themselves, if given the opportunity, would have said. He was speaking their language.

In the political sphere, every aspect is taken into account. His rating soared, and the next day, his photograph and speech had made it to the front pages of most of the newspapers. Even garrulous talk show hosts also portrayed him as the politician who was different from the rest of the flock.

For the party, this spelt good news as well as bad news. The party had taken a bad blow with the highest decision making body being portrayed as still subscribing to the old theory of religion and caste. On the good front, in spite of other shortcomings, internal democracy within the party was functional and voices of dissidence were not shouted down. This provided a silver lining because in present times, most of other political parties were dominated by strong and influential families whose dictatorial management style did not go down well with the electorate. Personally, for him, it was simply a win-win situation. He was flowing with the flow and had, by now, left everyone else far behind.

To evaluate the implications of the events that had taken place after the last meeting, party bosses had called for another immediate meeting of the Working Committee.Once bitten twice shy, this time they took every necessary precaution, and even mobile phones were not allowed inside. They wasted no time and voted for the resolution to expel Akhilesh, in absentia, for anti-party activities. However, it was not going to be easy because the present Chief Minister in the State was Akhilesh's protégé, and his rebellion could change power equations in the State. To quell the impact, a plan was formulated.

The party chief said, 'Before Mukhya Mantri ji (Chief Minister) asks for his pound of flesh and blackmailing starts, we should move forward and nip it in the bud.' Every member heard him attentively and many moved their chairs forward. One amongst them hesitantly asked, 'How?'

The party chief looked at him and said, 'I want to propose your name for the post of Chief Minister.'A sudden silence descended in the room, followed by murmurs. For many, it was not acceptable at all, sacrilegious even.

One rationalised, 'But the Chief Minister has not resigned yet. Why this hurry?' The party chief smiled and looked at him and said, 'Please repeat what you just told me.'

Nobody was allowed to bring in any phone but nothing was said about tape recorders, which Alam had brought. He took out the old fashion tape recorder from his pocket, and after pressing the button, kept it on the table for everyone to hear what was recorded yesterday. It was from a clandestine meeting that was called in the State capital by Akhilesh and his cronies and the Chief Minister was also a part of that meeting. They were plotting a conspiracy. Looking at the ashen faces of many members, he, the Nice Guy, started smiling. This was the first time that he had hit below the belt. Life is about survival of the fittest, and politics is no different. It is true that if all you have is a hammer, everything looks like a nail.

Although, he had brought a tape recorder inside, he had followed the rule and had left his phone outside. Many were trying to contact him via his phone, and Sheen was one amongst them.

IN GORAKHPUR, Shakti's attempt to gather information from his house failed miserably and landed him in jail for a few days. Luckily, Shakti got out without even going through the rigors of the trial as the intrusion in his house was not persuaded with zeal. Besides, no one had time to take this seriously, when too much was going on elsewhere. The same happened for Nazma also. The evidence proving her complicity in Javed's murder was not produced in court, and as a result, the police file related to Javed's murder was closed without any logical conclusion.

But, Shakti was not a happy camper since then. Shakti saw Alam as an obstacle because he was on the rise while Shakti's political career had taken a nosedive. For Shakti, the old classic theory, which says that if you can't beat them, join them, had also failed because of his silly move to intrude in his office.

Elsewhere, he was quickly put in the campaign mode, and was travelling hundreds of miles every day and addressing as many meetings as he could. He had put all ducks in the row, and had put in his resources to bring about the change that everyone awaited. The legislatures were coaxed one way or the other to be on his side. The legislatures were no fools either; everyone wanted to bet on the winning horse. Because of his soaring popularity and acceptance by all sections of the society, everybody was ready to salute the rising star. A few decades back, who would have thought that a Muslim could even be considered for the coveted post of Chief Minister of an important State of India?

Today India was on move. It had left behind the baggage of religion, caste and creed and was ready to look into the eyes of the world as an emerging super power. The world was anxiously watching India and recognising the potential of this new kid on the block. Who would have thought that the country, which in early decades after its independence, was at the mercy of America or the Soviet Russia was locking horns with China to gain influence in neighbouring nations Sri Lanka, Bhutan, Bangladesh and Nepal.

The campaign caravan stopped at a dhaba near Aligarh where a public meeting had been organised. He sat on a cot and took out his phone to surf the internet. Lately, he did not have much time or even the luxury to sit idly and check his social media profiles. A message on the screen drained all colours from his face and he almost screamed, 'What?' #GetwellSheen was trending on the social media. On further search, he found a news item that said that Sheen was going through serious bouts of depression and thousands of her admirers were worried about her.

He sat back in his chair and started sulking. He could not get over the fact that he had been so engulfed in the mechanics of power play that Sheen got out of his radar screen completely. How many times had she tried to call him, but he could never find the time to return those calls. The last time Sheen called him was when his phone was not allowed in the meeting where his coronation was in the works. Politics is addictive. It robs you of who you want to be and that may be the reason it is not fit for everybody.

He was struggling with his own inner self. His conscience continued to chide him and increase the guilt that he was already feeling. You cannot be an escapist all the time. Sooner or later, one has to face the challenges, and dilemmas which are staring you in the face. Sheen would definitely understand why her father's life could not be saved, but could she understand why he was avoiding her? She had trusted him so many times, but he had failed to deliver.

He tried calling her, but she did not pick up the phone. He started feeling restless and unable to fight with his own angst. Anxiety and guilt were gnawing his insides. He sat in the next flight that was destined for Mumbai.

It was not too difficult for him to find Sayeed's house in Mumbai. There was complete silence at the house. He was informed that Sayeed's wife was not interested in meeting anybody, at least today, and interestingly, nobody was willing to talk much about Sheen either.

Sheen was still not answering his calls. Not knowing what to do, he called one of the prominent politicians from Gorakhpur, who was notoriously famous in his hey days to be an insider in Bollywood affairs and it worked. Soon Alam was heading towards a famous hospital near Bandra.

Because of privacy laws, hospital staff were not at liberty to give him any information about Sheen's health, and told him to wait so that information of his arrival could be conveyed to one of Sheen's friend who was staying with her in the hospital. That is how he met his Facebook friend, Laila.

Laila was surprised to see him. In fact, she was the one who had once unknowingly introduced him to Sheen by sharing one of his posts about Kashmir. He noticed that Laila looked tired and weary. After the customary Salam, she came and sat next to him.

He asked hesitantly, 'How is Sheen?' Laila answered with a frown on her face, 'Poor Sheen, I don't know what to tell you. She talked about you a lot, but lately she is not talking at all.'

He didn't know what to say next. He sat quietly. Laila continued, 'As a kid she used to be bubbling with energy, but how much can she take?'

After taking a long breath, she continued, 'Sayeed uncle committed suicide and the blame went on her. That was too much for her.' At that time Alam was not even aware of what had happened to Sayeed. His confusion was evident in his expression. He asked, 'What are you talking about?'

Then Laila told him the whole story. She told him how Sayeed's wife blamed Sheen and her deceased father for all the misfortunes that had fallen on the family. Sheen was not able to take the harsh words of Sayeed's wife. At one time, she even attempted to kill herself and that was when Laila came to Mumbai.

Guilt, a thousand times more powerful than before, slapped him. He sat there like a stone, his face devoid of any reaction or expression. Probably, he was cursing himself. His practical and rational mind told him that he had no reason to take this on himself. After all, there are numerous things around you that you have no control on you have to let them go. That is how life should be. But he could not remove the burden of guilt from his shoulders with all his rationality and practicality.

Then upon his insistence, Laila took him to Sheen. He was not prepared for what he saw; it was not the same Sheen whom he had met before. She looked like a living dead. Her face was empty and devoid of any expression. There was no colour in her cheeks and the light seemed to have faded from her eyes. When she saw him entering the room, she looked at him as if she was trying to recollect something.

Then suddenly, her lips moved. She wanted to say something, but was not able to do so probably she was too feeble to even speak. He moved his hands towards her and gently patted her hand. She again moved her lips, and this time he could hear what she said, 'I want to live. Please help me.'

His hold on her hand tightened and he said cautiously, 'Yes, you will.' He was sure about what he had just said. He was happy that at least Sheen had still not lost all hope and wanted to feel alive again. If you have hope, then your abilities to surmount obstacles are intact.

His daily visits to Sheen helped her to recover. One day, he was sitting on the beach and was watching Sheen and Laila playing with the waves like little children. He looked at the girls patiently and was lost in thoughts. Even waves are not free to come and go as they wish, just like humans. Like waves, we are also controlled by circumstances that take us towards our destinies. Faraway, the sun was slowly sinking in the ocean, but with the resolve to rise again the next day.

But life was not as easy as the setting of the sun. Once gone, the process is unfortunately irreversible. His frustration was written on his face when he thought, 'How can I bring Sheen's father back?' And then, very quietly, he recited a prayer.

Sheen was slowly on the mend and they made it a point to come to the beach every day. One day she asked him to go a little further in the water, which he reluctantly did. In the past, he always enjoyed the waves. He used to feel exhilarated when waves would come rushing towards his feet and sweep the sand from under them. Sheen was standing not very far from him when the waves started retreating. People around him were screaming with joy, but the shifting of sand from under his feet did not feel the way it used to earlier.

He was feeling perfectly fine when the waves rushed towards the shore, but his injured brain could not comprehend the retreating waves. His brain still was unable to process any data which was sudden and which was contrary to usual.

The signals from the bottom of left feet to the right side of his brain got muddled and he started feeling dizzy, and his head started to spin. Not knowing what to do he raised his hand, as if seeking help, and finally dropped his hands like dead weight. God knows what would have happened to him if Sheen had not grabbed him by his hands.

He was standing there, unconscious, with Sheen holding him from his waist. The bystanders rushed to them and helped in laying him on the beach bed with his eyes still closed.

Even in his State of unconsciousness, he was mumbling short sentences, 'Oh! Thanks. Thanks for saving…Thanks Sheen. Thanks Bitia...'

His voice was faltering and Sheen was trying to listen to every word that he said. On hearing him say Bitiya or daughter,

Sheen's face became dismal and many colours came and went over her face. Finally, she gathered herself and looked at the man in front of her. He was absolutely right in what he had just said. Although not in his full senses, but even in that condition, he had given a name to the relationship between him and her. What else could be more appropriate other than what he had just called her?

Sheen kept looking at him with eyes that were filled with tears. Her thoughts started to saunter into green lush valleys of Kashmir. She saw herself in her house with her father and suddenly the dam burst. She became hysterical and started crying like a little kid.

She moved forward, put her head on his chest and kept on crying. Today, she felt better after a long time. Her miseries were still there as before, but today something had changed, and that change was visible on her face when she slowly wiped her tears.

She had found an anchor that had been snatched away from her since her father's arrest. It is all about perception, and she had understood that in order to live, she needed just that, a change in perception.

TODAY CATHY was at odds with herself. She was on the horns of a dilemma over what she should do next. She was a meticulous planner, but her own self surprised her. She was struggling because of her uncanny fancy for him. Throughout her college life, she was never off the mark. She was the one who was very unpopular for not tolerating irrelevances. She was direct, efficient and practical to the core, and that was the reason her love life had been dismal in the past. She had thought of herself to be beyond these worldly deviations. Apart from that, she had high expectations and there was hardly anyone who could be her Mr Right.

Today she was feeling unsure about herself. The game plan orchestrated by her was more or less foolproof. She kept reminding herself that it was all for the sake of the country. But then, what was this hesitancy all about? She was smart enough to see the pitfalls that might come in the future. And this was all because of him. To some extent, she was losing control and that was where she felt she was vulnerable.

Her career as well as her upward mobility was at stake. There was nothing more important to her than fulfilment of her dreams. She wanted to run the State Department and she was confident of doing it. However, today she felt that if matters of the heart were to take precedence, then she would consider herself to be a failure. And, for her, failure was not an option at all.

She decided to nip it in the bud. She would do whatever it takes, even if that included taking an assignment somewhere else. She would get herself transferred to China. After all, China was not a bad place to work. That was where Shuttle Diplomacy was initiated and the infamous Iron Curtain started showing what could be there on the other side of the great wall.

'What would he think of her?' She could not stop her thoughts from going to him. And then she chided herself, 'See, this is what the problem is. Why it should matter? Why should I give a damn about him? Who is he to me?' She was at war with herself. Whatever she had to do must be done quickly. India had been a great learning experience, but there were other experiences waiting for her. She realised that she had to cut the cord here. Never in her life had she been so confused and so at war with herself as today.

The events of the last few days were heavy on her mind. It all started when she was requested by the higher ups in the National Security Agency to lead a task force which was dedicated to gain influence in the Indian subcontinent. In the quest to exceed their expectations, she had started looking outside the box and started had meddling in the political process of India. The initial results were encouraging because she was blessed with a young officer Nancy Johnston in her team. Nancy had believed that the affairs of the State should be taken as a marathon, rather than a quick sprint. It was all going well until the complexities of human relationships, especially the one which operated on the unconscious level, overtook the task and for the first time in her life Cathy found herself like the rest of the flock, vulnerable and fragile.

To find an appropriate parting gift, she looked at the souvenirs that she had bought last week for her friends back home, and for some reason she got stuck on a replica of the Taj Mahal. It was quite different from the ones she had seen before. It was uniquely made of a see-through glass, rather than the customary marble. It was one of a kind; the craftsman had been very careful with each minute detail. What also made it special and unique was the fact that it also contained cavities of the two graves, of the king and his queen, their bodies wrapped in white shrouds. The openings of the graves were joined by hinges to the base and one could open and close them. If kept on a shelf or table, one could also see the shrouds due to the transparency of the small replica. At first, Cathy had found this piece weird and had thought, 'One must be quite sick to put this in his home and feel refreshed by looking at the shrouds.' But since the other details were impeccable, in spite of this creepiness, it was worth the money.

Cathy looked at the glass Taj Mahal and then precipitously started smiling. She opened the lid of the cavity of the male grave, took out the shroud from there, and closed the lid. The Taj Mahal was sent to him by Embassy Courier Service.

His trip to Mumbai had robbed him of precious time and excitement and fun that accompany election campaigning. He had a lot to catch up with. He noticed the box that was sitting on the table. For a minute, he thought of paying attention to it after returning back, but when he looked at the sender's name, he opened the box.

He took the Taj Mahal replica out of the cardboard box. Most of the replicas he had seen were made of marble, but this, for a change, was made up of transparent glass and that made it unique and quite different. He could not peel his eyes away from the grave cavities in the replica, and was surprised to see that the shroud was missing from the male cavity. He looked at the cardboard box again. There was a picture of the Taj Mahal on the box and he could distinctly see both shrouds, male and female in their respective cavities, in that picture. Someone had intentionally removed the male shroud from it.

That meant there was nobody buried in that cavity. The grave must be empty. What was the message that Cathy was trying to convey to him?

His head started to spin fast. Because of the stress that was building in him, his left side had started feeling numb. When was the last time he had heard of somebody who had died and had been buried? Images flashed before his eyes rapidly. He sat down on the floor. He had not heard anything related to dying or burying for quite some time. There had been no burial for Sadia and Nancy's body had been handled by the embassy itself. Then who could that be?

His hands went up to his head as realisation dawned on him. His breathing became heavy and quick. He had just unlocked the puzzle behind Sami's hanging and the hush-hush burial inside the jail. The first picture that flashed before his eyes was of

Sheen. After all, his belated prayer at the beach was heard. Prayer is the tool that we all have in our armour, but many amongst us are unaware of its potential, until it works.

All he could say was 'Thank you Cathy'. But Cathy was on her way to Ukraine, where new challenges were waiting for her to tackle. By now, she must have completely forgotten about the glass Taj Mahal.

While this was going on, there was an alert received at the American Embassy which Stated that Shareef had crossed the border and was now somewhere in India. This alert was forwarded to Cathy, who ignored it, because she was no longer interested in the affairs of India.

SAMI COULD vaguely remember what had happened to him on that fateful afternoon. From the beginning itself, there was something unusual about the day. After fajr, he had noticed that several curious eyes were occasionally looking at him. They were of the fellow prisoners as well as of guards. Everybody was cognizant of the hot topic being discussed in the media and that was the rejection of his mercy petition by the President of India.

Sami had had his afternoon meals, and completing his Zuhar or afternoon prayer, he had gone to his jail cell.

In spite of so many hardships he had faced in his life, his faith in Allah was still intact. His faith was derived from the first Kalimah, or Kalimah Tayyibah, 'Laa ilaaha illallaah'. (There is no one worthy of worship but Allah.) He knew that Allah is the most powerful and merciful, and if things were not working the way he wanted them to, then definitely there must be something else which had been planned for him. His naiveté would forbid him to see it.

He was lost in his thoughts, sometimes picturising himself

with his younger brother, Sayeed, then with his son. He even saw himself with his parents, playing outside his house as a little boy and was shrouded with peace and tranquility. He could hear his mother talking to the neighbour, his father listening to the radio, his wife asking him to go and fetch Sheen from school. Everything was so blissful. His beautiful reverie was suddenly replaced by loud noises, bullets all around him, dead bodies scattered, thumping of army boots and suddenly a loud shriek. He was shivering on the cot when someone grabbed him by the head. There was another person who had held his legs. They were carrying his body somewhere and finally there was darkness all around him.

He wanted to open his eyes but he could not. There was heaviness and pain when he tried to pry his eyelids open. The first question that came to his mind was whether he was dead or alive. Was he hanged? If yes, then the angels of the grave, Nakir and Munkar, should be around here somewhere and they would ask him three basic questions, 'Who is your Lord? Who is your Prophet? What is your religion?'

Then he heard voices. So he was dead indeed, he thought, and the angels have descended from the sky to ask him those questions. The thought frightened him and he held his breath, and waited for the questions to be thrown at him.

But the questions never came. It looked like there were people in the room who were talking amongst themselves. From the accent, they sounded Hispanic, or maybe one of them was Hispanic and other one with the heavy accent was probably British. They were talking about how much they hated their job. One with the British accent said, 'Such a nice day outside, and we are stuck in this room for the last four hours.' To this, the other man replied, 'O Man! I wanted to go straight to the beach, but my wife wants me to pick up some grocery. I hate this job as well as the wife.'

On hearing this conversation Sami forgot everything, and slowly released the breath that he had been holding. Then again, he started thinking, 'If they are not Angels of Death, then who they are?' A cold chill ran through his body and timidly he opened his eyes, one at a time. It seemed like a hospital room, and going by dresses of the persons around, one of them seemed like a nurse and the other was a security guard. They looked happy that he had woken up.

They monitored Sami for vital signs, gave him some food and told him to wait until Boss came to see him. After eating, Sami started feeling better and waited for the Boss.

The Boss was a middle-aged lady, who upon entering the room said, 'Hi, my name is Martha. I work for the Attorney General's office and I am your case coordinator. Welcome to the United States of America, Mr Ullah.' Sami looked at her as if she spoke an alien language. Gauging the puzzled look on his face, she said, 'I am talking to you sir, you must have forgotten your last name. It must have been quite some time since you looked at your birth certificate. When was the last time you saw it?'

To Sami, for a moment it seemed as if a crude prank had been played on him. But he regained his composure rapidly. He looked at the person sitting in front of him and asked, almost pleadingly, 'Please tell me what is going on.'

The answer that he received was the least expected. 'What is the hurry? You are here for good. I don't know whether it is by any compulsion or it is voluntarily your choice, you don't have to tell me this. But you are a participant in the Witness Protection Program administered by the United States Department of Justice.' Sami stammered, 'But, I don't understand.'

Martha said very politely, 'As per the laws, we are going to provide you a new identity and from now onwards, you will live the rest of your life under government protection. Again, I am not privy to all the information, so don't ask me. You must have done something good, or have intentions to do something good for the United States, that's why.'

Then Martha showed him a briefcase and said, 'Sir, in this briefcase you have all information you will ever need. Basically, you can live at any place of choice in the country. We will assist you in finding employment, but until then, your needs will be taken care of.'

Sami looked at the briefcase which had so many papers including his birth certificate. As per that paper, Sami was born in Brigham and Women's Hospital in Boston.

Yes, Sami's parents had lived in the United States of America when India had gained freedom from the British, and because of his birth in that country, he was an American citizen by birth.

Sami's grandfather had occupied a very high position in the princely State of Kashmir and Jammu. He was one of the personal assistants to the Maharaja or the king. The period when the British departed from India was a very turbulent era in Indian history. The Maharaja had found it difficult to make a decision, whether to stay in India or to side with Pakistan. There was tremendous pressure on him from the denizens of his State; a majority of them were Muslims. But in his heart, he wanted to side with India. It was alleged that a stage came when he had secluded himself in the confines of his palace, with orders to one of his trusted aide to shoot him to death if invading army from Pakistan ever reached him. One of the aides was Sami's grandfather, who with help from others, had sent a SOS to the Indian administration, as a result of which, the Indian government had sent the army and found an excuse to force the Maharaja to sign papers declaring allegiance to India. This was the reason that the natives were not very happy with Sami's grandfather and later they killed him.

The Indian government wanted to save his family, so they transported his only son first to England, and from there, they moved to the United States. Sami's father had settled on the Eastern Coast in Quincy, Massachusetts. He had lived there for quite some time, but he got homesick. So after Sami's birth, he decided to return back to India with his young son and his wife who was pregnant at that time. Later, Sami's younger brother, Sayeed was born in India.

It may be nothing more than an old-fashioned sibling rivalry that Sayeed always resented the fact that he was an Indian born, but his elder brother Sami, who was born in the United States, was an American by birth.

But, since Sayeed's latest movie was a major flop, one day under tremendous financial pressure, he made a grave blunder. In usual circumstances, he was a casual drinker, but on that day, he had drunk a lot.

He was examining the faltering revenues from his movie, and started blaming Sami for his misfortune. Out of sudden impulse, he grabbed the phone and dialed the American

Embassy and started yelling, 'You know what? It is all because of my brother. He will die, but before that, he will ruin me too. Why am I telling you all this? No, I am not kidding. You all Americans are idiots, like my brother. My brother is like you, idiot. He was born where you were born. Where? In America, of course. Go and check it for yourself. in Boston, the year... I know it was 1960 something…' In his inebriated State, Sayeed kept on screaming on a line that was recorded by the Embassy.

After receiving Sayeed's call, the Embassy staff sprang into action. There were round the clock meetings between Indian and American officials. After long deliberations, they agreed to pool their resources together in an effort to combat terrorism, which was getting patronage within the country as well as from outside. Sayeed's information became useful because now they had the tool that they could apply to Sami and put him into 'sleeper mode', which meant to be aroused only if needed in the future. This could only be made possible because Sami could be characterised as a US citizen; otherwise, it would have been difficult to get the approval for doing such a thing by the US Congress.

Everything worked as per plan, and as a result, Sami found himself in the United States of America. Unfortunately, for Sayeed, it could not be a happy ending and he was buried in India, the land where he resented to be born in the first place.

HE WAS slowly making enemies and was well aware of it. After putting the decades old political doctrine of religion and caste on the butcher's block, he had brought everything back to the drawing board again and many were not pleased with him for doing that. But in any case, public opinion is that what mattered the most in politics. If the public is with you, then you have the luxury of tossing the coin in the air as many times you want, and you can repeat the calculation with numerous permutation and combinations and as many variables, until you get what you want. As a matter of fact, if you are the darling of the masses, you even have the luxury of reinventing the wheel itself.

With his popularity spiraling high, the party wanted to seize the moment and they were willing to pay the price in form of the coveted position of Chief Minister of the State. If you make the world need you, then the world will give you bread. But in spite of having numbers in his favour, he was not willing to take any chances and hence, every trick of the trade was employed because life had taught him that nothing should be taken for granted. His personal staff and recently recruited sleuths worked overtime in combing the dossiers containing information about the legislatures who would vote for the Chief Minister's post, to get acquainted with their vulnerabilities.

He was speaking on the phone with someone and his voice was laced with authority and confidence.'Get the IP addresses of all the machines they have ever used and go to the guts of their laptops to list everything they have ever downloaded. Yes, all the porn they ever watched and all the games they ever played. Yes, do it for their children too. Do it for their sons and daughter, especially for the daughters. Figure out how much time they have wasted. Place it on spreadsheets. There has to be something. We have not given computers to them to write Java scripts or programming languages. Hire more people. Time is of essence.' Everything is fair in love, war and even in politics and for him, this was one battle which he wanted to win at any cost, and for him the struggle would not be over until he won.

With his aggression, there was an element of fear in the political circles. Information was selectively being leaked every now and then and this was giving sleepless nights to many. He overheard his personal staff talking amongst themselves, 'It is not as difficult as we were anticipating; everywhere you look, there is filth. It would have been really difficult if they were saints. Today most of them are crooks.' Another one added in chaste Urdu, 'Koyle se bhari kothri mein safed kameez ko saaf rakhna mushkil hai.' (In a room full of coal, it is difficult to keep your shirt white.) There was no contest for the post of Chief Minister. Nobody dared to challenge him because he was playing the game with vengeance.

Shakti's face had paled. His political future was in shambles. He had tried meeting his mother but she had simply said to him, 'You have to ask for forgiveness for the sins you have committed in your life. I am an ardent follower of Kabir, and I constantly live in shame because of what you did. What you did cannot be forgiven.'

On hearing this, Shakti's face burned with rage. He frowned at his mother and said, 'Main usko bhi dhwans kar doonga. Samajhta kya hai apne ko.' (I will demolish him too. What does he think of himself?) He returned home and that night he drank a lot.

Shakti woke up late in the afternoon. Though his head spun because of all the liquor he had consumed the night before, he switched the television on. The news was about the Chief Minister's visit to his hometown and he was not alone. He had a guest with him this time, andit was Bollywood actress Sheen, whose father was hanged by the government for being a terrorist. Her father was considered a martyr in Kashmir but for the Indian government, he was simply a terrorist. A freedom fighter is a terrorist if he is not on your side.

In that festive atmosphere, where the whole city was euphoric over the idea of having the Chief Minister amongst them, nobody paid much attention to Sheen except Shakila.

Shakila had seen misery and poverty throughout her life. Her parents were no saints either. They were involved in all types of vices and petty crimes. At Sahib's house, she had found a perfect heaven. Then gradually, she started yearning for more. Elements of greed had started creeping into her and with that, her ambitions also soared. She started believing that she had some right over Sahib, and started visualising herself to be the owner of Sahib's house after his lifetime, knowing well that Ahmad and Amna would never return to India to claim their inheritance. And Sahib would not mind because these things are trivial for a person of his stature. Moreover, Sahib always treated her better than how her real father ever treated her. But Shakila was not aware how and to what lengths he had gone to finally secure this house for its lawful inheritors, his children.

Recently, Sahib even looked to her to share his feelings. One day he was talking to her about Shakti, 'Aazmaye huє ko dobara kyun azamaana?' (Why test the one who has already been tested?) These trivial and simple things were of great value to Shakila. Nobody had ever treated her the way Sahib had. But today, Sheen's presence had made her feel insecure.

Somewhere along the Nepal border, Seema Suraksha Bal, the wing of Indian paramilitary force responsible for guarding the borders, received some damaging information. It was reported that Shareef, who was wanted by India and Pakistan both, was seen around the border area in the Doma range and informers noticed that at the time of sighting, he was totally intoxicated. Later, it was confirmed by other sources that he was successful in entering India from Nepal side.

TODAY, SHEEN'S arrival was not the only concern that Shakila had. She had other things to worry about too. And what could be more worrisome for her than the arrival of her mother back in her life? To her disappointment, Nazma had showed up at her door one day with some of her possessions hurriedly stuffed in a rusty tin box. During the trial period when she was in jail, her belongings were thrown out from the shack where she lived with Javed, and then her place was rented out by the landlord. After coming out of jail, Nazma stayed with a relative for a while, and then she found out about the whereabouts of her daughter.

Nazma had imposed herself in her daughter with a promise that she would not live there forever. It was surprising and pleasing for Shakila to find that her mother had changed a lot. She no longer seemed ill tempered and nasty as she used to be before. Shakila was overwhelmed when her mother asked for the prayer mat to offer namaaz; Shakila had never seen her mother praying before.

After reaching Gorakhpur, throughout the day Sheen had kept to herself. She wanted complete solitude because events of the past had taken a very heavy toll on her. She was attended by a physician, who checked her for wellbeing and agreed that she needed complete rest for a few weeks. She informed her producers in Mumbai that she was fine but they should not call her, rather she would call them when she would be ready to resume work.

It had been a hot summer day in Gorakhpur and it was getting dark outside when he knocked at the door. Sheen was still tired and drained out, but somehow she managed to stand up, and open the door for Alam. She was delighted to see him. It had been quite some time since they had spent some time together.

Sheen smiled and said, 'Aap? Mujhe bula liya hota.'(You? You should have rather called me.) To this, he replied, 'Nothing much. I checked with the doctor. You need rest. I want you to feel at home. You should take it easy.' Sheen was raw with emotions and said, 'I will try.' Silent tears of gratitude made her eyes wet. He went near her and tapped gently on her shoulders.

Sheen took a deep breath and said, 'For me, life has always been a struggle. I don't know if there will be a normal life for me. Every day I hope that this is the last day which is bad, and after this there will be no bad days. It can't be true that every misery has my name on it. Even when I feel happy and laugh, I am scared that something must be wrong in this picture. For every happiness that ever comes to me, I say wait a minute, what is the catch? In my childhood, nobody wanted to play with me because they thought that I was unlucky. Am I really unlucky?'

She continued, 'I have never hurt anybody in my whole life. I always try to be good with others. I am kind. I am God fearing. Why do people who are nasty and bad get all the goodies in life? Why do honest and simple suffer? Why?'

Looked like Sheen had not talked to anybody for a long time, or maybe after a long time she found someone who she felt, she could pour her heart out to.

The time for Isha had long passed, but Sheen was not willing to stop. She did not even realise that she was talking to the Chief Minister of an important State of India whose time was precious, and who at this time was supposed to be in a very important meeting with the agenda of Gorakhpur's development.

The television set placed in the corner was on and a pre-recorded debate in which he had participated was being telecasted. He could be heard saying, 'This area has the potential to be the sugar bowl of the country, but since sugar mills are based on primitive technology, they are not running at full capacity. As a result, the sugar cane is often left stranded at the gates of these mills to rot, resulting in farmers not getting full return for their crops.' In response to someone's question, he was saying, 'Today Gorakhpur is developing, but at a slow pace. But when I was a child, Gorakhpur was a sleepy town; far away and aloof from the fast pace life that was threatening the peace and tranquility of other nearby places.'

There in the room Sheen continued, 'I used to dream that my brother would come back. Then I would wake up from the dream, thinking whether he would still play with me, because I am a big girl now.' Her voice was raw with emotion and she choked on her words.

She tried to compose herself and said, 'In another dream, I saw myself buying a house on Juhu in Mumbai. I saw empty rooms in that house and when I peeked in those rooms, you know what I saw? I saw a grave in each room, right in the middle of the room. Yes, my mother's, my brother's, and I got so scared that I did not even looked inside the third room; there would have been my father's grave.' It had started raining outside and clouds had started thundering. They looked at each other and realised that it was time to go and watch the rain. They both were in dire need of some fresh air. Sheen put her foot outside the door and there was some faint movement in the darkness of the courtyard. And then, a shot was fired. Alam jumped in front of her, taking the second shot on his chest.

He fell on the ground. Sheen was looking at him in disbelief. There was blood coming out from his chest where the bullet had pierced. And suddenly, the whole universe stopped for a moment, except for the television set.

The debate still continued on the news channel. His voice echoed in the empty room as he identified methods for the development of Gorakhpur. He was saying, 'Apart from this, another promising venture can be utilisation of the seeds from Sakhoo trees to extract oil, which can be used as fuel.'

And then, even the debate was stopped midway for a very important announcement. All Television channels in India flashed the Breaking News that was coming from Gorakhpur.

THE NIGHT passed quickly. Ahmad was looking at the blinking screen of the old computer. The room turned sombre. The twittering of birds outside heralded the approach of a new day.

The butler brought some food and left it on the side table but Ahmad was so overwhelmed in decoding the machine that the food was left unattended for a while. Later, he served a big plate of biryani for himself, and started taking lazy bites from the plate lost in thought.

He looked at the old computer as if to say thanks, but now the machine looked totally different. There were no emotions on the screen, as they were there before. Probably, after handing over to him the essence of the 'Backroom Diaries' maintained by his father, it was resting in peace. Its mission was accomplished. Ahmad noticed that rather than being connected to the web, this computer was connected to an external device that most likely was the handset which his father carried with him all the time. He smiled and said in low voice, 'Dad, you were a genius.'

There were voices resonating from outside the room but he

was not interested in meeting anybody at this time. He flung himself on the bed, and went to sleep.

Shakila wanted to go and see Chhote Sahib (Junior Sir), but she was unsure about the timing. What if he was resting? Recently, she had abandoned her quarters and had started living in the main section of the house. She took this step after one of her mother's visitors had started coming in too often for her liking. The visitor was the infamous Ratan Gupta, who at one time was her father's closest buddy and his partner in petty criminal activities.

The butler came to inform Ahmad that many visitors waited outside to meet him and that included the men from the city administration, as well as party officials. He felt uneasy over the very thought of meeting those people. He thought, 'So finally the moment has come. I wished Dad was here too.' But then his spirits dampened further when he remembered that he had to go through all this because his Dad was not here. And now never would be. He reluctantly opened the door to go, but was caught by surprise to see Sheen, who stood on the other side of the door, along with Shakila.

Ahmad had known about them from his father. On seeing him, they both tried to smile but their efforts were in vain. Probably, like Ahmad, they too were also going through crises in their lives, and like him, they were too young to face the challenges which they were swamped with. These challenges were not of their choosing either, but they were there to prepare them for greater rewards. People, being short-sighted, once faced with challenges are so submerged in the struggle to keep their nose above the water that they miss out the rewards waiting for them at the shore. Often the pressure we face in our lives hardens us, and this way many of us glitter like a diamond in the end.

Sheen put her hand forward towards Ahmad, whereas Shakila adjusted her dupattata to cover her head properly. Shakila was the first one to start the conversation. She spoke hesitatingly, 'Aap ne theek se khana khaya?' (Did you eat properly?) Ahmad simply nodded his head. Then he turned towards Sheen who was saying, 'You may not know me.' Ahmad cut her in the middle and said, 'I know you. Sorry to hear about your father.' Hearing this, a strange expression swept across Sheen's face and Ahmad noticed the anguish and pain she was going through. Sheen said quietly, 'Sorry to hear about your father too.' Shakila did not know what else to do and started sobbing. The butler showed up and pointed them towards the hallway. It was his way of telling that Ahmad should hurry.

Ahmad noticed that the drawing room was simple as well as magnificent, and unlike the living room back home in the United States, had seen fair share of use. The rugs on the floor were worn out and cushions on the sofa had lost their firmness. The first person he met was the police commissioner, who after paying condolences for his loss, briefed him about the high-level inquiry that had been initiated. The District Magistrate was also present with a message of condolence from the new Chief Minister, who had replaced his father after his death. Other local party officials had also come to pay tributes. Ahmad was struggling to keep the conversation in the local language and after the initial stutter, he looked around in desperation. At that point, Sheen came and sat next to him, just in case he might need some help.

After the visitors had left, he looked at the stack of newspapers and sorted a few of them that were in English.

In these newspapers, there was ample coverage of his father's death and all headlines were screaming in unison 'Who Killed the Chief Minister?' Ahmad could not control his emotions any longer. He quietly got up, and went to his room, with Sheen following him.

When Sheen entered the room, she found Ahmad in a bad shape. He was crying for his father, crying to mourn the void that had been created in his life with his father's death. He had cried in this manner only once before in his life when his mother had not returned back from her work and lay crushed in the rubble that once were the majestic Twin Towers. He cried again today because he was now an orphan. There was another orphan standing close to where he was, and she understood his tears. Sheen came closer to the bed he was sitting on and put her hands gently on his shoulders. Ahmad turned his head towards Sheen, looked her in the eyes and could only say, 'Thanks'. Sheen struggled to find the right words and simply said, 'You are welcome.'

After a few hours had passed, Ahmad turned on the television. A serious debate was being shown discussing the possible reasons behind the death of his father. There were many theories that floated and those on the panel were having a field day. Shakti was also there. He was saying, 'It is very sad indeed. The deceased was my mentor and guide and he was trying to change the system too fast. When one tries to change status-quo, status-quo strikes back.' Another one from the intelligentsia, a popular political commentator, was yelling, 'You don't have to be a rocket scientist to figure this one out. Tell me, who benefitted most from this unfortunate incident?' To answer this, the gentleman sitting on the left side of the panel screamed out,

'Who was the one who took oath the next day?' Without really naming anyone in particular, these men had given enough juice for the news channels to dig up as much dirt as possible.

Sheen walked to the television set and turned it off. Ahmad said, 'Thank you Sheen. They want to improve their TRP ratings over the dead body of my father.'

Ahmad stared at the television set for long. He felt as if the whole environment around him was asking the same question 'Who killed the Chief Minister?'

SHAKILA WAS busy in the kitchen since early morning. Today she wanted to make breakfast for Chhote Sahib herself. The weather was pleasant, so Ahmad had gone outside the house and was strolling in the garden. He was surprised to see that there were at least a dozen varieties of mango trees in the orchard. He remembered that back home in the United States, choices were limited and one could only select amongst the four varieties of Mexican mangoes, which were available there round the year. He had never cared much for the Indian varieties which were now imported there after the ban on import was lifted. His chain of thoughts was broken when a couple of vehicles entered the premises and he saw the occupants making enquiries with the security staff, who pointed them towards Ahmad.

They were officers from the Special Investigation Team which was formed to investigate the murder of his father. The incharge of the team was a young inspector who introduced himself as Fateh. He was there to record Ahmad's Statement. They sat on the chairs in the lawn and Fateh asked Ahmad some simple and routine questions. When asked if he had in his possession any documents or information that might throw some light on the mystery, he replied in negative. He deliberately did not mention the contents of the Backroom Diaries, which he believed was for him only.

Fateh told him that he had made a copy of the hard drives of all the computers that his father owned and that also included the primitive computer that was gathering dust at the back of his father's room. Then Fateh jokingly said, 'We were surprised to find that old machine had nothing on it except some old family pictures. And yes, you were cute when you were a little child.' Ahmad thought his joke to be lame, but he laughed anyway. He felt proud of his father's computer skills which had tricked the task force constituted to investigate his murder.

Ahmad said, 'Thanks a lot for working hard to solve this. I truly appreciate this.' Fateh replied, 'No, you don't have to say this. We are just doing our job. Your father was a gentleman. He was my hero.' Ahmad kept quiet. There was too much going on in his mind at that time.

Fateh looked cautiously around to see if there was anybody about and then whispered to Ahmad, 'It is a mystery but we will crack it. There are tonnes of surveillance data from CCTV cameras which you might want to look at. I will burn a few CDs for you. It captures the moments before the tragedy happened. The house was fully monitored but we are yet to find what we are looking for.'

Ahmad interrupted, 'But how can I get the CD?' Fateh placed his hand on Ahmad's shoulder and replied, 'Don't worry; I will get it delivered to you in half an hour. Please take my number and feel free to call me any time. It was nice meeting you.' Ahmad shook hands with him and replied, 'The pleasure was mine. Thanks.'

Ahmad returned back to his room to check his e-mails and to take some rest. The heavy breakfast which Shakila had prepared this morning was making him lethargic. He was also contemplating what to do next. Tomorrow he would visit the graveyard one more time and then check out return flights to go back. He was convinced that there was not much he could do here. The investigation would take time and he could monitor it from the US also. The local media wanted to interview him and they could do it tomorrow, and then he would go home. He started feeling homesick and lonely and did not want to stay any longer in his ancestral home.

There was a knock on the door and Sheen poked her head inside and asked, 'Can I come in?' Ahmad replied politely, 'Yes. Please come on in.' Sheen came to tell him that she was also looking for flights to return to Mumbai because she had a lot to catch up with.

While they were talking, Shakila came in with the CDs that Fateh had sent. They hobbled around Ahmad's laptop to understand the order in which the information was stored on the CDs. Shakila excused herself to go and make some tea.

Sheen said, 'I couldn't believe when I heard the shot fired, and before I could realise anything, he was lying on the floor. It took a fraction of a second for him to realise that an assassin was hiding there. The room opens to the courtyard and at that time it was dark. With the help of darkness, the assassin came closer towards the room's door and then waited in the dark for us to get out.'

Sheen closed her eyes, as if she was visualising something and then she continued, 'The assassin was waiting for me because everybody knew that as per his schedule he was supposed to be in the meeting. He had cancelled the meeting last minute and had not even informed anybody about the cancellation.' Her voice chocked when she said, 'He was killed because he wanted to save me.'

Ahmad knew that there was not much he could say and changed the topic, 'Let's see what is there on the film.' By this time Shakila was back, and soon they were watching the recording from the camera, which was focussed on the courtyard. All they could see was darkness. Ahmad adjusted the volume and they could all hear Alam.

He was on television and was answering somebody's question. The sound quality was dismal and his voice could barely be heard because the recording device must have been too far. He was heard saying, 'Today Gorakhpur is developing, but at a slow pace. But when I was a child Gorakhpur was a sleepy town; far away and aloof from the fast pace life that was threatening the peace and tranquility of other nearby places.'

There was some movement in the darkness. The shade of darkness changed as the door opened the contours in the darkness took shape as light from the room poured out but still, it was not enough to make any sense. Then the shadow moved and that was it. One powerful gunshot was fired. Ahmad opened another window on his laptop, and now they were watching recordings from two different cameras at the same time.

From the recording of the camera focussed on the door, it all seemed just the same. His father was lying on the floor and

Sheen was bent over his body. Ahmad was concentrating on the window that showed the events that took place near the door but Sheen was looking at recordings from the camera, which was still focussed on the darkness of the courtyard. She had no reason to look at the happenings at the door because she herself was a part of it. Everybody who was watching the recording was making the same mistake. They were focussing on the door where the action seemed to be and not on the dark courtyard.

His last few moments were very intense. He was mumbling something, which was hard to decipher because of the poor sound quality of the recording. Sheen recounted it for Ahmad, 'During his last moments, he looked strangely calm. He had held my hand and had said that he wished Ahmad could be here to give his shoulder to his coffin when he would be carried to the graveyard. He was missing Amna and Sadia. Then he whispered something by taking Sadia's name and then he recited verses from the Qur'an. He knew that his last...' Sheen did not complete her sentence because she had noticed something on the screen which the others had overlooked. She pointed her finger at the screen where there was nothing but the darkness of the courtyard and said, 'Oh! That shadow walks with a limp.' And Ahmad started sweating because from the 'Backroom Diaries' he knew someone who walked with a limp. All he could say was, 'OH!'

They turned around to look for Shakila but by that time she had already left the room.

AHMAD LOOKED at Sheen and said, 'It is getting crazy. I can't believe it. You would be surprised too.' Sheen was totally confused because she was yet to decipher who walked with a limp. With a dry mouth, she said, 'I wonder where Shakila would be. That person in the dark, I wish I could see more. Could we change the settings to get a better picture?' Although Ahmad looked calm from the outside, but a thousand questions had waged war in his head. And he knew that the answers to those questions were etched somewhere on the hard drive of that old machine. To answer Sheen's question, he said, 'I don't think there is a need to get better resolution. I think I know who killed my father.' He was gasping for air and his face was full of rage. Sheen came closer to him and asked, 'Who?'

Before Ahmad could say anything, they heard some commotion coming from the far corner of the premises, and then somebody fired a gun. Sheen, who had gotten used to the sound of guns since childhood, got scared this time and nervously asked Ahmad, 'Did you hear that? I think it was a gun shot.' Without wasting any minutes, Ahmad grabbed her hand and said, 'Let's go.' They came out of the house and started running towards Shakila's quarters. By then, the whole compound was flooded by flood lights and security guards who had taken positions were visible everywhere. Some of them were also rushing towards Shakila's quarters.

The scene inside Shakila's quarter was heartrending. Shakila was standing near the bed and was holding a pistol in her hands. She had just shot her mother, who was lying on the floor in a pool of her own blood. She was taking her last few breaths. Shakila's face was pale and she was trembling with fear, panic and anger. In the corner of the room there was Ratan, who was sitting on the floor and his hands were on his head. He looked agitated, tired and confused.

Shakila was crying. She came closer to her mother, and said, 'Mujhko maaf kar do. Mujh ko maaf kar do. Tumne aisa kyun kiya? Kyun maara Sahib ko? Kyun Ratan ko aane se mana nahin kiya? Tum to janti thi maa. Bachpan se kya karta tha mere saath woh? Phir bhi tum ne aane diya? Sahib ne mujhe beti ka maan diya maa. Jo mere Baap ne nahin diya. Mera Baap to... Tum ko sab maloom hai Maa.' (Forgive me. Forgive me. Why did you do that? Why did you kill Sahib? Why did you not stop Ratan from coming? You knew what he used to do with me when I was a little girl. Still you allowed him to come. Sahib gave me the honour given to a daughter. Which my father never gave me. My father... You know it all mother.)

Nazma's face was slowly turning white. She could barely speak, she said, 'Maaf kar do. Main andhi ho gayi thi. Saari umar gunah mein lipti rahi. Socha tha ab achchi insaan banoongi. Ratan ki baat mein aa gayi. Kashmiran ko maarna zaroori tha, nahin to tumhari jagah wo le leti. Tumhare Sahib se bhi Shakir dada ka purana badla bhi lena tha.' (Forgive me. I became blind. I had spent my whole life in sins. I had thought that now I will become a good person. Got carried away by Ratan. It was necessary to kill the one from Kashmir. Otherwise, she would have taken your place. I also had to take revenge for Shakir from your Sahib.)

With that, Nazma departed from this world. Shakila threw the pistol towards Ratan and embraced the dead body of her mother, and started crying.

Sheen came close to Shakila and put her hand on her shoulder. Inspector Fateh had also reached the crime scene. He nodded to Ahmad. Ahmad was trying to console Shakila. He was saying, 'Tum ko kuch nahin hoga.' (Nothing will happen to you.)

Shakila looked at Ahmad with disbelief. Fateh asked the woman constable to arrest her. Shakila did not resist the arrest. She put her hands forward. Ahmad patted her on her hands, and said, 'Hum tumhaara intezaar kareinge.'(We will wait for you.) And Sheen nodded her head for a yes.

Ahmad turned to Sheen and said, 'Go and finish your work in Mumbai. I will wait for you here in Gorakhpur.'

Around the globe, approximately three billion passengers would take to the skiesin aeroplanes this year, but for the near future, Ahmad was not going to be amongst them.

AHMAD AND Sheen were on their way to the airport. Sheen had to catch the flight to Mumbai but for that she had to go to New Delhi first, because there was no direct flight from Gorakhpur to Mumbai, but a phone call from the butler changed their plans, and now they were coming back to the house.

Upon entering the premises, they found a couple of vehicles in the porch. The guests were given their places in the drawing room to wait. One of them was Officer Ratna Ahuja. She was from the prestigious Central Bureau of Investigation and this was her first assignment.

Ratna was of medium height and was dressed in full police regalia which included a sleek pistol stuffed in the holster attached to her belt. There were many other subordinates with her but they were already inside the house.

On seeing them enter the Drawing Room, Ratna stood up from the sofa and put her hand forward for a shake. She said, 'You may be surprised to know that last night the Home

Minister disbanded a Special Investigation Team that was headed by Fateh because there was conflict of interest. I cannot reveal the exact details but there were allegations that the investigation so far was sloppy. Now we are entrusted to re-evaluate from the beginning. My officers are inside the house and so far we have found a few discrepancies that needed to be looked at from a fresh perspective.' Ratna was talking very fast and Ahmad could only look at her.

She continued, 'See, nobody paid attention to the fact that the two bullets that were fired were from two different bores. The first which hit the door frame was not even considered, so we are evaluating the spot on the door frame and doing thrust analysis to back fit it and find the bore of the first gun. Then we will compare it with the post mortem report. I hate to say that the crime scene was not properly sealed off either and even the floor of the courtyard was not preserved. It was wiped off and now we cannot find any footprints there. I am very upset but at this stage can't do much.'

Ahmad hesitantly asked Ratna, 'Why did it happen this way?' Ratna took a deep breath and said, 'I don't know, I have been into this case only for four hours.'

Then she looked at Ahmad and said, 'I know you must be feeling lousy over all this, but believe me, the State agency is not that bad and Fateh is a very competent officer. We went to training together. I wish he could have started the investigation earlier.'

Sheen interrupted her, 'What do you mean?' Ratna was quite for a while and then she said, 'I guess you don't follow the news. Two different political parties are involved. The government in

New Delhi and the one ruling the State are not by same parties. So there are lots of allegation and counter allegations. I mean the blame game. Well, I have to leave. See you in the evening.'

A lot happened after Ratna left the premises.

Ahmad got a call from Ratna and she asked him to watch the news at 6. She did not say anything else and disconnected the line. Sheen and Ahmad waited for the clock to strike 6. But before that, two officers from Ratna's team came back again. This time they wanted to take some measurements inside the house. Then another party of four came and they barged them selves into Shakila's quarters but did not stay there for long. Ahmad and Sheen continued to watch all this with amusement.

At six, the news broadcast for which they had been waiting all day began. The title of the story flashed in big bold letters. 'Breaking News. Don't go away. Stay Tuned for the rest of the story behind the Murder of Chief Minister.'

And then on the screen flashed the picture of Ratan, who had confessed killing the Chief Minister earlier in police custody. When Nazma had fired the first shot which hit the door, Ratan who was with her, had fired the fatal shot that took the life of the Chief Minister.

Ratna's face came up on the screen and she was talking very fast in her signature way, 'Ratan had taken the contract to kill the Chief Minister from the party chief, who had doubts about playing the role of King Maker and started dreaming to be the King himself.'

Ahmad and Sheen looked at each other and realised that there was a dangerous world outside and they were better off in sticking together in each other's arms.

After marriage, it was their first night together, and Sheen asked Ahmad, 'What is love?' And Ahmad chuckled, 'It is like photographic plate and needs darkness to develop.' Like Sadia, Sheen also preferred the lights to be turned off and when it was total darkness all around, Ahmad looked outside the window and far, very far away, he saw two eyes staring at the windows and he turned his attention away from those eyes, because the onus was now on him that the Lions of Gorakhpur should not cease to be. He looked at Sheen, who was patiently waiting for him in the bed.

# Epilogue

Due to population explosion, the forests are dwindling in the Terai region and new townships, which are mushrooming, are erasing from the memory the places that were there before.

Now there is a thriving community of dwellings in the Doma region where decades back were dense forests. This area, in the past, was a hunter's paradise, but today animals are sparse and chances of finding them are minimal. This area has seen significantly more development compared to others areas in the region, because of the efforts of Ahmad's father, who because of his political clout, got significant amount of funds diverted to this region. Recently they also opened a High School which is named after him. According to the folklore, decades back Ahmad's father, along with one of his cousins spotted a tiger in this region, which he mistook for a lion.

Today, on the occasion of the Seventieth Republic Day of India, Ahmad and Sheen are visiting the school with their child. After unfurling the Tricolor, the Indian flag, they visit one of the class rooms where there is a poster of a tiger on one of the walls. One may call it a coincident, but the wall on which the calendar is hung is at the same spot where the tiger was sitting on that fateful night.

The child asks his father, 'Is that a picture of a lion father which lives here in the jungle?'

Ahmad thinks for a while, and then replies, 'No that is the picture of a tiger son. There were lions in this region before, but not anymore.'

The child's father was wrong. He was talking to someone who very well could be one of the future Lions of Gorakhpur.